What reviewers have said about this story:

Kirkus Reviews:

"A tense and unsettling portrait of a family torn apart by a predator in its midst."

Judge's Commentary
Writer's Digest Self-Published Book Awards:

"I could not put this book down."

Running Away

Away

Maggie's Story

A NOVEL BY

Sheri McGuinn

Durare
Publishing

Bullhead City, AZ

Cover Credit: Photo of Girl by Steve DeShazer

Cover Design by Sheri McGuinn

Interior designed with Microsoft Office Professional 2010

ISBN 978-1-942069-041 Paperback
ISBN 978-1-942069-058 EPUB
ISBN 978-1-942069-072 Kindle

Library of Congress Control Number: 2020914860

HUMAN
AUTHORED
Authors Guild

7993722

Table of Contents

RESOURCES

THANK YOU

BEHIND THE STORY

ACKNOWLEDGMENTS

ALSO BY SHERI MCGUINN

DISCUSSION QUESTIONS

Thursday: May 25, 2000

1: Maggie

May 25, 2000

Someone who doesn't even know me noticed before Mom or Lizzie.

Chip, the quiet guy who sits next to me in third period, stopped me after class Tuesday & asked if I was okay. I totally fell apart. He took me up to the projection booth above the theater. No one was there. Can't believe I pulled down my collar to show him the fingerprints. He asked about a doctor, I told him no. No doctor. No talking to teachers. No making phone calls to anyone. He understood. He's got a friend who ended up in foster care. Safe, but her mother didn't believe her & won't talk to her anymore.

Mom won't believe me. Not after everything I pulled trying to break up their engagement. And I can't live like this—Chip said he'd help me & he really came thru. We're gonna pretend I'm camping with his family for the holiday weekend.

So I'm out of here. This is my last night in this house.

I slap my diary shut as Lizzie barges into the room.
"Hey, why don't you knock!" I complain.
"It's my room, too, remember?"
"I had the door closed for a reason."
"Yeah?"
"Yeah, I wanted some privacy. I coulda been changing."
"Okay, Maggie." She sighs, backing off. "I'll knock next time."
"So close it already."
"It's like being in a box."
But she shuts the door while I get up from the desk we share. I know she'll want to start her homework. We never had to share a room at home, but that's sixty miles away—and Mom sold it.
This is Richard's house.

I don't feel like talking. Just toss my diary into the top bunk, climb up, and stretch out facing the wall. *He* painted this room white over wallpaper. It's cracked next to my mattress. Picked through three layers so far. This one's green. My room in *our* house was deep-sea blue, with tropical fish my friend Chandra painted and furniture that Mom and me sponge-painted to look like coral. This furniture's junk.

At least I got first pick on the bunks. Lizzie wanted the top, but I'm two years older. She can have it once I'm gone. It'll be like I was never here. No. Lizzie'll miss me.

"Maggie, how do you do this?" She's pointing to a math problem.

"I always louse those up. You better go ask Mom."

Can't pack yet, but while she's gone, I look around to see what needs to go. There isn't much of me here. Just my clothes, a few books, my old CDs, and the sleeping bag I'm using for a comforter. It's a summer bag, but it'll hafta do. All our other camping gear is in storage, except Lizzie used one of the big framed backpacks to move a bunch of her stuff. Maybe it's still here. No, not in the closet—Yes! There it is! Under her bunk. Good. Don't know what I'd use for my gear otherwise. It's too big for a weekend, but I can say I don't want my school pack to smell like a campfire. Lizzie's coming back. I shove it under her bunk.

"Mom wants us to clean up and help get dinner on the table," she says as she puts her math book on the desk.

We wash up in our bathroom. Mom doesn't like people washing their hands in the kitchen sink while she's cooking. Wonder if I'll eat dinner here tomorrow? I don't know when they're coming for me.

Mom gives the orders soon as we get to the kitchen. "Lizzie, take care of the place settings. Maggie, help carry the food."

She's made this whole big pot roast, with potatoes and carrots— gravy, even. We eat way more meat now she's cooking for Richard. I like salads. We used to make a whole meal of a salad, with nuts and cheese and lotsa different veggies, not just lettuce.

"Smells good," Richard announces to the room when he comes up from his office in the basement.

When he washes his hands in the kitchen sink, Mom doesn't say a word—not to her *husband*. We all sit down and Richard stops us to say grace. Hypocrite.

"Lord, bless this food." At least he keeps it short. "Maggie, how much meat do you want?" he asks in his phony sweet voice.

"Just that little piece, please." I try to sound nice, but it's hard. I nod silently for how many potatoes and carrots.

His fingers stroke mine as he hands me the plate. I drop it.

"That's okay," he says with that smile. "It didn't break."

I scoop some carrots off the table and put my plate in front of me. Mom's rushed to the kitchen and is back with a damp cloth, wiping up my mess.

"Maggie, you need to be more careful."

"Yes, Mom."

My fault. Again. I can feel him watching me, smiling. I hunch over and focus on eating.

My plate's clean while everyone else is only half done.

"May I please be excused? I've got a lot of homework."

"Okay," says Mom, but Richard says "No" at the same time.

I stay put and keep quiet while they sort it out. I don't want any trouble. Just twenty-four hours to go.

"She shouldn't gobble her food down like that," he says. "It's rude. She'll only learn if she stays at the table until everyone is finished."

"Maggie, Richard is right," Mom says—no surprise, she always goes along with him. "It's rude to rush through your meal. But I'm glad you're so concerned about your grades now, so go study. Just be more polite next time."

Amazing. Figures. Now that I'm leaving, she starts to make her own decisions. Or she just wants me to study.

Alone in the bedroom, I look through my stuff. Gonna sell my CDs, if anyone wants them. Probably won't take anything but clothes. And bathroom stuff. Lizzie comes in, so I lie up in my bunk doing my homework. Don't want any phone calls home tomorrow! Richard walks past our room a couple times. Wish Lizzie would leave the door shut.

"See ya later."

Her voice startles me. She's in her jacket, with her backpack slung over her shoulder. I sit up so fast my head bumps the ceiling.

"Where're you going?"

I need Lizzie out of here to get things ready for tomorrow, but I don't wanna be home alone with *him*.

"Sitting for Petersons."

"The people right down the street?" I demand.

"Y-yuh," she drawls. "What's got you in a knot?"

"Just wondered. So you're walking over there?"

She looks at me like I've lost it. "Duh—it's four doors down."

"Mom going anywhere?"

"Don't think so, but it's not my turn to watch her." She shakes her head. "You are so bizarre. See ya later."

She closes the door on her way out. I want to make *sure* Mom's still here, but if I hafta go near Richard he might find another excuse to touch me.

I open the door a crack. They're talking, just voices, no words, but Mom's here. I let my breath out, blowing it up my face so it catches my bangs, then take another breath and let it out real slow. Learned something from that stupid counselor.

Gotta take care of things while Lizzie's gone. He won't do much while Mom is here.

2: Peg

"Peg, honey, come on, you need a break." Richard coaxes me. "I rented one of your favorite movies. A real chick flick."

It's *Sabrina.* The girls and I must have watched it a thousand times. I think we sold our copy at the yard sale. But he was trying to do something nice.

"I really need to get these papers graded." I sigh.

"You didn't have to work this much at your old school."

His remorse pours into me through his hands as he rubs my shoulders.

"I wish I'd known they were going to cut my position," he says.

At the time, it seemed more sensible for me to change jobs than have him commute sixty miles through the snow belt, but I never would have agreed if I'd known he'd lose his job a few months later.

He keeps talking.

"I feel so guilty, having everything fall on you. I'll make it up to you, once my business gets going. I promise you."

"When are you going to tell me what you're doing?"

"I don't want to jinx anything, sweet pea. I'll tell you when the money starts pouring in. Hey, can I help you grade papers? Would you have time to watch the movie with me then?"

Richard is so loving and supportive. He's trying to help with the girls. I just wish I had more time for everyone.

"Come on, you need to relax," he urges. "You push yourself too hard. You don't have to be perfect."

"Maybe I do need to kick back and watch a movie," I concede. "The first two classes are done." Besides, finishing my work after the movie will give me an excuse to wait up for Lizzie. "Okay. It'll just take a few minutes to record these grades."

"Great. I'll ask Maggie if she wants to watch it with us."

I give him a big smile for that. Lizzie's accepted him, but Maggie's still resistant. He keeps trying, though. As I alphabetize papers to make recording grades easier, I hear him down the hall by the girls' room.

"Maggie, would you like to watch *Sabrina* with us? I'm making popcorn."

Maggie just says, "No," but her tone is vicious.

She never used to be rude. I hope Lizzie doesn't get this impossible when *her* hormones kick in.

As Richard comes back through on his way to the kitchen, he shrugs and gives me his half-smile, "Just you and me, babe."

He is so patient with her.

3: Maggie

Richard opened my door without knocking and asked if I wanted to watch the movie with them. His voice was all sweet for Mom to hear, but the way he looked at me made me feel naked. I hate him.

I'll stay up 'til Lizzie's home. Mom always waited up for me when I babysat; she doesn't for Lizzie. Guess she doesn't care about *either* of us anymore. Wish Lizzie could come with me. I'll come back for her when I'm set. She'll be okay 'til then, I think.

I'm gonna be fifteen this weekend, but I can pass for eighteen. Need to get some phony ID to get a job, but that's gotta wait. Money comes first. Chip's mom is letting him take some out of his bank account for the phony 'camping trip' he's taking with 'a bunch of the guys' this weekend. Don't like taking his money, but I'll pay him back later. If he can't get enough, there's Lizzie's babysitting money, but she worked hard for that, so only if I can't get it other ways.

I take my CDs out of their cases and put them into my carrier. There's almost fifty. If they sell for five bucks apiece, I'll be in good shape. Passed the word around today—gonna hook up with people in the morning before school. I stuff the carrier into the bottom of my school pack. Don't want Mom to see it.

The smell of popcorn makes my stomach grumble. When they're settled with the movie, I'll go make some for myself.

Right now, I go through all my clothes. There's a couple white blouses we got a few weeks ago 'cuz mine were getting too tight again. Can't believe I was worried about being flat just a couple years ago. I try on my good black slacks—they still fit. My black skirt's tight, but it'll do, to be a waitress or work in an office. I pick out jeans and some T-shirts, my hoodie, underwear and bras and socks.

Then I put everything that's going into one big drawer, even the dressy stuff. Just fold it carefully. It'll all fit in the pack. Can't load it now. Gotta wait 'til tomorrow when I've told Mom about the imaginary last minute invitation to go camping with Chip's family. If I give her time to talk about it with Richard, she'll never let me go.

We thought Mom needed a man in her life—WRONG! He ruined everything, even *before*.

She hasn't had time for us since they first started dating.

My stomach rumbles again. I open the door part way. Harrison Ford's asking Sabrina to bring back "one of those little Eiffel Tower paperweights." I listen a few minutes, then stop stalling and walk down the hallway. They're snuggled up on the couch. I move so fast thru the living room that I'm already in the kitchen when Mom calls out.

"Maggie, sure you don't want to watch the movie with us?"

"Nah, I'm reading."

"Okay."

That's how it is now. We never talk face-to-face except when I'm in trouble again, and she always watches movies with *him*.

Me, Mom, and Lizzie used to stay up every Friday and Saturday watching movies on our big old comfy couch. We usually fell asleep on it. Now we don't do anything together, and we sold the couch.

While the popcorn's nuking, I get two cans of cola from the fridge and fill a glass with ice. Lizzie and me used to argue which was better, Pepsi or Coke. Now we get the store brand. Can't even remember who liked which one.

When the popcorn's finally done, I dump it into a bowl and shake a little salt and some Parmesan onto it. Gotta be careful. I throw away the bag and wipe the counter, check the kitchen—there's no excuse for him to bother me. I stick the cans under the arm with the popcorn and pick up my glass of ice.

As I pass thru the living room, Richard gives me a smug smile over Mom's head. She's totally into the movie and doesn't notice. I pretend to look at the movie too, but he knows I see him. He pulls her close, then gives her one of those fake love kisses on top of her head.

I hate him so much. I wanna run, but make myself walk, even tho' I can feel him watching my butt all the way down the hall. It's a relief to shut myself into my cell.

4: Peg

Richard pulls me closer as Maggie comes back through the room. Even now we're married, I don't like being demonstrative in front of the girls. I pretend to be absorbed in the movie and ignore his kiss on top of my head. When she's back in her room, I lift my face for a real kiss. It's much better than the movie. As his lips travel down the side of my neck, he starts undoing my blouse.

"Richard!" I chastise him in a hushed voice as I stop his hand. "Not here! Maggie could have forgotten something in the kitchen. She could come back."

"She won't."

"She could," I repeat as I adjust my clothing. "I have to set a good example."

"There's nothing wrong with fooling around with your husband." He kisses my forehead, then smoothes the worry lines with his thumbs. "They have two parents now."

I smile and caress his cheek. "I don't know what I would have done without you, the way Maggie's been. It took me by surprise. We were always so close, I thought we'd skip the rebellion stage."

"Not many do."

"I wish you'd known Maggie better before she got so mouthy."

"So do I, but she'll come out of it eventually."

I stop his hand as it moves under my shirt again, "Richard . . ."

"Come on, teach. Quit being such a prude," he teases.

His calling me 'teach' reminds me of the work I should be doing. I won't have a moment to breathe tomorrow if I don't finish. I could grade papers while we watch the movie, but it's the couch foreplay Richard's after. That would be tough with a red pen in hand.

He's giving my face feathery kisses that *should* be making my body respond. What's wrong with me? I should be thrilled that he wants me so much. I certainly waited long enough for this. I didn't even date when the girls were little. He's my white knight.

I make myself kiss him back, deeply, then use my sultriest voice to warn him, "Just keep it PG13."

5: Maggie

Doing homework's pointless, but if I don't, some teacher could call home tomorrow.

When fall grades came, Mom gave me a pep talk how she understood having to move into such a big school was hard, but I could catch up in summer school, as long as I did better the rest of the year. Didn't tell her I'd rather repeat ninth grade than go to summer school. So I pretended to try harder, but planned on bombing the last few weeks. Now it's not an issue. I'll be gone.

I wonder how much money Lizzie's got. It's in her bottom drawer, in a kitty tin box. A hundred and forty dollars, and she's making more tonight. She's got a little Valentine Whitman Sampler box in there, too.

We used to get those from Mom every year, then use them for treasures—special stones and notes and stuff. Mine are all in storage. I leave Lizzie's alone. It's private.

But she's got a bag of Milky Ways. I love Milky Ways. The bag's open and there's empty wrappers in it. She won't miss one. I eat the bottom off first, then the thin layer of chocolate from the top, so there's just caramel left. Get that stuck up behind my front teeth and suck on it. Wonder how much it'll cost to get ID. Might take awhile, too. Need enough money to get out of town and last 'til I can work. It'd be easy to take Lizzie's.

If I'm thinking of stealing from her, I should take money from *them* first. They won't hafta pay for my food or stuff when I'm gone.

Finish off the cola and open the door a crack. Sabrina's back from Paris. Tiptoe down the hallway and peek around the corner. They're both on the couch, not looking my way. I stand with my back to the wall, breathing slowly for a moment, then straighten up and cross to their room. Wait—no, they're not coming. They didn't see me.

Heart pounding, I look for cash. There's a few coins on top of their dressers. I take some quietly and leave some, too. Don't want them to notice. I check *his* drawers first. Grosses me out to touch his clothing, especially his underwear—move it aside with the tip of one finger. I'd rather steal from him than Mom, but there's nothing but clothes and some cards she's given him.

Mom used to keep emergency money in her underwear drawer. We never bothered it. Hate to take it now, but—there isn't any! They're laughing at the movie. I need to get out of here. Do a quick check of her other drawers. Nothing but clothes, 'til the bottom. No money, but there's a stack of old school spiral notebooks with stiff tan covers. The top one says "Harrisburg, Pennsylvania"—it's a journal she wrote.

On the first page it says she's fourteen. Mom never mentioned any trips when she was a teenager. She was an only child. Our grandparents died before I was born. The only person who ever told us anything about Mom was Aunt Jan, Mom's best friend, but the only stories *she* ever told us were when Mom was little. Of course we were little ourselves then, before Jan married that Italian guy and moved to Europe.

Richard's voice startles me.

"Pause it, would you? I need to use the bathroom."

I close the drawer quiet as I can with shaking hands, then scootch under the bed. Moments later, Richard's feet walk past me, inches away from my face. He closes the bathroom door and I hear him taking a leak. I wriggle out and move into the hallway. I peek down toward the living room—Mom's nowhere in sight. Get back to my room and let out a sigh of relief. That was entirely too close for comfort, and all for a handful of change. No one should hafta live like this.

The journal's still in my hand! No way it's gonna go back in there tonight. I stuff it into my pillow with my own diary, just in case Mom decides to come say good night. Sometimes she does. Then I stretch out on my bunk to wait for Lizzie.

Chip said it's easier to hide in a big city, 'cuz no one notices anyone else, and the cops are busier. He's probably right. Won't stay here in Buffalo, tho'; they might find me. Harrisburg might work. Far enough away, but close enough not to cost too much to get there. It's pretty close to a bunch of other cities, too. If it doesn't work out, it'd be easy to move on to another place. I'll check bus schedules online at school tomorrow. Can't do anything more tonight.

Open the paperback I've been reading at school—always carry one with me now so I look like a loner, not a lonely loser. Chip's the only friend I've got. Never hear from Chandra or my other friends, and I can't call them. I ran up the phone bill in September, so Richard stopped all long distance service. We're the only people I know without cell phones. Mom bought into the brain cancer bit. Can't email, either. The only place I have access to a computer is school, and they block email. Mom's computer died and Richard's is for his use only, in his private cave downstairs. Doesn't matter. I'd end up telling Chandra why I was running away, she'd tell her parents, and they'd tell Mom.

I can't let her know. No matter what, it would hurt her, and I couldn't stand it if she ended up hating me. Better to make a totally clean break.

6: Peg

While Richard's in the bathroom, I take the empty popcorn bowl out to the kitchen. Maggie left everything neat and clean. That's a nice change.

The movie scenes in the harbor town reminded me of the trip the girls and I took to Maine. That was almost two years ago! We spent most of that summer camping. The summer before, we made a major trip out west and camped in the Rockies. Last summer we didn't camp at all until that awful beach trip. A sense of loss washes over me.

Maybe we should go back to Rollin's Pond this year. It was our special summer place when the girls were little, in the middle of the Adirondacks with wolves howling at night. We'd camp on the water, canoe through all the little lakes, read by the campfire at night. Every year we met interesting people, a lot of them from Canada, eh?

We should go to Rollin's this summer, just the three of us. We need to reconnect.

Richard comes up behind me and kisses the back of my neck, then goes to the refrigerator. He won't want us to go without him. The last time the girls and I camped, I ended up in the hospital and he flew down to Rehoboth Beach to take care of me. I'd always had to manage on my own with the girls, no matter what. It felt so good to have someone else take charge and take care of us. But lately, I'm feeling a little claustrophobic with his excessive attentiveness.

"I'm going to have a beer. Want one?" he asks.

"No thanks, I'll pass."

He misses or ignores the concern in my tone. He only drank on weekends, moderately, before he lost his job. In five months it's gotten so he drinks several beers every day and sometimes tequila, too. He's not like my father. I never realized my father was an alcoholic because he never seemed to be drunk.

Richard gets argumentative when he's drinking tequila. I need to talk to him about it, and about my plan to camp with just the girls, but not this weekend. This will be a nice three-day holiday.

Maggie's birthday is Monday. We'll spend some time together as a family, even if it's just playing board games.

Richard and I go back to watch the end of the movie. Harrison Ford's asking his secretary to get tickets to a show. Richard's embrace makes me feel cozy and loved. It's only one beer. I shouldn't fuss at him for that. He *is* an adult. His ardor increases as Harrison Ford unites with Sabrina and the credits roll. I take care of our glasses and then straighten the pillows on the couch while he locks the door.

"What if Lizzie forgot her key?" I ask. "Maybe I should wait up for her. I could get those papers graded."

"She has her key. If she didn't, she could ring the doorbell or come around and knock on our bedroom window." He turns me around and pulls me into his body. "We haven't been married long enough to have separate bedtimes."

Warmth spreads through me in response to his slow, caressing kiss. It *would* be a shame to waste all that couch foreplay.

He nibbles on my neck between words as he says, "Besides, if you stay up, Lizzie will think it's because she's out babysitting. You want her to know you trust her."

He's right. I need to let the girls grow up. If he hadn't sided with Lizzie, I wouldn't let her babysit so much on school nights, but they were right. It hasn't hurt her grades a bit. She's still on the honor roll.

Light kisses on my collarbone are making me tingle now, like they should.

"I guess you're right," I gasp. "I'll just say good night to Maggie."

7: Maggie

Mom pokes her head in my door. "Still up?"

"Yeah."

She tucks the sleeping bag under me and gives me a little pat.

"Want me to turn off the light?" she asks.

"Nah. I'm still reading." I hold out the book for her to see.

"Okay, but lights out as soon as Lizzie gets home."

"Okay."

"Goodnight."

" 'Night."

She shuts the door. That's how it goes now. No more bedtime chats. She didn't even ask me about the book. She won't miss me.

Can't believe how excited we were when she started dating. We got her to try the internet thing. Total role reversal the first time she went out! We watched her get ready, told her she looked great. She actually wore makeup! She'd set it up to meet in a public place and she had a friend there, in case the guy turned out to be a weirdo. But he was just boring. She was about to give up when she met Richard. They were always going out—dancing, movies, ball games, concerts. She was so happy, and at first he seemed okay, but we only met him a few times before they got engaged. The more we saw him, the less we liked him. Mom acts weird around him, like she can't think for herself.

They'll be glad when I'm gone. I really blew it after she got hurt at the beach. We went without *him*—the first time we did anything without him since they started dating. He said he was worried, but he was really ticked that she was going somewhere without him.

Before when we went to Rehoboth, Mom would drive straight through to get more beach time and save money. *He* made her promise to stay in a motel on the way, and they talked on the phone so much, he might as well have been with us. When we finally got camp set up at the beach, things started to get better. Mom was out there body surfing with us and we were having fun. The waves were great.

Then Mom caught one wrong, or it caught her. I heard her scream for help. She was covered in blood, her swimsuit and T-shirt shoved up under her arms, so everyone was staring at my mother's bloody—well, it was really embarrassing. She saw me, pulled the shirt down, and I got it together to warn her another wave was breaking behind her. She managed to keep her feet, then staggered out of the water before the next one. The lifeguards put her on a backboard while Lizzie and me grabbed our beach stuff. Mom talked them into letting us ride in the ambulance. The guy in back asked for a local number to call for someone to help, and when she didn't have one, he said, "What were you thinking, coming down here all alone with your kids?"

Before Richard, my mom woulda told that guy "alone" was the only way we did anything. But she gave him Richard's work number to call, as if she'd done something wrong.

Lizzie and me sat in the waiting room for hours, playing cards and planning how we'd stack up all the air mattresses, so Mom could be more comfortable in the tent. She had a broken nose and a wrenched neck. They were checking that nothing else was hurt. Then right before they decided she could go, Richard got there. He'd talked his way onto a charter flight. He totally took over, took us to a hotel, and made us leave Mom alone to rest. He wouldn't let *us* do *anything* for her, as if it was our fault she got hurt! He got a separate room for Lizzie and me. After Lizzie fell asleep, I went outside for a walk.

It was drizzling and like three in the morning, so I didn't see anyone, 'til this homeless dude came out of nowhere and I screamed so loud he ran away and I ran all the way back to the motel and stood out front, panting. The clerk came out on his break and started talking to me, like it was perfectly normal for me to be out there by myself in the middle of the night. I told him why I was panting and he made me laugh about it. He was smoking a joint and I tried it so he'd think I was cool. Told him all about Mom and Richard. He asked what I was doing to stop them. Told him Mom was too far gone to even try, so he said to convince Richard he didn't wanna get stuck with us kids.

So I tried. Got mouthy. Punched any boy who wouldn't cream me for it, then I'd say they were making sexual comments. Mom had to go to conferences on my behavior, I had to work on "issues" with the counselor, and the boys started avoiding "psycho bitch." I never explained anything to that stupid counselor. She was totally annoying.

Then Mom and me had a big fight one day when we were packing to move, and I went to the creek and got drunk and it was a mess and she hasn't trusted me at all since then. So I know if I tried to tell her what's happened now, she'd think I was lying—either it didn't happen, or it was my fault it happened. She'd end up hating me either way. If I leave without saying anything, maybe she'll miss me a little.

Lizzie's a half hour late. She's supposed to be home from sitting by midnight on school nights. Hope she's okay.

She'll be safe here 'til I send for her. Richard likes her. She's the good girl; I'm the bad girl. He only punishes bad girls. So she'll be okay. I should leave her my diary tho', just in case.

8: Peg

The lovemaking is good.

As we cuddle together afterwards, his breathing deepens. I try to slip out of his embrace unnoticed, but he's immediately awake, laying a guilt trip on me.

"You aren't getting up to work all night, are you?" he asks pitifully.

"No. It's past midnight and Lizzie hasn't come in yet. I was going to call her."

"You'd wake up the kids she's watching."

"Maybe I should get dressed and walk down there."

"You're being ridiculous, sweet pea. She's only a few minutes late, and she'll be mad if you embarrass her by going over there. Come back to bed."

I'm not being ridiculous, but he's probably right that she wouldn't want me to go over there or wake up the children by calling. "I'll just work on my grading until she gets home."

"And make her feel like you have no confidence in her? She's not Maggie. Lizzie's a good, responsible girl."

"I know she is."

"You've got to let her grow up. She doesn't need you to tuck her in like some little kid. She's *babysitting* for little kids."

"I like to be up when she gets home."

"And it doesn't matter that I won't sleep until you come back to bed? Are you *always* going to put them first?" He looks miserable.

I've been just a mother for so long, maybe I don't know how to be a good wife. I slip back into bed. Richard wraps his arm around me and falls asleep again immediately. I can't move. I lie awake, worrying about Lizzie, Maggie, my job, and my marriage.

9: Maggie

My last good day was less than a month ago, when I had strep and Mom stayed home with me and made chicken soup and we played cards all afternoon. If it could be like that—but it can't.

Lizzie finally gets home.

She sees I'm awake and whispers, "Waiting up for me?"

"Yeah, right," I snort. I let her take off her pack, then ask casually, "So, how'd it go? Why're ya so late?"

"The kids were fine. They were ready for bed when I got there. But their parents locked the keys in the car, and didn't realize it 'til they were ready to come home. It took them forever to get the car unlocked with a coat hanger someone gave them."

She puts the new money into her tin. I'm glad I didn't take any of it. She trusts me. Of course, she trusts me not to eat her candy, either. She doesn't notice the missing Milky Way.

"What'd you do all night?" she asks.

"Been reading."

"Okay if I turn off the light?"

Sometimes Lizzie's so nice it gets on my nerves. But I tell her to go ahead and turn off the light. I lie on my bunk in the dark, picking at the wallpaper—scared to leave and scared to stay.

10: Peg

It's almost one when the front door closes.

Lizzie is very quiet. If I hadn't been lying here awake, I wouldn't have heard her. I'd like to find out why she's so late, but I don't want to squabble with Richard again tonight. If I got up to finish my work, I'd probably get to sleep sooner. But he'd wake up and insist he can't sleep without me. So I have to lie here awake instead of getting something done.

Sometimes I feel like crawling right out of my own skin.

I should have insisted on staying up so I could talk to Lizzie. Grades aren't everything. She's hardly ever home anymore. Richard makes me feel unreasonable, but sometimes it's better to follow gut instinct than reason. He's influencing too many of my decisions. I didn't want to sell my house. I grew up there. It was the only link the girls ever had with their grandparents. I liked teaching high school, too.

Getting married was supposed to make things easier. Instead, for the first time since I had the girls, I'm raiding my savings every month to pay the bills. Richard has two mortgages, no savings, and bad credit. With my income alone, we can't refinance, and I haven't gotten my contract renewal for next year. I'm afraid to ask about it because my evaluations haven't been very good. I've been scrambling like a novice all year. It takes a special breed to teach middle school and I don't think I'm one of them. I don't know what we'll do if I lose my job, too.

I should tell Richard I *know* he got fired. He would have gotten a severance package or at least unemployment if his company downsized. But it's obvious he feels awful about it. What's done is done. But did he see it coming? Usually people get warnings and a chance to correct a problem. If he knew his job was in jeopardy in July, he should have said so and moved in with us.

If he'd sold this house, he could have paid off his debts and he'd have had money to start his business, too, whatever it is. I wish he wasn't so secretive about that.

My house was paid off. My paycheck wouldn't be eaten up with mortgages every month. One more person wouldn't make that big a difference. We could be building savings instead of spending them.

If we'd stayed there, I'd still be teaching high school, I'd still have tenure, the girls would still be in a nice small school with the friends they've known all their lives, and we would be in our own home if this marriage fails.

No, I'm not going there.

Before the girls, I was in and out of too many relationships too fast. I'm not that person anymore. I stayed away from men altogether while the girls were little, to give them stability and to focus on having the close kind of relationship that would protect them from the errors I made when I was young. Maybe I should have waited longer, but the girls wanted me to date.

Richard was wonderful when we first met, and when I got hurt. It's hard on a man to lose his job, and he's given up his privacy by having us move in here.

We just need to clear the air, then there's nothing that can't be worked out. He only had one beer tonight, and he'll drink less when our financial issues are resolved. There's really no reason to give up on our marriage. He's very loving and tender, and he is doing his best to be a father to the girls, even when Maggie's been awful.

But she's getting better. The last week or so, she's been polite to both of us, most of the time. I don't know what sparked the change, but after almost a year of outrageous and rude behavior, it's a relief.

I wish I had more private time with her. Lizzie's in my building, so we have opportunities to chat every day. But I hardly ever have a chance to talk with Maggie without Lizzie and/or Richard right there. Maybe I should take her out to lunch this weekend, just the two of us, for a birthday present.

Friday, May 26, 2000

11: Maggie

Today's the day.

I'm the first one up, have been all week. Wear my sweats out to the kitchen—that's what I sleep in anymore.

I pull out a big container of peach yogurt. Dump like two cups into the blender, add as much milk, and hit the blend button.

Mom insisted on keeping our blender. Everything else is *his*.

I pour myself a big glass, leave the rest for Mom and Lizzie, then get out some blueberry bagels and cream cheese. Fix myself one and leave the rest by the toaster, all ready for them.

Want Mom happy with me, so she'll say I can go when I ask her about the 'camping trip' after school.

When Mom's alarm goes off, I'm already done in the shower and drying off. Put my sweats back on and I'm brushing my teeth when she calls "Good Morning" through the door.

Lizzie's awake, but still in bed when I go back to our room.

"Morning," I greet her.

"Morning," she yawns. "How come you're up so early?"

"I dunno. Birds woke me up."

"Babysitting's getting to me, but don't tell Mom!"

"Money hungry! Hey, could I borrow some from you?"

"No."

"Why not? You've got a bundle."

"I'm saving up." She's got a smug little smile on her face.

"What for?" I can tell she's got a secret.

"Remember I was upset we moved here too late to sign up for that trip to Mexico this summer? Well, one of the kids moved away, and I can have her spot. If I earn the money, Mom's gotta let me go."

"I still don't think she'll let you. You're only twelve."

"It's a school trip, I'll be thirteen by the time they leave, it's only two weeks, and I've earned it!"

I can tell she's been practicing this line for Mom's benefit.

I reassure her, "That might work. Good luck."

Now it'll really be lousy to take her money. Wish I'd found some last night. I wait for her to go to the bathroom, then get dressed for school. Maybe I'll make enough from my CDs to leave her cash alone.

12:Peg

"I've already hit the snooze button once."

Richard is nuzzling my neck. I pull away and turn off the morning D.J. "We'll be late if I don't get up right now."

"Fine," he sulks, and he puts his pillow over his head.

He can go back to sleep because he doesn't have to get up and go to work. I do, and I'm tired. I hate starting the day feeling so irritable. I put on my robe and head down the hallway. One of the girls is running water in their bathroom.

"Good morning," I call, trying to shake off my mood.

"Morning," Maggie replies through the door.

In the dining room, my work for school is still spread out across the table. I put everything back into the file box and put my purse on top. I'll have to rush all day.

Breakfast food is out and ready. Maggie must have done that! There is hope! I don't want a bagel this morning. I ate too much popcorn last night and it always bothers me. I just pour myself a yogurt smoothie and take it back to our bathroom. Between sips, I get my clothes ready, turn on the water and let it run to get hot. I finish off my liquid breakfast, then take a quick shower.

When I get out, Richard's still in bed. He's always in the basement with his computer after school, but when does he get up? Some days he's smelled of tequila when we got home. I don't want to spoil the holiday weekend, so I'll wait until next week, then I'll insist on talking through all the issues. I could cut some of the pressure by paying off the second mortgage with my savings, but not until my name is on the deed. This marriage *will* work, but I'm still going to protect myself and the girls. Richard starts snoring while I finish dressing.

Next week, I promise myself, I *will* get some answers, we'll work out the financial issues, and we'll discuss the drinking. If we're going to fight, we may as well get it all over at once. I'll drop the girls off at a movie after school Tuesday so we don't argue in front of them.

I leave the bedroom door open. He should get up, anyway. Lizzie's in the kitchen eating a bagel and drinking her smoothie, but she's still in her pajamas.

"Lizzie," I tell her as I put my cup in the dishwasher, "If you can't get up and going in the morning, you can't babysit on school nights."

"I'll be ready in two minutes." She takes a big bite of bagel.

"Why were you so late last night?"

She answers around the bagel, "They locked the keys in the car. They said to say they were sorry and it won't happen again."

"It better not. Or you won't be there on school nights."

She passes me her cup and heads back to the room she shares with Maggie. As I put her cup in the rack, I hear her shout, "Hey, I gotta get dressed, too!" They got along better when they had their own rooms. Maggie comes in, ready to go.

"Thanks for making the smoothies. Did you eat a bagel?" I ask.

"Yup."

"Good. I was beginning to worry you were going anorexic on me."

"Nah." She grins and grabs my file box. "I'll take this out to the car for you."

"Thanks, honey." I hand her my keys and hold the front door open. "Put my purse up front."

Two years ago, her offer wouldn't have surprised me. Now it's a welcome sign. Maybe we're through the worst of her teenage years!

"Lizzie," I call, "Hurry up! We're running late!"

Richard hates it when we call from one room to another. I don't care. I *want* to wake him up. I really am crabby when I don't get enough sleep. Lizzie comes rushing down the hallway, still zipping up her backpack.

"Did you get all of your homework done last night?"

"Yeah. The kids were ready for bed when I got there."

"Remember, if your grades slip, no more babysitting on school nights."

"Yeah, Mom, you've told me a thousand times. I've got it under control."

She's beginning to sound like Maggie. I lock the house and follow her out to the car. Maggie's in the front seat. Usually she rides in the back because she gets out first. Lizzie surprises me by getting into the car without complaint. She pulls out the MP3 player she bought with her babysitting money.

"You're not supposed to have that at school," I remind her.

"I'll leave it in my pack. Everyone does."

She cranks up the volume and turns away from me. I'll deal with that later. As we head down the street, I try to get some conversation going with Maggie.

"Isn't it a beautiful day?"

"Yeah."

"I'm glad all the snow banks are finally gone."

"Yeah."

"I hated how black they got from all the exhaust."

"Mm-hm," Maggie mumbles her agreement.

"Would you get lunch money out of my purse for everyone?"

"Sure," she replies, picking it up off the floor by her feet. She pulls out my wallet and opens it. "There aren't any ones or change."

"What is there?" I ask as I change lanes.

"A ten and a five."

"That's all?"

"Yep."

"Okay, you take the five and give Lizzie the ten. She can bring me the change after she gets her lunch, in case I want to buy anything."

Maggie gets out at the high school and I drive as quickly as I can through the rushhour traffic, but by the time we get to our school, there's a line inching into the staff parking lot and parents stopped all over the place, letting their kids out to meander across to the school's main entrance. Most of the kids are too busy socializing to watch for teachers trying to park or parents trying to leave.

"This is why I hate being late," I complain, but Lizzie's still listening to her music. I shout sharply, "Put that thing in the back! You are not allowed to have it in school and I do not want you carrying it in your pack!"

"All right! You don't have to yell." She puts it behind her seat. "You *will* cover it up, won't you?"

"Always do. Here, put this back there, too," I say, handing her my purse. "Sorry for shouting; I hate this mess."

Finally, I'm able to get into a parking space. Lizzie's got her door open as soon as I've stopped.

"Maggie gave you the ten?" I ask.

"Yup, I've got it."

"Bring me the change as soon as you're done with lunch. I didn't eat much this morning."

As she gets out of the car Lizzie asks, "Want me to pick anything up for you?"

"No, I may eat out of the machine in the faculty room."

"You'd get mad if I did that."

"I'm not growing."

"You still need to be healthy. There's Serena. I'll see you later."

She slams her door shut and takes off across the lot. I'm not sure I like Serena, but it's tough to make friends when you're the new kid. Especially in middle school.

I get my file box out and pull the cargo cover over Lizzie's MP3 player and my purse. Odd . . . I thought I had a twenty left yesterday.

13: Maggie

Soon as Mom turns the corner, I head across the street. A bunch of people are already waiting to buy my CDs—guess the word spread. The first few go for five apiece. Gotta drop to three bucks on the rest. Get stuck with eight crappy ones. With the twenty from Mom's purse, that's like a hundred and fifty. Don't take time to count it exactly—just fold it up and stuff some into each of my pockets. Can't be late to any classes today. Can't get into any trouble or have any phone calls home. Everything has to go right so Mom'll let me go tonight. Besides, she might miss me a little if I'm being good when I leave.

Morning classes seem to last forever. Chip walks down to lunch with me after third period.

"You set?" he asks, all nerved up like he was the one running away.

"Pretty much. My first period class went to the library, so I got on the computer and checked out bus schedules for different places."

"Know where you're going?"

"Not sure yet. There's a few buses leaving tonight."

"You packed?"

"No. But the pack's under Lizzie's bed and everything's ready to load it up quick. My CDs went kinda cheap."

"How much did you get?"

"About a hundred and fifty. Didn't think I should count it here."

"Good point. You don't want anyone to see you with that much cash. I've got another hundred for you. Told my mom I was buying all the supplies for the 'camping trip' and 'the guys' would reimburse me next week. I'll bring it this afternoon."

"I don't know when I'll be able to pay you back. What'll she say when you don't get the money next week?"

"Don't worry. She'll probably forget. It's money my grandma left for me. I already paid for the computer camp I'm going to this summer, and there's lots left. I just wish I got more out for you."

"Well, that'll make it $250. I can leave Lizzie's money alone."

He shakes his head. "You don't know how long it'll take to get a job, or what else might happen. Take her money. You can always mail it back if you don't need it."

"I guess so." Hope it doesn't ruin her trip.

"My cousin Amy gets off work early today. She'll pick me up right away, so we'll be at your place around five or five thirty."

"Okay. I'm gonna talk to my mom right after school. I'm pretty sure she'll let me go—especially if he's holed up in the basement and doesn't know about it 'til she's said yes—but she'll definitely wanna talk to a parent. Are you sure Amy can pass for your stepmother?"

"Don't worry. She graduated college in drama, and she said she'd have a good story worked out so she doesn't have to pretend to be a bunch older."

"Good." I'd been worrying about that. Mom's not stupid.

"Well, I'm going straight home after school. My dad's really psyched about my camping with the guys like he used to when he was my age. Almost makes me want to do it for real sometime, if I knew any guys who were into camping."

"Whacha gonna do all weekend?"

"Amy's got some awesome video games at her apartment. I'll chill there."

"Okay. See you around five or so."

"Here's my number, in case anything goes wrong."

I give him Richard's, too, then we split up.

If Mom doesn't buy this camping story, I'm gonna hafta sneak out later tonight. That'll be a lot harder to do, but I've gotta get away.

14: Peg

Every spare moment during my morning classes, I grade papers. When the lunch bell rings, I rush students out the door and make a quick trip to the restroom. The papers for my last class still have to be graded. If I get them done during lunch, the afternoon will be less hectic. But when I get back to my room, Lizzie's waiting for me.

"They let you leave the cafeteria with your lunch?" I ask.

"I told the monitor I had to meet with a teacher. I figured you'd need the change right away." Lizzie follows me into the room.

"Is that how you got your food so fast, too?"

"No, the kids told the sub the teacher lets us out before the bell."

"And you didn't tell her that's against the rules?"

"Get real, Mom."

Of course not. She'd look like a teacher's kid.

Lizzie puts her lunch on a student desk near mine, and digs into her pocket. "Here's your change," she says as she puts it on my desk.

"Thanks." I sit down and get out the trail mix I keep in my drawer.

She slides into the student desk and starts unwrapping her sandwich. She's about to take the first bite when she says, "I wanted to talk to you, anyway."

These are words every parent wants to hear, yet also dreads hearing.

"What's up?" I ask casually, putting aside my work.

I pour some of the trail mix onto a napkin while she chews and swallows, then takes a sip of milk. At last she continues.

"I'm worried about Maggie. She hardly ever comes out of our room, and she was really bizarre last night."

"Bizarre?"

"Like wanting to know if you were giving me a ride?"

"To the Petersons? They live right down the street."

"Exactly."

"You know, she was probably confusing them with those other kids you sat for, remember, about a month ago?"

"It was more like she wanted to keep tabs on you. Really weird."

"We've been getting along better the last couple of weeks. Maybe she wants to talk to me or something. I'll ask her after school."

"Don't do that. She'll get ticked off at me."

"I won't say you said anything."

"Okay. In case you haven't noticed, she doesn't even come out of the room to watch TV."

I'd always limited the girls' television. When we first moved, they overdid it with Richard's big screen, but the novelty wore off quickly.

"You're not watching it much anymore, either," I remind her.

"I'm busy with homework and babysitting, and I also do stuff with my friends. Maggie never goes anywhere. She just stays in our room."

"Well, what's she doing when you go in there?"

"Reading, or writing in her diary. Or doing homework."

"She needs to get her grades up. And we all need private time."

"Maybe. I thought I should say something, though. Back when that thing happened at the creek, I felt bad 'cuz I knew she'd been drinking down there before and I never said anything."

"She had?" I try to sound calm, but I'm shocked.

"Yeah. Not much, though."

"At the creek?"

"Last summer, when you were with Richard all the time, Maggie would buy stuff for me with the pool money you gave us, so I'd keep quiet and go to the creek instead. She said they teased her at the pool and it was more fun at the creek. No one hollered at us for running, and there wasn't any chlorine to sting my eyes."

"So she'd been drinking all along?" I feel like I'm strangling.

"Not much, just a little a few times," Lizzie tries to reassure me.

She's probably covering for Maggie again because she can hear how upset I am. The day we were packing to move, Maggie and I had a terrible fight and she took off. A fellow teacher brought her home hours later—puking drunk, making no sense, her wet T-shirt practically transparent. He'd found her down at the creek. Maggie had apparently been making out with a twenty-one year old man when she got angry and clubbed him with a full bottle of beer. I'd thought it was an isolated incident. Apparently I was wrong. Richard's always telling me that what we know is probably only a small piece of what she's been doing.

The bell rings. So much for a calm afternoon.

"Later, Mom." Lizzie gathers her things and leaves quickly.

"Later."

She'll come to my room when her friends have all left school.

I wonder if I should look in Maggie's diary, but I've never invaded the girls' privacy like that. I wouldn't like it if one of them got into my old journals. I don't want them to know half of what I did when I was young. I probably shouldn't keep those notebooks in my dresser, but I keep thinking I'll start to write again and use them for material.

I finish recording grades for my last class as they arrive. When they leave, I lock up and step across the hall. Evan is the only teacher I've really had time to get to know. We both have last period prep. He talks about his students as we walk down to the work room and he watches as I get two Cokes out of the machine.

"Must have been a rough day," he says.

"I'm exhausted. I didn't get all of my work done last night, so I didn't have a spare moment. I need something to keep me awake."

"What happened? Not more trouble with your daughter, I hope."

"No. I just didn't sleep well."

"Anything you want to talk about?" he asks.

I've shared a few of my worries about the girls with him before, and problems with Maggie, but the main thing bothering me last night was my marriage, and I'm not discussing *that* with a male colleague.

"Just a little bit of everything," I tell him.

"How *is* your older daughter?"

"Actually, things are going better the last couple of weeks," I say, my energy suddenly returning. "Maggie even volunteered to carry my box out to the car for me this morning, and sat in the front seat where we could talk. Of course she didn't say much, but at least it felt like we had *some* sort of connection, more than usual, anyway. She spends most of her time at home in her room."

"I hope that's normal. My son does the same thing. We have to pry him out for meals, especially if he's in the middle of a video game."

"But he plays sports, doesn't he?"

"Only wrestling. Once that's over, he doesn't socialize much."

"So you don't worry about him spending so much time alone?"

"Not as long as I know what he's doing. Not every kid is a joiner."

"Ms. Lewis?" a woman interrupts us. Richard's not happy that I use Lewis for work, but it's on my credential and degrees.

"Yes?" I reply.

"I'm the school psychologist. We met last fall?" When I nod she continues, "We have a new student. She'll be in your class next week."

"I'll have to use her transfer grade. We're about to go into review. It wouldn't be fair to test her on the year's work."

"She doesn't have transfer grades. She's had a really tough time. We're having a meeting in ten minutes. Could you possibly be there? I know it's terribly short notice, but everything just fell into place."

"Okay. Where?"

"Conference room one."

"I'll be there."

I spend a few minutes chatting with Evan about his summer plans, then go directly to the meeting.

15: Maggie

There's a close call fifth period. Suddenly the teacher's looking right at me and I know she's asked me a question, but haven't got a clue what it was. The girl behind me whispers the answer and gets me off the hook.

Then, thirty-six minutes before the last bell, I'm called down to the office. One of the girls who bought a bunch of my CDs is sitting in a chair outside the principal's door. I'm told to sit in the chair next to her.

"What's going on?" I whisper.

"Julie's in there. She had her ear buds in. Thought the sub wouldn't notice, but she had the music so loud, he heard it. It's a stupid rule."

"So why're you here? And why me?"

"She must've said she bought them from you, and that I bought some, too."

"It wasn't on school property."

"I'm pretty sure that doesn't matter. They've busted people for smoking over there."

My heart sinks. The principal hates me. He called me in the first week of school to review my history—the stupid stuff I did trying to scare off Richard. He warned me that sort of behavior would get me suspended in his school. They were already married, so there was no point in trying to get rid of Richard, and here no one knew how fast I changed, so they wouldn't call me balloon boobs. Thought I'd be fine.

But right away I got a bunch of tardies to Gym and English 'cuz I'd wait to change in a bathroom stall for some privacy. They suspended me a day for that!

Then some jerk kept bothering me with stupid sexual comments, then one day he pinched my butt and I told him to keep his f-ing hands to himself. Only I said the whole word and the teacher heard me, but didn't see the pinch. With my history, they didn't believe me. He got one day; I got two. That was before Christmas, before Richard got canned or whatever.

Then there was the punch, week before last. The poor kid didn't mean to touch me *there* but he was already on the floor holding his stomach before I realized it was an accident. Got three more days—and that's why I've gotta leave now.

Finally it's my turn.

"Miss Lewis, you have been in and out of this office since you got here," the principal says. "You've been suspended three times. Tardies, language, and less than two weeks ago, for punching another student. Now this."

"I didn't know . . ." I start, but he cuts me off.

"It's in the handbook. Students are not to buy or sell *anything* at school." He's not even looking at me, he's writing.

"We were across the street. I thought that was okay."

"The handbook specifically states school rules encompass all areas within the drug-free zone."

"I didn't mean to break any rules—Please, really I didn't . . ."

"Who else bought them?"

"I don't know their names. I don't know many people here."

"Do you have any left?"

"Yes, sir." I get out my CD carrier and show him.

"Was that full?"

"No."

That's almost a lie. It was almost full. But maybe he'll let me off if he thinks I only sold few.

"How much money did you get?"

"I'm not sure. I spent some of it on lunch already."

He pauses, like he's deciding whether to check for the money or not. If he does, I'm sunk. Then he holds out his hand. "Give me the case. You can have them when your mother comes in and talks to me about this."

He's only taking the CDs. I might have a chance. I politely hand him the case. They're crap, anyway. The good ones sold. As long as he doesn't call Mom today, it'll be okay. I put on my very best responsible voice. "When do you want to see her?"

"I'll call now."

"She's at work." I'm still using my polite voice, but inside I'm screaming *Not today! She can't know I'm in trouble today!*

"Well, I can call your house, then."

"My stepfather is out of town." My heart is pounding with the lie. I want to scream that *he* picked me up the last time, and *you* sent me home with him even though he reeked of tequila. You let me ride home with a drunk, and that's not nearly the worst of it. But I can't say that out loud.

Maybe the principal did notice the tequila last time, because he doesn't try to call home. "I'll call your mother at school, then. She's at the middle school, right?"

I nod miserably and sit in front of his desk, trying not to cry while he picks up the phone.

16: Peg

The new girl is not present at the meeting. Neither is her mother. That doesn't seem right to me, but maybe they couldn't make it.

The woman who asked me to come starts.

"I'm Mary Parker, the school psychologist, and this is Andrea Sills, probation officer for our new student, Rose Carlson."

She has the rest of us introduce ourselves, then she continues, "Rose will be starting Tuesday. She does not have transfer grades, and she'll need some special handling. I'll let Andrea give you the history."

"I like this girl. Her mom's a single parent, working two jobs. At ten, Rose was picked up for curfew violation. She'd taken her little brothers to the playground at midnight, while their mother was at work, because their apartment was too hot to sleep. She was put into a program to prevent juvenile delinquency. Unfortunately, she made the wrong friends. She started drinking. By thirteen, she was sexually active with males in their late teens and early twenties. She got involved with a meth user and then started using herself. Her mother kicked her out and she moved in with the boyfriend. That was last summer. Rose ended up in the emergency room a month ago. Her boyfriend beat her up and she was suicidal. She was admitted to the psych ward, got into counseling, and got clean. Her mother still refuses to have her anywhere near the other children, so we've put her into a group home temporarily."

The psychologist takes over. "Rose wants to finish school. She knows she won't get credit for these weeks. They're to help her adjust better in the fall because she hasn't attended regularly since fifth grade. She'll be tutored over the summer."

I am so lucky I don't have to parent alone anymore. Even if Richard and I disagree sometimes, it's better than not having that second person there to help.

The meeting runs past the last bell. When we're finally done, I go straight to my room. Lizzie's waiting outside my door, impatiently. I leave everything at school. This weekend is for my family.

17: Maggie

Mom still hasn't called back. The secretary at her school doesn't know where she is, so they leave messages on her phone and in her mailbox. The last bell's about to ring and the principal always stands out front while the buses load. He holds out a paper and tells me to have her sign it and bring it back to him Tuesday morning. I won't be admitted into classes until he talks with Mom.

I *can't* back out of leaving, not now. No way am I gonna stay and be suspended. Can't live thru that again.

I stay clear of the principal while I wait for Mom.

It's a three-day weekend. The principal and most of the teachers take off as soon as the buses leave. Hope Mom didn't call him back before he got out of his office. She's later than usual. Everyone but me is gone when she finally pulls up.

"Sorry I'm late," she apologizes. "I was tied up in a meeting."

"That's okay." She must not have gotten the message! Things are starting to go right! Relief makes it easier to sound excited as I ask, "Hey, can I go camping this weekend? Chip's family is going and said he could invite me along."

"Who's Chip?"

"I introduced you a few days ago, Mom, remember?"

"Oh, the skinny kid, Chip like microchip?"

"Yeah."

"I was thinking we could do some things as a family this weekend."

Lizzie helps me out. "I'm babysitting half the weekend, Mom, and Sunday Serena and I have to work on our English presentation."

"Oh." Mom sounds disappointed, even though we haven't hung out together in ages.

"So I can go camping?"

"I need to talk to his parents."

"Knew you'd say that. His stepmother's coming over after work."

"I haven't said yes yet."

"It's *camping*, Mom. We haven't been camping forever."

"I think we should go to Rollin's this summer, just the three of us."

"When?" asks Lizzie anxiously.

"I'm not sure. Maybe as soon as we get out for the summer."

"No," moans Lizzie. "We can't go then, Mom."

"Why not?"

"You know that trip to Mexico my Spanish class is taking?"

"The one you were too late to sign up for?"

"Marissa moved and I can take her place. I know money's a problem, but I've already saved over a hundred dollars from babysitting, and the only real cost is the plane ticket, 'cuz we'll stay in people's homes, and Spanish Club is paying for tours and things. I'll pay for the ticket. Please, you gotta let me go."

"You're only twelve."

"It's a school trip, I'll be thirteen by the time they leave, it's only two weeks, and I've earned it!"

"Did you know about this, Maggie?" Mom asks.

"She told me this morning. She has been working really hard."

"I'll want to know more about the arrangements, who screened the family you'd stay with, who's chaperoning, things like that."

"No problem," says Lizzie, practically bursting. "There's a meeting next week about all that, but they need the ticket money then."

"I'll bring my checkbook. You can pay me back as you earn it, if I decide you can go."

"You are the greatest!" Lizzie exclaims.

"Camping, Mom?" I ask. "I'm not asking to leave the country."

"Where are they going?"

"I forgot to ask, I was so excited. Probably someplace close."

"Monday's your birthday."

"He said they'd be back Monday afternoon."

"I'll meet them, then decide."

"Okay. I love you, Mom."

I do. I just can't stay here, is all. Even if you're really going to Rollin's without *him* this summer.

18: Peg

I stop at the grocery store for milk and eggs and get some granola bars in case I let Maggie go camping. The store is crowded with people stocking up for the holiday weekend, but with the girls having their own plans, I only need a few things. So much for family time.

I'll go into school tomorrow and get my plans done for the rest of the year, with no interruptions. That should only take one good work day, so I pick out a Dean Koontz novel I haven't read before to fill in the rest of the weekend.

At home, the girls carry in groceries and Maggie stays to help put things away. I don't want to spoil her mood, but today's meeting and my conversation with Lizzie are weighing heavily on my mind.

"Maggie," I start, then pause, unsure what to say.

"Yeah, Mom?"

"You know, after that day at the creek, we talked about alcohol, and drugs, and how you can end up in bad situations if you use them."

"We've talked about that stuff a lot of times, Mom."

"Well, I just wanted to remind you, sometimes it's the friends you pick that determines what kinds of things you get into."

"Yeah, peer pressure. You don't hafta worry about that. Chip's the only one I hang with at school, and he's *totally* straight arrow."

"You haven't made any more friends like that group at the creek?"

"No, Mom. And I haven't had *any* alcohol since that day."

"None?"

"Not a drop. Not even New Year's, remember? You made me stay home, and I didn't even ask for a sip."

"Good. I just don't want you to get hurt. So much can go wrong when you're under the influence of drugs or alcohol."

"I know, Mom. You don't need to worry about me."

We hear Richard coming up the basement stairs.

"Got some homework to do before Chip comes."

Maggie's out of the kitchen in a flash.

She's still avoiding Richard and giving him her ice treatment, though at least she's stopped being overtly rude to him most of the time. I need to remember how much he's put up with.

"How was your day?" I ask him, as he goes straight for a beer.

"Pretty good. Still have some more work to do." He twists off the cap and takes a swallow. "What's on the agenda for the weekend?"

"Not much. Lizzie's busy and Maggie might go camping."

"You're not serious!" Richard exclaims. "Camping with who?"

I respond calmly, "The family of a friend at school has invited her to join them. I promised to meet them before making a decision."

"She got suspended for hitting a kid last week!"

"I know, but she admitted she made a mistake. She knows that boy didn't mean to touch her chest. She just didn't realize it fast enough." I'm annoyed by the pleading note in my voice.

"She always has an excuse."

"It's a reason, not an excuse, and she hasn't been in any trouble since she went back to school."

"It's been a week. Of course you should reward her for not getting into trouble for a whole week."

His sarcasm cuts because it's a valid point.

"You're right." My shoulders slump.

"Damned straight I'm right. You're too forgiving with that girl."

He doesn't usually talk to me like this; I'm glad I didn't specify that the friend is a boy. I want to calm him down. He's probably right.

"I'm glad I've had your help since she started acting like this."

"I wish I'd been around to help you before," he agrees. "Maybe she wouldn't have gotten so far out of line."

"She was really easy until she hit puberty."

"You never realized what she was doing."

I'm irritated at the way he's talking to me and the way he's making me doubt myself. Maggie's *my* daughter! I know her better than he does, and I made her a promise.

I assert firmly, "I told her I'd wait until I meet them, then I'll make my decision. I am not going to break my word."

He snorts his disgust. "They'll sucker you into letting her go." He opens the refrigerator again and stands there looking. If Maggie held it open as long, he'd complain. "What's for dinner?" he asks.

"Stir-fry."

"You know I don't like rabbit food. I'll make some nachos." He pulls out the salsa jar and cheese. "I can eat while I work."

I don't try to dissuade him. I don't know what's going on with him, but I'd rather have a peaceful dinner. I definitely don't want Richard talking to Maggie while he's like this. She'd probably mouth off at him and then I *couldn't* let her go. This camping trip may be the best birthday present I can give her.

While he melts the cheese onto a bowl of chips, Richard starts up the conversation again. "I thought you wanted a family weekend for the holiday and Maggie's birthday."

"I did. But camping's a good activity that she's been missing."

"Right. Except when you land in the hospital."

"I always camped with the girls. That's the only time we ended up at a hospital."

"I don't understand why you like it, but if that's what you want to do, we can go sometime this summer."

Oh no, will he ruin Rollin's Pond by insisting on going with us? I have time to deal with that. This argument is about this weekend.

"It's not just camping. Maggie's made a friend and she's been asked to join a family outing."

"You really believe this is an innocent family outing? After what happened at the creek?"

He brings up that incident every time Maggie does anything. I think about my conversation with Lizzie at lunch, and wonder if I *am* being naive. He sees that I'm faltering and he keeps pressing.

"You know she looked and acted like a drunken slut."

He's right. I don't like hearing it, but it is the truth.

With her clothes wet, I realized for the first time how much she'd developed. She definitely wasn't a little girl anymore. Maggie claimed nothing happened, but she was so drunk, would she even remember? She didn't make any sense at all that night. I just put her to bed.

Richard takes my silence as a sign of capitulation and pushes on.

"I hope she doesn't get herself into a situation she can't handle this weekend." He shrugs with a worried look on his face. "Do you know this kid she wants to go camping with?"

"He looks like a nice nerd, and they're friends, nothing else."

"You're letting her go with a *boy?* Peg. Think this through. Her way of dealing with boys, or men, is to flirt, then lash out at them if they respond at all. That's why she hit all those boys at school and that's how she got into that situation at the creek."

I don't like his tone. He's taking a few incidents and making terribly broad judgments from them. And he's drunk. I don't want to argue with a drunk. When I don't respond, he finally gives up.

He gets another beer out of the refrigerator and makes one last dire prediction.

"Just don't ask me to help when she gets knocked up."

I don't take the bait. He can have the last word. I'm done. He sighs as if my stupidity has exasperated him, then he goes back to his office in the basement. I work on dinner. I should probably ask the girls to help, but I want some time to myself to think. Do all married couples argue like this? We've been married less than a year! Could he be right about Maggie? She didn't seem to be flirting with this boy when I saw them at school. Is she really that manipulative? She did get Lizzie to lie about the creek.

I hope I'm not making a mistake if I let her go this weekend.

19: Maggie

When Richard comes upstairs, I leave the kitchen, but stay where I can hear. I knew he'd try to talk Mom out of letting me go! I leave them arguing and slip out front with the portable phone from the living room.

A man's voice on the other end says, "Hello?"

"Is Chip home?"

"Just a minute."

When Chip gets on the phone we talk about school, 'til there's the click of the first line being hung up.

"He's trying to talk her out of it. Can you hurry?"

"Okay, I'll take my stuff out front and say goodbye to my folks, so I can hop in the car as soon as Amy gets here. Thirty minutes maybe?"

"Thanks. Oh, and Monday's my birthday. I told my mom you said we'd be back early enough for dinner."

"Okay."

"And she wants to know where we're going to camp."

"Should I say that Rollin's Pond place you were talking about?"

"It's too far away. Lakeshore State Campground would be good. It's on Lake Erie down by Dunkirk. It's too cold to swim, but we'd look for shells and driftwood and other stuff the winter storms threw up on the beach, and have a bonfire."

"Okay. So, back before dinner on Monday and we're going to have a bonfire at Lakeshore State Campground. I'll let Amy know, so she can sound like it's stuff we do all the time."

"And don't forget, it was a last-minute invitation."

I put the phone back and go to our room.

Lizzie's on her bed reading. I ask what happened to the pack she used for her stuffed animals. At first she doesn't remember, and it's hard not to tell her it's right under her, but finally she leans over the edge of her mattress and pulls it out.

"Mom said you could go?" she asks.

"Not for sure."

I can't pack in front of Lizzie. Can't let her see how much stuff I'm taking, or the dressy clothes. Or her money.

"Hey, wanna play cards?" I ask.

"Sure." She sounds surprised. Guess it *is* a long time since I suggested we do anything together.

She's beating me at Rummy when the doorbell rings.

20: Peg

"Mom! They're here!"

Maggie hasn't sounded this excited in ages. I'm so happy for her.

My smile fades when I see them. She can't be this boy's mother. It's a scam. I want to cry, it hurts so much. Especially after my argument with Richard. He's right again.

"Mom, this is Chip and his mom."

Chip looks safe enough. I knew that from seeing him the other day. His *mom*, however, can't possibly have seen thirty yet. But she's looking right at me and smiling, reaching for my hand.

"I'm so glad to meet you. I'm Sarah Smith. Chip can't stop talking about your daughter."

"Yes, it's a pleasure to meet you. You know, you look very young to be a teenager's mother."

"I'm actually Chip's stepmother."

"His stepmother?"

"Yes, I started sitting for Chip and his sister shortly after their mother passed away. Their father worked so late that the kids would be in bed when he got home. I'd stay and we'd talk about their day. Well, one thing led to another. He proposed when I graduated from college."

She's blushing a little. If this is a lie, she's a good actress. I smile at her. Encouraged, she continues.

"We decided to go last night, and when Chip told us how Maggie's been missing camping, we told him he could invite her. We've got a three-room tent, so the girls will have their own space."

She's so sincere, it's hard not to believe her. I look at Maggie. I'm still not sure this isn't a scam, but I can see that it's important to her. Chip pushes his glasses up with his index finger. If Maggie's been trying to awaken his sexuality, he hasn't noticed. He looks straight at me when he speaks.

"Maggie and I have been talking about Rollin's Pond. We can't go that far for a weekend, so we're going to Lakeshore State Campground down the other side of Dunkirk, on Lake Erie."

"We've been there a few times." I search Maggie's face. "You're sure you'll be back before dinner on Monday? It's Maggie's birthday."

"Definitely," his stepmother answers. "We'll probably be packed up and ready to leave before noon. We'll get her back whatever time you say."

"How about four or four thirty?"

"She'll be back by four."

"Okay, Maggie, you can go. But are you leaving right away? Our dinner's going to be ready in a minute. I was hoping Maggie could eat with us before she takes off for the holiday weekend."

"That's no problem at all," Chip's stepmother says. "We were going to get supplies for the trip. Pancake mix and marshmallows and such. We'll come back in about an hour. Make sure you pack enough for weather changes, Maggie. It might rain."

"I will," she says. "I'll be ready when you get back."

The lightness in Maggie's voice makes me realize I've made the right decision. For the first time in months she sounds happy.

"Lizzie, set the dining room table with the Haviland while Maggie's packing. If we're not going to be together all weekend, at least this meal can be festive."

Using my mother's good dishes is part of what makes it a holiday.

"Where are they?" asks Lizzie.

"In that box out in the garage."

I go into the kitchen and start the last minute preparations for our meal.

21: Maggie

First, I get Lizzie's money.

That makes it over three hundred I zip into the small pocket of my school bag. Pack the clothes next, fast, in case Lizzie or Mom comes in—can't let them see me packing a skirt to go camping! I get my fleece and Mom's poncho out of the hall closet. Won't have room for my winter coat. Can get by without it 'til fall. By then, I'll be working.

Lizzie's there setting the table.

"That's Mom's poncho," she says.

"I know. It might rain this weekend."

Back in the room, the fleece and poncho bring the pack close to full. I check around—remember my diary and dump it out of my pillow. Mom's journal is there, too. I put Mom's journal on top of my clothes, then my school bag, then I close up the big pack. I roll up my sleeping bag, then sit down at the desk.

I rip a page out of my diary and write a note to Lizzie, then put the note and the diary into her money box.

I'm ready.

22: Peg

"You shouldn't let her go." Richard says from the top of the basement stairs, making me jump.

"I didn't hear you come up." His breath reeks. "Is that tequila?"

"It's a holiday weekend."

"You've already had quite a few beers."

"Great. I think you're wrong to let your daughter go off and party all weekend, so you're going to pick a fight with me over tequila."

I shouldn't have said anything. I want to have a nice weekend. "I don't want to fight," I tell him, but tequila makes him argumentative.

"How can you be so naive? After all the lies she's told?"

He's drunk.

"I can't just assume she'll *always* lie to me." My tightly controlled anger shows by the way I clip my words. "It's a family camping trip. It's nice that she's been invited."

"Whatever." He pulls the beer carton out of the refrigerator and heads for the basement. "I'll be downstairs the rest of the night."

I wonder how much tequila he's got down there. This is temporary, a reaction to our financial situation, that's all. When you're married, you work through the hard times together. My parents certainly did.

"Is it safe to come into the kitchen now?" Lizzie asks.

"Of course," I reply, pretending that I don't know what she means. "Give me three plates and I'll serve up the stir-fry."

"Isn't Richard eating?"

"No."

Maggie comes in just as I'm about to call her.

"All packed?" I ask.

"Yup. I'm ready for anything."

"I'll say," Lizzie says. "Mom, she took your poncho out of the hall closet."

"That's okay, but you should have asked, Maggie."

"Lizzie didn't give me a chance. Thanks so much, Mom. This trip's really important to me. I love you. I just need to get away, you know?"

"Of course I understand, I was fifteen once."

Only when I was fifteen, I wasn't living at home. But the girls don't know about that. It was over long before they were born, and there's no extended family to tell them anything. Fortunately, gossip about my reappearance had died out before they were old enough to hear and ask questions, and I never told anyone about those years, not even Jan.

The three of us have a pleasant dinner. Lizzie talks more about Mexico and Maggie tells me more about Chip. He's in her third period class, he's very quiet, a computer geek with few friends, but very nice once you get to know him. As we clean up together, we talk about camping at Rollin's Pond and all the good times we had there, and our camping trips out west, too.

"That lake in Canada was awesome, Mom. And riding out on the glacier . . ." Maggie's enthusiasm is cut off by the doorbell.

"I'll get it," I tell her. "You go get your gear."

Chip is at the door.

He pushes his glasses up again and I feel confident I've made a good decision. Maggie's got her sleeping bag tied onto the top of one of the big framed backpacks we use for camping. It's stuffed. She's ready for anything, alright.

"Got enough for the weekend?" I tease her.

"I've got everything I need. Don't worry about me, Mom."

She gives me a hug and a kiss. It's the first time in ages she's done that without prompting. "I love you, Mom."

"I love you too, honey, be good and be careful."

Lizzie and I wave until they're out of sight.

23: Maggie

I stop waving when we turn the corner.

Chip's in the front and I'm riding alone in the back of the little red car. My pack's next to me, with the sleeping bag on top, jammed up against the ceiling.

"Maggie, this is my cousin, Amy. Amy, this is Maggie."

"You told my mom your name's Sarah."

"I'm over twenty-one. Don't want to get into trouble."

"Thanks for helping me."

"It's okay. Like my story?"

"Practically believed you myself."

"Thanks. Chip says you want to go to the bus depot downtown?"

"Yes, please."

"Did you decide where you're going?" Chip asks.

"Pittsburgh, to start. But say you don't know what bus I took."

"Not a problem," says Amy. "Why Pittsburgh?"

Actually, it's Harrisburg, but I never mentioned that to Chip and it's better if they *really* don't know where I'm going.

"Why Pittsburgh?" echoes Chip.

"We've been there before, so I know my way around a little."

"You don't have family there, do you?"

"No, we went there a few times 'cuz they have great museums."

"Do you have enough money?" Amy asks.

"Oh, yeah," says Chip. "I almost forgot to give you the hundred."

He hands me a neat stack of twenty dollar bills. I tuck them into my back pocket and thank him.

"That won't last long, especially buying a bus ticket," Amy warns me. "I know, I live on my own."

"I've got over three hundred more—sold most of my CDs this morning and stole my kid sister's babysitting money."

"Will she be okay with your stepfather?" Amy asks.

"You told her?" I accuse Chip.

"I had to, so she'd help."

"Don't worry," Amy reassures me, "I'm not going to tell anyone, but do you think he'll bother your kid sister?"

"I don't think so. But I left her a note and my diary just in case. Put them in the box where she keeps her money."

"When do you think she'll find them?"

"Probably later tonight, when she gets home from babysitting."

"When's your bus leave?"

"Not sure exactly, but I need to be there before seven thirty."

Amy stops asking questions and concentrates on driving. It's the Friday night of a holiday weekend, so traffic's really bad.

"What if they think you're too young to ride alone?" Chip asks.

"You only gotta be fifteen."

"How can you prove it?"

"She won't have any problem, Chip. She looks older," Amy says. "They'll assume she's at *least* fifteen, unless she acts like a kid."

"Did you have any trouble getting your stuff packed without anyone getting suspicious?" Chip asks.

"Mom had Lizzie set the table while I packed, so it was easy."

"What about *him*?"

"They were arguing about whether I should go—that's why I called you. But I musta missed something, 'cuz he gave up and went back downstairs to his office."

"Chip," Amy interrupts, "I need you to give me those directions you got off the internet. I'm not used to driving downtown, and there's a bunch of one-way streets."

"Okay."

Chip reads off one instruction at a time, and we find our way to the bus station.

"I don't know where to park," Amy says. "It's already after seven."

"That's okay, let me out at the corner. I need to get my ticket."

"Are you sure?"

She sounds worried, and I know why. Everything's rundown and dirty, with weird-looking people around. There's an old woman with a shopping cart filled with garbage bags.

"I'll go straight into the bus station," I say. Wanna sound confident, but I'm a small-town hick. I thought the 'burbs were city, and they're not even close to this.

Amy pulls as far right as she can at the corner. "You could crash at my place."

"No, thanks. They'd find me and you'd get into trouble." I pull my gear out of the back. "Thanks for all your help, Chip. I'll send you the money soon as I can."

"Don't sweat it."

"Be safe," says Amy.

The truck behind them honks. I close the door, step up onto the sidewalk, and watch Amy drive away. The little red car turns a corner, and I'm on my own.

24: Peg

Lizzie and I clean up the kitchen after Maggie leaves.

"How about a game of cribbage?" I ask her.

"Nah, gotta get my math done. I'm babysitting at eight thirty."

"Okay."

I'm disappointed, but she's being responsible, so I can hardly complain. I curl up on the couch with the paperback I picked up at the store this afternoon. Richard comes up to the kitchen. *Now* he's hungry. His movements sound clumsy. He's *never* gotten this drunk before.

My father drank beer daily, a lot of beer, but it never showed. He was always an affable guy. Of course, his drinking was the reason he had trouble supporting us and why house repairs ended up half-finished or poorly done. When I was little he'd take me along to get supplies and that always included a case of beer. He'd say, "This'll be a thirsty job." But he never got argumentative like Richard does. In fact, I only heard my parents argue once.

I don't want to deal with Richard right now, so I stay on the couch and read. I'm well into the story when Lizzie comes into the room.

"Hey Mom, I'm going over to Peterson's now."

"What on earth do they do every night?"

"They bowl and stuff. Last night they waited 'til the kids were in bed, then went to a late movie. Tonight they said something about dance lessons. Some club has free lessons before they open for regular business? Something like that."

"Have your key?"

"Right here." Lizzie pats her pocket.

"Okay. See you later."

I ignore Richard when he comes through on his way to the bedroom a little later. He's walking with his hand on the wall. The drinking's definitely got to stop before it gets any worse.

25: Maggie

The bus station's crowded for the holiday weekend. I get into the ticket line right away.

"Destination?"

"Harrisburg, Pennsylvania."

"That will be the 273, departing at 7:50, with a transfer in Syracuse to the 9002. Round trip or one way?"

"One way."

"That'll be eighty dollars and twenty-five cents."

I give her all the twenties Chip gave me. That leaves me with more change for machines. She keeps talking while she prepares the ticket.

"You'll have to store your luggage under the bus. That pack won't fit in the overhead rack. You need to fill out this claim ticket and tag with the address you're going to, so we can get the bag to you if it doesn't make the transfer."

"Does that happen very often?"

"Not if you move it yourself."

"Okay, thanks."

I make up 123 Second Street, Harrisburg for an address, and Linda Smith for my name. There's a Second Street in almost every town. Just hope they don't ask for ID to get the bag back.

The lady takes the claim ticket, keeps the original, and gives me a copy. Then she tells me to turn around. "I'll stick the tag onto your pack for you. Make sure you keep your claim ticket."

"Thank you."

"You're welcome. They'll start loading luggage in ten minutes or so. Next?"

I hike over to a bench and stand with my back to it. With my knees bent, the pack rests right on the seat. I can slide off the straps and tilt it against the back of the bench.

It feels good to have the weight off my shoulders, and it was only on a few minutes. Gotta get used to carrying it.

For now, I pull out my school pack and put everything for the ride into it, then make sure all the zippers are shut on both packs. Sleeping bag's strapped tight onto the big one.

I don't look at anyone 'cuz I don't want them looking at me. Hope the ticket lady won't remember me. Spot some snack machines and decide to stock up—I forgot to pack the granola bars Mom bought! I was too jazzed to eat much dinner, either, and the trip will take all night. I put on the big pack again—don't dare walk away from it—and carry the little one by the strap.

I get a couple cans of pop, then move on to the chip machine. Push the wrong button and get salsa chips. I hate salsa chips. There's an old homeless dude in a knit hat over by the drink machine, checking to see if there's anything in the change return.

"Hey, you want these?" I ask him, holding up the chips.

He looks me over, then comes and takes the chips.

"Thanks," he grunts.

"No problem."

He peers at me like a bird watcher observing a specimen.

"Runaway." He nods. He's talking to himself, not me, but it's scary for him to peg me like that.

"How can you tell?" I ask.

He shrugs. "Can't. You just told me."

He tricked me into saying I'm a runaway! Didn't think I was that dumb. Now I'm really scared. I can't get caught. I can't go back there.

"You gonna tell them?" I ask, nodding towards the ticket counter.

"Problems at home?"

"Yeah. My stepfather."

"Most people don't leave unless there's a reason."

We look each other in the eye, measuring each other up. I decide he's not gonna tell on me. He decides to help me.

"You need to know your story," he says.

"Huh?"

He shakes his head like I'm mentally challenged. "Make it up."

"You mean I should make up my whole life story?"

He nods.

"Do you think I can pass for a college student?"

He looks at me closely. It takes forever, then he nods again.

"Okay. I'm a freshman at Buffalo State, no, just State. Fredonia if they ask where."

"Right. Know where you're going. Don't lie, but be general."

"Pennsylvania."

He nods and smiles. "Why?" Then he shuffles away.

Get the chips I want, then sit and think about my story. Still haven't figured out the details when they announce my bus is ready to load luggage. I stop at a candy machine for a Snickers. The machine takes my money and gives me nothing. The old dude comes over, runs his hand over the side of the machine, picks his spot, then slams the heel of his hand against it. The coins drop. So do two candy bars. He gets them out and hands me one.

His hands are surprisingly clean. I take it and head outside.

The driver's stowing other stuff in the compartment under the bus. Finally, he checks my ticket and the tag on my pack, then slings it in so it slides 'til it runs into everything else. Hope my sleeping bag doesn't get messed up. So far it's still rolled tight.

"I gotta transfer in Syracuse," I say.

"That's a twenty minute layover. I wake everyone up. Have your claim ticket ready and you can transfer your own bag. I'll pull it out for you."

He sounds like a recording. I get onto the bus. It's pretty full. I find a spot next to a woman who's asleep against the window, even tho' it's still light out.

Wonder when they'll find the note. I hope Lizzie doesn't show Mom the diary unless she has to—hope Richard leaves her alone.

Suddenly I feel totally empty. I blink a few times, then pull out my paperback, a stupid little romance. You know everything is gonna turn out right in the end. Not real at all. Still, it might work for my cover story. I'll read it while there's enough light.

26: Peg

After hours of being lost in Koontz' story, I need to get up and stretch. I find Richard sprawled out on top of our covers, still dressed, snoring loudly. He always says he can't sleep without me beside him. With enough tequila, he can!

I throw a blanket over him, then go back to the couch and try to read, but find myself thinking about Maggie and how important this camping trip seemed to be to her. I try to figure out when and how we got so disconnected. The girls and I were always a team. We did everything together. They helped around the house, we painted their rooms together. I was soccer mom when they played.

I don't know if things changed because I started dating, or because the girls were growing up. Maybe a combination. They were the ones who pushed me to sign up for the online dating service. Richard and I dated for months before I was sure it was serious enough to introduce him to the girls. They seemed to like him. They didn't care much for the baseball game he took us to, but that wasn't a reflection on him.

Moving and changing schools last August was definitely hard, but Maggie had started acting out before that, and Lizzie said they were sneaking down to the creek all summer. There was that nice boy who took them bowling and to movies a few times. I can't remember his name; I'll ask Lizzie what happened.

I can't settle my mind down to read. I make myself a cup of tea, put on a jacket, and go sit in the back yard. Even with the city lights, I can see some stars. I miss camping, too.

27: Maggie

It's totally dark before I finish skimming the novel. It's not holding my interest and it wouldn't work for a cover story. Shoulda brought Mom's journal to read. It's in the bag stowed away below.

The bus is hot—already finished both cans of pop. I head back to the toilet, but it stinks from three rows away. Decide I can hold it.

I close my eyes and lean back. The woman in the seat next to me is still sleeping.

I'll be a freshman at college. No, that doesn't work. I'd have college ID. For that matter, I should have a driver's license. What makes sense is to wait 'til I get some ID, then that's who I'll be. In movies, there's always some guy who takes care of all that—wonder how to find one of them?

I musta fallen asleep.

"Syracuse. Twenty minutes. Transfers, make sure you have your claim ticket ready if you have baggage below."

It's after eleven. I leave the stupid novel on my seat. Maybe someone else will like it. There's no problem getting my luggage, just hold out the claim ticket. The sleeping bag's starting to unroll, so I tighten it up before I hand it over at my next bus. I ask that guy if there's still time to use the restroom in the station.

"Sure. Eight minutes. Don't be late, though. I don't wait."

I walk to the bathroom. If I ran, I'd wet myself. When I'm done, the driver's still standing by the bus, so I grab more pop from a machine. Show my ticket and board, and get lucky! One spot's left with two seats open. I take the window seat, lean up against the glass, and close my eyes. Won't get to Harrisburg 'til morning. May as well sleep.

28: Peg

Lizzie's home before midnight.

"How'd it go?" I ask.

"Okay. They were in bed when I got there."

"You smell like smoke."

"Yeah, Mr. Peterson walked me home tonight and he was smoking. He said Mrs. Peterson thinks he's quit, but he still needs one once in awhile." She yawns.

I should let her get to bed, but I want to ask before I forget.

"Lizzie, what ever happened to that boy who used to take you and Maggie bowling and to the movies?"

"John? The last time I saw him he was at the creek with his new girlfriend."

"Maggie wasn't really dating him. You always went with them."

"They used to make out all the time." Lizzie shrugs.

"What do you mean by making out?"

"They'd hold hands after we left the house, and he'd come over when they thought I was asleep and kiss and stuff on the couch."

"Why didn't you tell me?"

"They weren't doing anything extreme, and when you were out with Richard I kinda liked having John there. It felt safer." She yawns again. "'Night."

"Good night, honey."

What else have I missed? Maybe Maggie *does* only relate to boys sexually. But Chip's nothing like John. I knew there was chemistry with John and Maggie. That's why I insisted they include Lizzie, and always in the afternoon. Except when he was sneaking back to the house, apparently. I wonder if Lizzie really knows how far it went. I wish I felt better about Chip's stepmother. But Chip himself? No, Maggie's not having a sexual relationship with Chip. I'm sure of that. They're camping with his family, that's all.

Richard's snoring. He doesn't wake up when I roll him up onto his side. It takes awhile for me to get to sleep. I hope Maggie's having a good time.

Saturday, May 27, 2000

29: Maggie

The bus stops at a lot of little places.

I finally get used to it. The driver announces we're in Scranton and I go right back to sleep 'til someone sits down next to me. I jerk awake.

"Sorry, I was trying not to bother you," he whispers.

"That's okay," I mutter.

I close my eyes again and pretend to go back to sleep, but check him out through my eyelashes. There's a little light on him from the station, then from the streetlights as we drive out of town.

Studs, leather, chains, lip pierced, ear towards me pierced at least three times—total punk.

I hold onto my pack tighter. Most of my money's in there.

He notices me doing that.

"I'm not gonna jack your stuff," he says. His voice is hushed. Most of the passengers are sleeping.

I open my eyes a little, but don't ease the hold on my bag.

"Seriously, chill," he says. "Where're you headed?"

"Pennsylvania."

"This *is* Pennsylvania. I get off in Pine Grove. What about you?"

"Harrisburg."

"My dad's a prof at Pine Grove. Why Harrisburg?"

I panic—wasn't supposed to name the city and I don't have a story. "My mom lived in Harrisburg" pops out loud enough to get a glare from the guy across the aisle.

The punk waits until the guy settles with his eyes closed again. "So why are you going there?"

"To see it, maybe feel a little closer to her."

"You sound like she died."

"Yeah."

I've never been a good liar, but this is so far out there that it's more like make-believe. Mom and Lizzie and me used to make up all kinds of stories when we were on road trips. One of us would start it, then pass it on, and the third person had to come up with the ending. When he tells me he's sorry about my mother, I sigh and keep going.

"Yeah, I never knew her. I was adopted. It took years to track her down, then I found out she died when I was a baby. Couldn't find any other family, and she never told anyone who my father was."

Keep it simple. And quiet.

"How about your folks? The ones who adopted you?"

"Oh, they totally supported my looking for my birth mother."

"So where do they live?"

Now what? I don't wanna make up where I'm from, too, that's too much to remember. So, "They were killed in a car crash, a few weeks after I found out about my birth mother."

"Both of them?"

I nod and try to look like I'm fighting off tears. "Instantly. Wiped out by a semi."

"Whoa. That's tough. How long ago?"

"Last summer. Christmas really got to me. Couldn't stand college or my job, so I saved up, quit, and got on the bus."

I'm tough.

"So you don't know anyone in Harrisburg?" he asks.

"No." Back to reality.

"Where you gonna stay?"

"Gotta keep it cheap. I was thinking I might camp in a park or something."

"The police'll probably hassle you. It'd be easier to find someone who'll let you crash at their place."

"I never did anything like that. This is the first time I've traveled alone."

"Well, when you get into the bus station, head on over to the river. There's a park all along it where people go to chill. Talk to people there. Someone will help you out."

He made it sound so easy. "You've been there?"

"When I was a kid, I went down to Harrisburg with my dad a lot. He says you used to be able to crash out on City Island when he was in college, but it's all built up and everything now, so they probably patrol it too much to do that anymore."

"Thanks. I'll try talking to people."

"If you don't score a room down at the river, try HACC, that's the community college. It's on the main bus routes. The International House and Temple U are right downtown, but that's older students and Penn State's campus is way out."

"Does HACC have dorms?"

"I'm not sure, but I know there's apartments with lots of students living in them. Some of my dad's students transfer from there."

"Great. Thanks." I shift the conversation to him. "So, you're on your way home?"

"No, I live with my mom. I can't hack being with my dad for more than a few days. He was a hippie back in the day, now he's all uptight and embarrassed by the way I look. Like he's gonna get fired 'cuz I'm not prep."

"It sucks when parents change."

"Yeah," he agrees. "My mom gets a kick out of the way I dress and act, and she actually listens to punk once in awhile."

He goes on about punk music 'til I drift off, still clutching my pack, despite his insisting he wouldn't take it. It moves and my eyes pop open. It's okay. It's just one of his chains catching on a strap. He gets untangled and says goodbye. It's forty more minutes to Harrisburg. There's water on the windows and puddles spray the bottom of the bus.

I wonder if they know I'm gone.

I don't go back to sleep. We get into Harrisburg like five thirty in the morning. It's raining and dark. There's a forty-five minute layover, but the driver tells people to be back in half an hour. Says he's running late 'cuz of the rain. My pack's the last luggage he pulls out of the bus. The sleeping bag stayed on better this time.

"Looks like your ride's late," he says.

We're the only people around, except for some homeless old lady with the usual shopping cart full of garbage bags.

"He can't get here 'til seven," I say. Lying is getting easier. "Know a good cheap place to eat while I wait?"

He suggests a little place that sells omelets, less than a block away.

"It's not the nicest looking place, but the food's good and the prices are pretty reasonable."

I go into the station first to use the restroom. Take the handicap stall so there's room for both packs. Good thing the big one's got a frame—the floor's nasty. The smaller pack gets looped over one end of the sleeping bag. After, I wash my hands with both packs slung onto one shoulder. Gotta lean to the opposite side for balance. I walk that way out into the waiting area and put them down on the nearest bench to reorganize. Gonna stow the little pack for now. Things I wanna be able to reach go into the outside pockets of the big pack and the map from the internet goes into my fleece pocket. It's not very good, but it shows the way to the river. Once everything's set, I put the frame on the edge of the bench— makes it easier to slip into the straps. With the hip belt tight, it's still heavy, but I can handle it. Mom's orange poncho goes over everything—pack and me.

There are pamphlets at the counter, maps of the local bus routes. No good for walking, but I keep one for the route from City Island to HACC, the community college. Good thing that punk told me what HACC means.

It's trying to get light out, but with the rain, it's still pretty dim as I look for the omelet place. There's more homeless people, heading for the bus station. Hours on the door said it's open from five thirty in the morning to midnight. A dry place to stay during the day.

The restaurant is open and it's like at least half full. Hope that means the food is good. Might be the only place to eat this early. The waitress takes a look at my pack.

"Traveling, eh?"

"Bus driver said you have good omelets."

"That'd be Gus. I'll put you in a booth. You want coffee?"

"Do you have herbal tea?"

"Sure. Peppermint, lemon, or cinnamon apple?"

"Lemon, please."

She puts a menu on the table and goes for my tea. The poncho and pack go on one bench. I sit on the other side and roll my head and shoulders—didn't even walk that far and it's a relief to get the weight off. I definitely have to toughen up.

Out of ten omelets on the menu, I pick the one with veggies and cheese. Mom used to make omelets like that on weekends, before *he* came into the picture.

Hope she doesn't worry about me too much. As long as she misses me *some*.

"Sorry for taking so long," the waitress apologizes. "Here's your tea. A lot of the people from the art festival are eating here."

"The art festival?"

"It's one of the biggest in the country, three days. Front Street was closed down yesterday so they could set up."

"Like crafts and things?"

She nods. "It's all really good stuff. And they have music on two stages, and films being shown, too. There's fliers by the door."

She takes my order and helps another customer.

I get one of the fliers to see what's going on. The festival's along the river, all the way from Market Street to Forster Street.

According to my map, that's between two of the bridges that cross the Susquehanna—Market St. Bridge and M. Harvey Taylor Memorial Bridge. It starts in like three hours and goes all weekend. Hope I can still find a place to stay.

The waitress comes back with my omelet.

I tell her I'm gonna go to the art festival and ask if it's okay to sit here and read for a couple hours, 'til it'll open. It's still raining.

"Keep your tea going and the manager won't care, unless we get busy."

"Thanks." I smile, then pull Mom's journal out of my pack.

30: Maggie Reads Peg's Journal

Mom's journal is a spiral notebook, so it folds open to the first page. I make sure the table is clean and dry, then set it down to read while I eat my omelet.

Journal: Christmas 1971

Most of this house is older than I am – clean, but old – worn carpeting, patched wallpaper, ancient kitchen appliances. Mom doesn't care. She lives in her garden.

When Dad fixes anything, Mom repairs his repairs while he's at work. Before I was born, she hung baby animal wallpaper in my room. I got stuck with those little critters until I was ten. Then Mom finally let me paint my room pink and we bought café curtains with tiny purple flowers. She thought we should get the pink ones, but once she saw them on my windows, she decided the color mix looked good. It's kind of little girlish for me now I'm in high school, but at least it's not baby animals.

I have to convince Mom to let me go away to college. Northwestern is the best for journalism, but American University would help me get into a Foreign Service job, something where I'd get to travel and live in amazing places. She keeps saying how nice it is I can live at home while I go to Fredonia State. If she makes me do that, my life will be as boring as hers!

She did end up with a boring life, though. Until Richard, we still lived in the house where Mom grew up. And she's never traveled except for our camping trips. I've never seen her writing, either.

I keep reading—her mother got her underwear and school supplies for Christmas! I used to wish we had grandparents, but maybe we didn't miss much. Then she talks about her best friend Jan. I'm sure that's the Aunt Jan who babysat for us when I was little. I wish she hadn't married that Italian guy. She wouldn't have let Mom marry Richard.

Mom's first kiss was in the middle of a game of Twister.

December 28, 1971

That really was my first kiss. When everyone else had left, I told Jan and said it hadn't done a thing for me, that I thought it was gross, that his mouth was partway open and slobbery with spit. She laughed and said kissing doesn't count until you French.

She realized I didn't understand what she was talking about, so she explained that you actually kiss with your mouths open and do stuff with your tongues. She laughed at the look on my face and said I'll like it when it happens.

Wow. Mom's always been like a nun, but she didn't know *anything*. I keep reading while I eat. Mom was as boy crazy as I used to be. She tried to rationalize talking about boys so much.

January 12, 1972

Relationships are at the core of our existence, aren't they? Most successful men are married to smart, supportive women. So, as a woman, I need to find a smart, supportive man to be successful in my career.

When I was a kid, I'd sneak out of bed and make her cocoa. She never got mad. She'd smile and give me a thank you hug and tell me to go get some sleep. Most of the time she was grading papers. I wonder if she was writing sometimes.

The end of January, Jan got her license and she talked Mom into covering for her so they could go up to Fredonia to the college all the time. That's like twenty miles away! Mom was fourteen and not even supposed to be dating, and she was hanging out at the college!

Thought I was bad going to the creek with Lizzie. Some of those people were pretty old, but at least we were in the same town.

"How's the omelet?" asks the waitress.

"It's good."

The omelet reminds me of Mom more than this journal now.

Jan's boyfriend got his roommate Brian to hang out with Mom all the time so he and Jan could have time alone. Sounds like Jan wasn't doing it, either, but was thinking about it. Brian gave Mom a rose he picked on campus and she went off the deep end writing about how many kids they should have, then she turned around and worried that she wasn't ready to settle down, that she wanted to travel and everything. No duh! She was only fourteen.

So bizarre. If they were doing it, maybe, but it sounds like they were just going to movies and stuff together.

February 15, 1972

Susan threw it off so casually, "My mom's on the pill," like wouldn't everyone's mother be on the pill? I'm sure mine isn't. My parents never touch. I can't imagine them ever having sex. When I was little, I saw two dogs locked together and Jan told me that was to make puppies. I know it's not exactly the same with people, but still, it has to be even grosser than French kissing, and it definitely requires touching.

Boys talk like sex is all they think about, but why would a woman want something shoved inside her? To have children, I guess, but then the pill makes no sense. Unless married women are expected to let their husbands do that even if they don't want more children. But Jan makes it sound like women actually want sex too?

Maybe there's something wrong with me.

Clueless. Definitely not having sex.

She keeps wondering about stuff like that. Then Brian gets her a ticket to a concert and they actually kiss.

March 10, 1972

*On the way back to the dorm, we stopped in the Grove and Brian kissed me!!! It was French, and it **wasn't** gross! Not the least bit of slobber! We walked a little way, then he pulled me into a hug and kissed me again and I kissed him and we kissed for ages.*

I am definitely normal!

But Jan's mad at Steve. So now I'm in love but I don't know if I'll ever see Brian again. I can't even call him or write because I don't know how they get mail, and it's just a payphone in the hall there. And it's long distance, so if I had the number I couldn't call from home.

Poor Mom! Finally got a good kiss, and then she got cut off! I know how that feels. Richard took long distance off his phone after we moved in, and Mom doesn't like cell phones. We had internet, but Mom's computer got dropped when we were moving and school won't let us do email there, so I lost contact with all my friends. I'd already broken up with John, anyway.

When Mom was dating Richard and staying late, John would come over after Lizzie fell asleep and we'd make out for hours on the couch. We got really hot, but I never let him get my clothes off. He never pushed for it, either. Said he *liked* teasing each other. Then I caught him making out with a slut everyone knows about. That was the end of that.

I go back to reading. Mom finally called Jan's boyfriend and got them to talk on the phone, but they couldn't see the guys before Easter vacation. Her mother got her a job tying grapes over the break. Seems like her mother started connecting better with her.

I give the waitress my empty plate and ask for another cup of tea. It's still pouring outside. They're not too busy, so my sitting here reading's not a problem. Wish we hadn't moved. Maybe I coulda tied grapes this year. Coulda left Lizzie's money alone. Of course, I never woulda gotten suspended there, either, so I wouldn't be running away.

I wonder if they've figured out that I'm not coming back.

31: Peg

Richard's snoring beside me. I'm still tired. I try to go back to sleep, but my mind won't let me. What if that day Maggie came home so drunk wasn't the only time she went to the creek without Lizzie? What if someone got her drunk and took her virginity? Would she tell me? Or would she hide it? Could that be why she's been so aggressive with boys? She *might* be learning to use her sexuality manipulatively, if something like that happened. I have to get her to open up and talk with me. Maybe it's time to tell her about my past, but will she learn from it or use it as an excuse to do whatever she wants?

I'm not going to get any more sleep. I may as well get up and start the day. I manage to slip out of bed without waking Richard. He snorts, rolls onto his side, and stops snoring. I'm not going to tell him that I'm having second thoughts about Maggie's camping. It could be innocent. I'll make some private time to talk with her this week.

The house is quiet. I make some coffee, then sit by the window, holding the cup in both hands, warming them as I look out at the yard. It's pretty barren. I miss my mother's rose garden. She was a wonderful gardener. My parent's marriage is the only one I have to measure how things are going with Richard and me. As a child, I never realized my father was an alcoholic, but my mother stayed with him, through that and more. I don't think Richard's an alcoholic, but it scares me that he may be headed that way and that drinking makes him so irritable.

I need someone to talk to, to help me sort things out. Not Evan. And I've lost touch with Jan. After she moved to Rome, her life went such a different direction that we gradually quit emailing, and I lost all my addresses when we disconnected from our server. There was so much going on, I didn't think to write them down.

I could probably find Jan, but for now I'm on my own, as usual.

Lizzie comes out to the kitchen. She's already dressed.

"Hey, Mom."

"Good morning."

"Richard sleeping?"

I nod.

"Can we go out to breakfast, then?" she asks.

It would be cheaper to eat at home, but I'd enjoy having an outing with Lizzie. It's nice she's suggesting it. I used to take the girls out more often.

"Okay. Where do you want to go?"

"Denny's, I guess."

There's no wait. The waitress puts us in a booth and gives us our plastic menus. It doesn't take long to decide which picture we want.

"These chains are pretty much the same, aren't they?" I comment when the waitress has left with our order.

"Yeah. I miss The Diner. They were always so nice to us, even when Maggie and I went by ourselves. They have *the* best milkshakes."

"Did you know your grandmother worked at The Diner?"

"No way."

"Yes, she did. At first she didn't let us know . . . she only worked while I was at school. She even got me a job over spring break so I wouldn't find out."

"Why?"

"She knew my father wouldn't like it. He was supposed to be the breadwinner."

"That's dumb. How'd he find out? Did he see her working?"

"No. She had to tell him because she needed to go in earlier. He never went to The Diner. He said he'd gotten sick from a meal there and would never go back."

"Really?"

"Well," I pause. She never knew either of them. The truth won't hurt. "Actually, he was a wonderful father, but too charming for his own good. He avoided The Diner because he'd had an affair with the woman who owned it."

"Louise? That old lady?" Lizzie chokes out a laugh.

"Well, she wasn't an old lady then."

"Did your mother know?"

"Yes."

"How could she work there, and why would Louise hire her?"

"The affair was over, but it wasn't the *only* one. Mom told me about it after Dad died. Louise felt like he'd cheated on her, too. So, when Dad's business started sliding and we needed money, she gave Mom a job."

"That must've sucked. How'd your mom stand it?"

"There were bills to pay. But in the end she and Louise became friends."

"Your parents still stayed together?"

"Yes. Mom knew about his philandering for years before she said anything. Then when she did, they made up right away. Mom said he stopped running around then."

When our meals come, the conversation reverts to simple comments on the food, until Lizzie finishes.

She asks, "Was your mom home when you were little?"

"Yes, but she was always in her garden. Jan and I did our best to stay clear."

"Aunt Jan is pretty cool. I miss her brownies."

"I was so happy when she agreed to babysit for you girls when you were little. I never had to worry about you while I was working or going to school."

"Did she always watch us?"

"Pretty much. I started teaching right before Maggie was born. I stayed home with her until the fall, then Jan took over."

"You were married, right?"

"Yes, you know that."

"Well, what was he doing?"

"Tom was going to school."

"Was Tom my father, too?"

The question startles me. "Of course."

Lizzie's lips purse bitterly, like my mother's used to when she was upset. "You said he died before I was born, after the divorce. So if he really was my father, why did you get divorced when you were pregnant with me?"

When I told her that, I never thought how she would put the pieces together. She's hurting so much already, I can't tell her he's alive and simply never wanted to see her or visit Maggie. Instead, I build on the lie.

"I'd already filed for divorce when I found out I was pregnant."

"So why didn't you stop and make it work?"

The moment I told Tom I was pregnant with Lizzie flashes through my mind. He laughed and started packing his things into his car. He said the pregnancy was my problem. What can I say without making Lizzie feel worse?

I decide on part of the truth. It's long ago, but I still feel stupid.

"I paid for his classes, then he dropped out and partied with the refund. When I found out, I was ready to forgive him and try to make it work, but he was leaving me for an older woman with *real* money and they were moving away. I wanted the divorce to be final before I lost track of him."

"Did you even tell him you were pregnant?"

Which is better for her to believe? That he died never knowing or that he was still going to leave?

The waitress takes Lizzie's plate, but I put a hand over mine. I have a few bites left. The interruption gives me the time I need to choose. "I was going to tell him, but I never had a chance."

"Because he died in that car accident." Lizzie heaves a big sigh. "So maybe he would have stayed."

She looks so much more peaceful. The lie is much better than telling her he never wanted to see her. I finish my meal and pay the bill. As we walk out, Lizzie sounds like herself again.

"Mom, can we drive down for a visit with our old friends sometime soon? And get milkshakes at The Diner?"

"Sure."

We head home in good spirits. Richard would probably say I've told her too much, so I won't tell him about our conversation. On the way we talk about videos and how we haven't been watching many together. We decide we'll get a bunch next weekend and have a movie fest with Maggie. Or if it's nice, we'll go visit the girls' old friends, then do movies the weekend after that.

32: Maggie Reads Peg's Journal

This journal really doesn't sound like Mom, but it's as close as I can get to her right now. I wonder if she'll miss me. Probably not—I've been so awful.

Mom bought an ID bracelet and had it engraved with her name, a gift for Brian, but when they got to the college, he told her he got back with his high school sweetheart over the break. Mom got the "just friends" deal, so she could still cover for Jan. Then Brian crapped out on her and she ended up borrowing a school ID so she could hang at the Student Union.

That *does not* sound like my mother at all—fourteen and some guy at the Union invited her to a frat party!

Then things went bad at home, too. She overheard her parents arguing and found out her father had been running around on her mother for years. I guess having two real parents can be tough, too.

April 26, 1972

I felt so good this morning, but now? She forgave him!!!!!!! I can't believe it. She even apologized for yelling at him! I snuck out, so they still don't realize I was there. I think they're both disgusting—him for being a liar and a cheat, and her for putting up with it. She apologized!!!

Whoa.

This I can believe is my mom. She wouldn't put up with that kind of crap and she really hates liars. I wish I'd told her about the creek and why I acted like such a lunatic at school. She wouldn't think I'm so bad and maybe I could have told her about Richard.

She goes on ranting.

Money's not the only reason my mother wants me to live at home while I go to college. She's been afraid he'd leave her once I was gone!
I don't ever want to be that weak.
I will never need someone like that.

I guess that's why Mom never dated when we were little. She didn't want to depend on anyone. We should have left that alone.

Mom figured the whole town knew about her father way before she did, so she didn't talk to anyone about it. Probably right.

The next day, Jan asked her to pretend they were staying at each other's houses so she could spend the night with her boyfriend and finally go all the way.

April 27, 1972

Jan is so self-centered! She didn't even consider how I might feel sleeping on a couch by Brian. So I get to spend the night in her parent's car with the dusty old blanket they keep for emergencies. I'd tell her to go to hell, but I'm looking forward to that kegger. I've never even sipped Dad's beer, but he's always chilled out. Maybe it'll work for me. Maybe it'll loosen me up enough to kiss someone I don't care about.

Then there's an entry with shakey handwriting.

She went to the frat party all by herself—not smart, Mom. One of the guys she knew from the Student Union got her in. She had a beer, but didn't like it and just pretended to drink it. She danced all night with a bunch of different guys. It was cold out, so she figured she'd stay at the party 'til it ended—oh no!

When she went to leave, the guy who invited her gave her a cola to drink while he went to get his jacket. She woke up the next morning naked on the floor. She doesn't come out and say so, but it's pretty clear the guy slipped her a rufie and raped her. When she's dressed and about to leave, the guy tries to drag her upstairs, but a hippie dude named Joe rescues her. Most of the entry is about him. That's just like Mom – focus on the positive.

Joe has the greenest eyes I've ever seen. I got lost in them while he talked. He sounded like an adult, telling me about his family's restaurant where he works, but he was dressed in faded blue jeans and a tie-dyed shirt. He had a leather thong around his neck with a stone dragon dangling from it. He does stained glass and he's making a big piece that can be hung in any window, so he can take it with him when he moves. It's a dragon with a wizard in front of him, casting a spell on the dragon with this crystal. There are tiny flowers at the foot of the dragon, and the colors of the flame from his mouth. Joe's eyes were alive when he talked about his art.

She told him she was okay and he dropped her off around the corner from her house. He wasn't really a hippie. He was on his way to Canada to visit his draft-dodging brother, but then he'd go back to work at the family restaurant. He told her to look for it if she ever came to Harrisburg—the only Greek place on Third Street with a coffeehouse too.

Wonder if it's still here?

She writes more later that day—after Jan comes and takes her out to the Tastee Freeze. We used to go there for cones all the time. Mom didn't tell Jan what happened, she claimed she had too much to drink and fell asleep on a couch at the fraternity. Turns out, Jan chickened out of doing it with her boyfriend, anyway.

Jan asked about the guy who got me home and I told her about Joe and his family and his motorcycle, which totally amazed her. Me, the girl who just finally got her ears pierced, riding a motorcycle. So I told her how cool it was but that it left me kind of sore, like when you ride a bike too long. There's no way I can tell Jan or anyone else the real reason I'm sore. Jan can't even go all the way with a boy she's been dating for two years. I'm a drunken slut who did who-knows-what with who-knows-how-many guys I don't even know. Actually, I'm beginning to have flashes of memory, some of the things I did and let them do to me.

I did like it, at least some of it.

I'm such a slut. Who will ever want me?

Shit. Sounds like she was gangbanged, not just raped. And she didn't even realize she was drugged, or that it could make her seem to like it, even if she didn't really. And her parents are all over each other after making up. Guess her mother was really forgiving. Mom describes her as glowing and figures being a slut runs in the family.

And she doesn't have anyone to talk to. Chip guessed what was happening. I didn't hafta tell him much. Didn't put the details in my diary, either. Just wanna forget it. Guess that's how Mom felt.

I get back to her journal. She doesn't write any more about it, but two weeks later, she's PMSing, ticked off at Jan, sick of school, hating her teachers. She ends by wondering what Harrisburg is like, wondering how long that Joe guy's staying in Canada visiting his brother. That's why it says Harrisburg on the cover of this journal—Mom ran away, too! That's got to be it.

I wonder if she's pregnant? Her life sure fell apart in a hurry—I know how that feels.

There's an empty cup in my hand. Hardly noticed when the waitress refilled it, but it was at least twice.

Now she says, "Sorry, honey, but I really need the booth."

"That's okay," I say, closing the journal.

She hands me the check. "Just pay at the register."

"Can I leave my pack in the booth while I use the bathroom?"

"I can't watch it, but I'll ask my regular over at that table. I'm sure he'll keep an eye on it for you."

"Thanks."

She stops by the other table, and the man smiles and nods at me. I take the little pack with all my money with me and, inside the bathroom stall, split it up into different pockets. Back at the booth, my gear's like I left it. I nod a thank you at the other customer, put on the pack and poncho, then wait at the register to pay.

33: Peg

Richard's up and gone when we get home from breakfast. Dean Koontz is tempting, but I'd really like to have my lesson plans done for the rest of the year. The last weeks at school are always so busy.

"Lizzie, I'm going to go to school to get some work done today. Did you say you need to get together with Serena sometime this weekend?"

"Tomorrow. We're gonna work on our English presentation at her house. Can you give me a ride to the library today? I have more research to do online. It sucks that your computer's broken."

"I can drop you off on my way to school. I'm going to finish my plans for the year."

Lizzie frowns. "You won't want to leave to run me home."

"Not really. You could walk home from the library."

"That would take an hour. The library closes at five on Saturday. You won't work later than that, will you?"

"No. If I can't finish by then, I'll do it next week."

"Okay. I'll take my other homework with me and wait for you. As long as I can get back here before six. Petersons are going out to dinner and dancing tonight."

I leave a note for Richard on the kitchen table.

34: Maggie

It's still drizzling as I head down Market Street toward the river. Can't believe that stuff happened to Mom and she never told us any of it. At least it explains why she was so ready to believe Richard when he kept saying I was probably way worse than they knew—she was doing all *kinds* of stuff behind her parents' back. Tho' neither of us was really doing anything *that* bad.

It's weird to think of Mom having this whole other life. Maybe she came here and hooked up with that Joe dude. Maybe he's really my father. If I find that restaurant, he could be there and recognize me and go get Mom and Lizzie—no, that's stupid. Mom didn't have me until she was almost thirty, so it's not likely he'd be my dad, and Mom and Lizzie are not gonna come and join me. I need to get a grip. Gotta look out for myself now.

First thing's finding a place to stay.

Want to stay clear of cops, in case they're looking for me, but when I get to where Front Street is blocked off for the festival, there's a cop right there—gotta walk past him. Turning around would really look suspicious. I take a breath and try to be invisible. Glance over and he's looking right at me.

He smiles. "Quite a load you have under that poncho."

"My pack and sleeping bag. Keeps 'em dry."

"Going camping?" he asks.

"Traveling. Just passing through." Maybe he won't bother me if he thinks I'm not gonna stay around.

"There's no camping here," he says.

"Not a problem. Waitress up the street told me about the festival, so I came to check it out. Wasn't looking for a place to camp in town."

He stares at me at least a full minute before he says anything.

"You traveling the whole summer?"

He's not asking my age! Must think I'm a college student. That's good. That's very good. He looks pretty young himself. I relax and lie some more.

"Yeah, I've got the whole summer ahead of me."

"Where are you headed?"

It's fun passing for a college student. I start to get into the role.

"Haven't really decided. Figured I'd hit the shore first, you know, Rehoboth maybe?"

"I like Rehoboth. Do you body surf?"

"Yeah. Used to go there every spring with my mom and sister."

"Are you meeting up with anyone this trip?"

"Nope."

"What's your mother think about your traveling on your own?"

"She's chill with it—did some traveling herself back in college."

"You're not hitchhiking are you?"

"Oh, no. I'm not stupid. Rode in on the bus."

"How long are you going to be here?"

"Haven't decided."

"Do you know where you're staying? There's no camping in any of the parks in town. That includes City Island. Some of the vendors are sleeping in their campers by their exhibits, but that's an exception."

"I might crash with someone out at the community college."

"You won't find anyone between semesters, especially Memorial Day Weekend. Besides, it's not safe to go home with someone you've just met, even if they say they're a student. There are some inexpensive motels about five miles up the river, right on Front Street. You can take the number three city bus, if you don't want to hike it."

"Thanks. Sounds like a good idea."

"You'll want to go early. I'm not sure how late the buses run, and the motels may fill up quickly with the art festival."

Someone comes up to ask him a question and I walk away. That went pretty good. Still feel better as the distance between us increases, and I won't be wasting money on a motel. My cash has to last 'til I get settled with a job. But he's probably right about no one being at the college this weekend. Better find someone here.

The exhibits are set up in the middle of the street. The first ones are a bunch of stuff for little kids. I cross the street onto the grassy area and walk to the edge of the river.

The bank's high above the brown water. A small tree races along with all kinds of trash caught in its roots. The Susquehanna is huge!

Most of the festival customers are middle-class women or couples. There's no one to ask for a place to crash. I stop to look at some lockets made with real flowers, then there's a flash of lightning, a boom of thunder, and rain hits me like a pail of water. I help the vendor pull her table under her canopy. It's awfully crowded, but customers can still look at everything. I turn and my pack bumps into someone.

"Sorry!" I apologize.

"I'm fine. Isn't this rain something!" exclaims a cheerful gray-haired woman.

I smile back, but the weather sucks. In a little bit, the rain lets up to a drizzle and I move on. There are rivers running down the street and the grass is soggy—like walking on a sponge—no good for sleeping outside.

Amazing how many people are still out looking at this stuff. One vendor's pushing up on his sagging roof to make the little lake pour off it, like we had to do when it rained at Rollin's. Then volunteers come around with bales of hay and make pathways with the stuff.

The next booth I like has awesome photos of people. There's one of an old guy with a winter coat tied around his waist, pulling cans out of the garbage and another of a bony woman in a flowered skirt and a plaid shirt—it's in black and white but you know the colors clash. She's got a spacey smile and she's holding out her hand with the palm up. There are pictures of street kids, too.

"You like my work?"

"Yeah. I mean, mostly you never think about homeless people, but these really shove it right out there. You know what I mean?"

"Yeah. That's what I'm after," he says. He looks at my pack, then my face. "Where are you headed?"

"I'm not sure."

"A lot of these people started out that way, then ended up nowhere."

"I'm just looking for somewhere to crash for a few days, 'til I get work and my own place. That's all."

I'm not going to end up nowhere.

"I'm sleeping in my camper. It's parked right up this side street, so I can be close to my booth. I pack up all the photos for the night and put them in there, too. It's crowded, but if you don't find anything better, you can come back. You could sleep in the cab of the truck."

"Thanks. I may take you up on that."

He doesn't ask my name, but gives me one of his cards. I write the name of the side street on it, so I'll remember. Barbara Street.

"It's an old Dodge pickup with Illinois plates. The camper's white with a beige stripe around it. Maybe I'll see you later."

I move on up the river. There's a totally soaked old woman with a red bandana on her head, walking around waving something a few inches above the hay. Guess it's a metal detector like people use on the beach. He should get her photograph.

The rain stops, so I take off the poncho and wrap it over my gear. It's still cloudy. Keep the fleece on for warmth. Past the festival there's still a grassy park area between Front Street and the water.

I pass two ladies headed towards the festival. They each have a little kid by the hand and they're busy talking. They never make eye contact with me, but they pull the kids a little closer and leave plenty of room between us as we pass. I turn around to watch them. They've let the kids out again. When they pass a grubby old man coming my way, they pull them back in as if they're on leashes. When they've passed him, they let the children back out. He comes on by me, and I still watch the women with their kids. When a prep jogger runs by them, they don't pull the kids close.

I nearly leap out of my skin when a voice comes from behind me. "They're careful to keep their distance. Might hafta admit we exist."

The old man's clothes say he lives in them. His stringy hair is so greasy, the rain didn't even get it wet. He hasn't shaved in months. I just stare at him, speechless. This man is talking to me like we're the same. That gives me the creeps.

"Your sleeping bag," he says. "They know you're on the street."

"I'm not," I start to say, then the jogger runs wide around us.

It hits me. I *am* one of them.

I turn away from the old man and stare out at the rushing, muddy water. Tears push into my eyes. I blink and force them back—can't start feeling sorry for myself. I won't be homeless for long. I'll get a job, soon as I get some ID that says I'm old enough to work. Maybe the old guy knows where to get some. I turn back to ask him, but he's disappeared.

I keep walking up the river. The jogger stops up ahead near a guy in jeans and a camo jacket, then he turns around and jogs back past me. The other guy lifts a hand as if he's greeting someone. I look behind me. No one's coming, so I lift my hand the same way. When he gets close enough to really see me, he stops and takes a second look. I know he didn't mean to wave at me, but I still say hi first. Maybe *he'll* be able to help me.

"Hi," he answers. "Thought you were someone else."

"With this outfit?"

"Yeah. Friend of mine's been traveling."

"Sorry. Didn't mean to fool you."

"No problem."

"You live around here?" I try to sound casual.

He nods. "You?"

"Just got here. Know anyplace I could stay 'til I get a job?"

He looks me over carefully. "Maybe."

I wonder if I should offer to pay, but he starts asking questions.

"How old are you?"

"Eighteen."

"Yeah, in how many years?"

"One. And a half." Lies are coming easier.

"What kind of trouble you in?" He's staring at me, assessing me.

"None."

"Yeah, right." At that moment, the wind blows hard and the rain starts up again. "Come on," he yells, and he takes off up the side street.

It's hard to keep up. He's not running, but he's taller and walking fast, and I've got the pack. At least that's covered with the poncho. My fleece is soaked before we've gone one block. Two more and he's way ahead. He steps through a door and waves for me to follow.

Inside, I shake my head to get rid of some of the water. The place is heavy with incense. A girl not much older than me sits on a dirty old couch, smoking a cigarette and watching cartoons. There's a grimy toddler eating something off the floor. The girl is ignoring him.

"What the fuck?" she says, looking at me. "Who the fuck is that?"

"Found her by the river. She needs a place to stay for a few days."

"You're not gonna let her crash here."

There's disbelief in her voice. He hadn't sounded sure before the rain started, but he doesn't like this girl telling him what to do. His tone puts her in her place.

"Yeah. She's staying here."

"Fuck." She turns to really look at me. "So, what, you've run away from home? Mommy and Daddy mean to you? Shit, Charlie, you can't let her stay here."

"I said she's staying, bitch."

I'm not sure I wanna stay. The language is no big deal, but it looks like he's gonna hit her, 'til she shrugs and says, "Whatever."

He motions for me to come after him up narrow stairs.

Where else would I go? I follow. We stop at the second floor.

"You don't go up there," he says, pointing to a closed door at the top of another flight. He takes me into a narrow hallway with two doors and opens one. "You can crash in here. Other door's the bathroom."

My nose clogs with the smell of mildewed dirty laundry. Most of the floor is covered in piles of clothing. A stained double mattress is on the floor by the only windows. They look out onto the street.

It's pouring harder than ever. At least I can be dry here.

"Whose room is it?" I ask.

"Nobody's. People crash here when they need a place. You can stay as long as you need to—you aren't a Bible thumper or a narc, are you?"

"No."

He pulls out a joint and lights it. He takes a toke and passes it to me. I take it. Don't wanna look like a narc. Glad I tried it at that motel on the way home from Rehoboth—I know enough to suck in and hold it. Pass it back to him.

I let my breath out with just a little cough and say, "Thanks. But your girlfriend would be happier if I found another place."

"Don't worry about Crystal. She'll get over it. Besides, it's fucking pouring out there again." He takes another hit.

A gust of wind shoves a sheet of rain into the windows.

I take off the pack and lean it against the wall, then pull my fleece off over my head. "Just 'til I get a job."

"You have ID that says you're eighteen?" he demands.

"No."

"Tough to work then. Tough anyway. There ain't shit for jobs around here. But you definitely need ID."

"Know where I can get some?"

"Maybe. But it'll cost."

"How much?"

He takes a deep hit and holds it, then he passes it back to me. I take another hit but make it a small one, and hold it in my mouth. He lets his breath out slowly at the same time I exhale.

"Fifty or a hundred for a good one," he says.

I'm smart enough to not let him know I've got the money. Instead, I say, "I'll figure out how to pay, if you can get one for me."

He nods and looks me over. All of a sudden, I'm very aware of my wet shirt clinging to my body. My nipples are totally headlights.

"Yeah, you can get cash if you need it."

I feel like a cow up for sale.

He says, "Matt's coming by later. Sometimes he's got something."

"Thanks."

I'm not clear if Matt is a pimp or someone who has IDs. Don't really wanna know right now, just want some dry clothes.

Charlie puts his arm around me and talks in a hushed voice. "I better go downstairs, or Crystal'll figure we're fucking and get all pissed off again. You just chill up here for awhile. Let her get used to the idea you're staying."

Alone, I open my pack and change. I use a dry shirt to wipe myself off—didn't think to pack a towel, and can't use any of the smelly stuff on this floor. Clean jeans, a T-shirt, and my hooded sweatshirt warm me up. Glad I didn't depend on just the fleece. It's soaked.

I take out my cash and count it carefully. Just over three hundred left. It's not a good plan to leave it in my pack or carry all of it in my pockets. I count out two piles of one hundred each—fold each pile crossways, then lengthwise, then push one pile into each sock, all the way 'til it's by the arch of my foot. Put another hundred in my left back pocket and the rest in the right. Now I can pull some money out without showing anyone how much I have.

I take my wet clothes across the hall to the bathroom. I've been in outhouses that were cleaner and smelled better! The tub's black with greasy-looking grime. I wring out everything, then take it back to the other room. Hang my fleece on one side of the doorknob and my shirt on the other. Find a chair on its side, lying half buried under a pile of clothes. Set it up as a drying rack for the rest of my stuff, then go back to use the bathroom. I squat over the crusty toilet. It takes concentration and I start to giggle. Toilet paper on the floor's the cleanest thing in the bathroom. That makes me giggle, too. Must be the pot hitting me.

Dry my hair with the shirt I'm using for a towel, then comb it out. The mattress doesn't seem to be buggy, but those big yellow stains are gross. The other side's worse. I shove it against the front wall, then push the piles of clothes away from it. There's a quilt, but it stinks. Good thing I've got my sleeping bag.

There's one can of pop and a little bag of chips left. I get them and Mom's journal, sit down on the mattress, and lean against the front wall between the windows. A trickle of water's leaking around the edges. It makes a cold draft, but it's fresh air in the stale room, so that's okay. Keep my hood up. The chips are good, but there aren't enough of them. Finish the pop, too.

I hear voices downstairs, then footsteps coming up and on to the third floor—voices up there—then footsteps back down. No one's bothering me. I settle in to read. The daylight's dimmed by the rain. The wind picks up again and throws water against the windows— sounds like waves. Glad I'm inside. I find the page where I left off, but it's hard to keep my eyes open.

35: Peg

As soon as I get to my classroom, I start working. First, I finish up next week's lesson plans in detail. I should have turned them in Friday, but I got caught up in that meeting. There are two weeks after that, then exam week, then summer vacation. None of my classes are going to cover everything in the syllabus and still have time to review. I pick the most important material and make lesson plans for that. Then I go through the year's plans for each subject, highlighting points to review. Then I plug the highlighted items into activities I've used before for review. As I finish, I feel one weight lift off me.

If I get issues with Richard settled Tuesday, the only major problem will be if they don't renew my contract. I'll still have paychecks and medical coverage through August. If I haven't been notified one way or the other by Friday, I'll ask about it.

Lizzie's waiting for me at the library. Richard's car is still gone when we get home. It's only three thirty, so I challenge Lizzie to a game of cribbage before we fix dinner. She sets it up on the dining room table while I get colas.

"We didn't sell the backgammon and other games, did we?" Lizzie calls out.

"They shouldn't have been sold," I answer as I bring in our drinks. "They're probably in the storage unit. We labeled those boxes in detail. We'll just have to take a day and go search for the games."

"We've gotta have backgammon for Rollin's."

"Let's not talk about that this weekend. I haven't told Richard yet."

"Okay."

We're still playing when Richard comes home with Mexican food. "I saw your note and wasn't sure how late you'd have to work, so I thought I'd surprise you by getting dinner," he says.

"Thanks, it smells great. My plans are done for the rest of the year."

"Wonderful! I'll make Margaritas so we can celebrate. Finish your game. I'll get everything set up to eat in the kitchen."

"That is so thoughtful. Thank you. What did you do all day?"

"Oh, I did some work downstairs, then ran a few errands."

He goes out to the kitchen with the food.

I'm five points away from winning, with a twelve point lead. But it's my crib, so Lizzie counts first. I turn over a seven at the beginning of play and a huge grin cracks her face.

"Don't ever play poker, Lizzie."

I only make one point in play. She has a pair of sevens and a pair of eights, a twenty-point hand. She creams me.

"Winner puts away the game," I tell her.

I go out to the kitchen, where Richard hands me a Margarita. I've had more to drink in the last year than the previous ten. I've been careful because of my father, and my own history. But a drink or two on a holiday, or to celebrate finishing my planning, is not excessive.

I'm still on my second Margarita as Lizzie and I clear the dishes. Richard made them a lot stronger than the first batch and he's already finished his. He gets up to make more. When I suggest we've had enough, he waves away my concern.

"Let's enjoy ourselves while the troublemaker's away. At least we have one good girl around."

He gives Lizzie a squeeze and a wet kiss on her cheek.

She shrugs him off and says, "I gotta go."

She grabs her backpack and leaves to go babysit.

Richard makes himself another drink and makes amorous advances while I finish cleaning up. I encourage him just enough to keep him going, until the counter is clear and wiped. Then I make my own moves and we head for the bedroom. It's over in a few minutes, for Richard. He just rolls away from me and starts snoring moments later. I'm left frustrated. It's the Margaritas. This never used to happen. He always took his time and made sure I was satisfied. When we talk about his drinking, I'll use this as one of the reasons for him to cut back.

At least I can get up without waking him. I make a cup of tea, curl up on the couch, and continue reading my new Koontz novel.

36: Maggie

I wake up curled on my side in the dark. There's a murmur of voices downstairs. It's not raining now, but it must be cloudy 'cuz there's that yellow-gray light you get in the city on cloudy nights.

I shuffle through mountains of clothing and grope by the door for the light switch—nothing happens. The bulb must be dead. Hallway's totally dark. No windows. Hafta feel my way to the bathroom and grope for a switch. When the light goes on, there's a bug on the wall, then it's gone so fast I'm not sure I really saw it. I check the toilet for bugs before using it, then rinse off my hands and shake them dry.

Leaving the bathroom light on helps me find my way down the hall into the stairway. There's a dim bulb down at the foot of the stairs, but no other light or switch. I feel my way downstairs step by step. The incense smell is stronger than it was earlier.

No one's on the couch. The voices I heard are the television. Back in the next room, there's a big dining table. At one end, two guys are playing cards. One's dark with long dreds. The other looks like he's never seen the sun. At the other end of the table, Crystal's changing the toddler's diaper. She tosses the dirty one into a garbage can a few feet away. It lands with a heavy thud—musta been soaked.

The kid's bottom is an angry red color and has dried poop on it. I can see now it's a little boy. She wipes a paper towel across his butt, then tosses it toward the garbage can. It misses, but she doesn't seem to notice. She sticks a new diaper on the kid, then lifts him up and holds him on her hip.

She sneers in at me. "Thought you were never gonna wake up. Lightweight. The weed Charlie's got now ain't all that strong."

"Didn't sleep much the last week. Needed to catch up."

"Yeah, whatever."

The two guys playing cards finish their game.

"Later," says the one with dreds. He sounds Jamaican.

They start for the front door.

"Hold up, I'm coming too," says Crystal.

She pushes the little boy into my arms. All he has on is the diaper. He's filthy, his hair is matted, and he smells sour.

"Watch him for me, would you? I gotta get out of here for awhile."

"I guess so," I stammer.

"Will Charlie be okay with that?" asks the white guy.

"Charlie's the one who invited her to stay, so if there's a problem it's his own fault."

"He's gonna shit," says the white guy.

"Tough," says Crystal. "I need to get out and have some fun, too." She turns to me and points as she says, "Diapers, kitchen. Soup's on the stove. Help yourself. Don't use the microwave. It blows the fuse."

The white guy snickers. He doesn't seem quite right to me.

"What's the baby's name?" I ask.

"Jimi."

"When's his bedtime?"

She laughs. "When he crashes. He just ate, so he should fall asleep pretty soon."

She laughs again, and so do the other two. I'm not sure what the joke is, but I'll be glad when they're gone.

"Lock the door, all the locks, and don't let anyone but me or Charlie into the house. Nobody. Anyone who says Charlie's said they can come in without one of us here is lying."

"Okay."

They leave. I set the two deadbolts and lock the knob as well. This must be a rough part of the city.

My stomach growls. The pop and little bag of chips is all I've eaten since my omelet this morning and I walked a bunch with all my stuff.

I plunk Jimi down on the couch. TV's on Cartoon Network. That won't be appropriate for him this time of night, but I doubt Crystal cares.

The kid hasn't made a sound—not even when she was rubbing his butt with the dry paper towel, and that had to hurt. He just sits and stares at the screen—doesn't move around much, either. Maybe he's retarded or something.

I go out to the kitchen to get myself some soup.

The bathroom was nasty, but the kitchen's worse. Smells of rotting food. Cold soup's in a pot on the stove with a layer of fat on it. I turn on the burner to heat it up and look for some clean dishes. Don't find any. Everything's dirty. Dishes, glasses, pots, and pans are piled all over the kitchen.

There's another bug like the one in the bathroom. It's on a dirty pan in the corner, but it disappears into a crack when I go to kill it. There's dishwashing liquid by the sink, just doesn't get used much. Find a drawer full of towels and dishcloths, too.

I fill up the sink with hot water and suds and start by washing out a bowl and spoon for myself. Check on Jimi. He's tipped over, sound asleep. My soup's not hot yet, so I keep washing dishes.

How can people live like this?

37: Peg

I'm still reading when Lizzie lets herself in with her key.

"Hi, honey, did Mr. Peterson walk you home?"

"Yup. Why are you up so late?"

"Oh, I started this book and it's really hard to put down. You know how I am."

"Yeah, but you haven't been reading all that much since Richard."

"Since Richard. You make him sound like an event."

"Well, yeah. You've like, well, changed a lot. Since Richard."

"Marriage does that, honey. You both have to make changes."

"It seems like you've done most of the changing, and he's creepy when he's been drinking. You saw the way he kissed me."

"He was a little drunk and sloppy, but you're just not used to any man giving you a hug or a kiss. It wasn't inappropriate or anything."

"If you say so, but I didn't like it and mostly I don't like him."

"That's not true. You and Maggie were all excited about our getting married."

"We were excited 'cuz you were happy. We never really liked him."

"Why didn't you say something before?"

"Well, we didn't see him much 'til you were already engaged and had the date set. And he's tolerable when he isn't drinking and he just started that the last couple of months. Besides, you were so happy—we didn't wanna hurt you."

"Well, it does hurt to have you act like he's doing something wrong just because he gives you a hug and a kiss on the cheek."

"Sorry, Mom." She's staring blankly past me.

"You should head to bed. You don't want to get so far off schedule that you have trouble getting up for school Tuesday."

"Okay. Anyway, I've gotta go to Serena's tomorrow morning, about eleven. If you give me a ride there, her parents will bring me back when we're done. And then I'm sitting again, starting at five."

"Okay. I guess we better both get to bed."

"Yup. Love you, Mom. Want me to wake you up?"

"If I'm not up by ten thirty, you better knock on the door."

"Okay. Good night."

I throw away my tea bag and start to put the cup in the dishwasher. But I'm not really sleepy. So I heat up another cup of water instead, and put in a new tea bag. Soothing herbal tea, not black.

The girls have never had any male relatives to show them affection, so of course they're not comfortable when Richard gives them a hug or kiss. We probably should have waited longer to get married, but living so far apart was too hard. And the move hasn't been easy on any of us. Richard's had his home invaded by all of us, he's lost his job, and he's had to adapt to living with teenagers. That's tough for anybody. But even Lizzie has noticed his drinking is becoming a problem.

Tuesday. We'll clear the air Tuesday.

I remember why I fell in love with Richard. He was so much fun. He took me out all the time, opened doors for me. He took care of me when I got hurt. Most men get scared off by kids or want their own. In Richard's first emails he talked about being too old for babies or little kids, but he liked teenagers. He used to coach girls' softball. I wish I could find those letters and read them again, but I lost my email when we changed servers. I wish I'd printed copies.

A yawn catches me. I've got to get some sleep.

While I was reading, Richard must have gotten up and ready for bed. I try not to disturb him as I slip under the covers, but he rolls onto his side, pulls me up to him, and mutters, "Love you."

He's still asleep, or mostly asleep. I feel guilty for doubting him. I need to be supportive. He's depressed because of losing his job. We can't afford to go out like we did before and I even chewed him out for spending too much the last time he bought me a present. It's no wonder he's started drinking. He's probably wondering why he married *me*! And on top of that, there's all the trouble Maggie's put us through this last year. I hope she's not lying to me about this camping trip.

38: Maggie

I wash all the glasses, dishes, and silverware—stack 'em high in the drainer, then wipe off the shelf with the soapy rag and pile the rest on a towel. Just fill the pots and pans with sudsy water and leave 'em on the stovetop to soak. I clean the table and wipe out the refrigerator, too. That should make up for my eating and sleeping here.

It's after midnight when the kitchen's clean. Gotta heat my dinner again. I take a bowl of soup into the living room, find an action movie, and sit on the couch next to the baby. He starts to roll over in his sleep and I gotta catch him so he doesn't fall. That's probably why he was napping on the floor earlier. The carpet's filthy, but he's probably safer there, so that's where he goes. It's kind of cool now, so I look around and find a blanket shoved in a corner—smells like pee. I move him away from me some and cover him with the stinky blanket. I won't have kids 'til I can take better care of them than this.

The soup tastes kind of funky, but maybe that's 'cuz I just smelled that blanket. Figure I'll be up all night watching movies, after sleeping away the afternoon, but soon as my soup's gone, I start feeling drowsy and doze off.

Sunday, May 28, 2000

39: Peg

Richard wakes me up with kisses. We make love the way we used to, and we're enjoying the afterglow when Lizzie knocks and calls through the door.

"Mom, it's almost ten thirty."

"Okay, I'll get a quick shower," I call. I snuggle close to Richard. "She needs a ride to her friend's house. They're working on a project for school."

"We'll have the rest of the day to ourselves?" He smiles. "Just the two of us?"

"Yup."

Richard's stomach growls loudly, making us laugh.

"Let's go to brunch," he says, "then we can come back here and be as noisy as we want to be!"

"Sounds good to me."

Having the girls in the house does inhibit my response when we're making love. Maybe that's part of our problem. We shower together, but still manage to get Lizzie to her friend's house shortly after eleven.

Richard drives to a riverside cafe we frequented when I first started staying over at his house. We haven't been out for ages.

"Sit tight," he says when he's parked. He opens the car door for me and we hold hands as we walk into the restaurant. The hostess seats us by a window. We sit across from each other, rubbing feet under the table while we look at the menus.

"You like the Eggs Benedict," he reminds me.

"I was thinking of trying the blueberry pancakes today."

"Those are easier to make at home."

"I suppose you're right."

When the waitress comes, Richard orders the Eggs Benedict for me and country fried steak for himself. When she's gone, he reaches for my hand and looks deeply into my eyes.

Yes, we need time alone sometimes.

Breakfast is wonderful.

When we get home, I expect Richard to whisk me off to the bedroom, but instead he's got a pensive look on his face.

"What's wrong?" I ask.

"There's something we need to talk about. I hate to ruin a beautiful day, but I'm afraid it can't wait."

He pulls me down onto the couch, but not playfully. He takes both of my hands in his and we sit face-to-face. What can be so serious?

"Peg, I love you. You know that."

"Yes, and I love you."

"I've been thinking about Maggie, and I have a suggestion. Please, don't get mad, just think about it, because I think it might be the best thing for all of us."

"What is it?"

"I think we should let her go live with that friend of hers, Cheri?"

"Chandra? What are you talking about?"

"Chandra. I think we should consider asking her parents if Maggie could live with them for awhile."

"Why?" I try to pull away, but he holds my hands more firmly.

"Please, don't reject the idea without thinking it through. Maggie is obviously unhappy here, not doing well in school. She might do better if she were back in familiar surroundings."

"She's made a friend, and she's been working hard this semester."

"She also hates me."

"She does not. She's still adjusting."

"It's not just that. I feel like she's setting me up. She, she's been *suggestive* with me, for months now, whenever you're not looking."

I jerk my hands away. "What do you mean, she's been suggestive!"

"She'll wiggle her butt, or give me a look. A sensual look."

"For months? Why haven't you said anything, why now?"

It's not possible. He's out of his mind.

"I was hoping you'd catch her at it yourself, but she's very sneaky. I was afraid you'd think I was imagining it. But the way Lizzie reacted to my hug yesterday, I'm afraid Maggie's telling her lies about me, the way she lied about those boys she hit last year, making accusations against them after she was the one making the advances. That is a very scary position for me. I mean, I used to coach girls' softball! And I was never accused of anything improper, never."

"Maggie hasn't accused you of anything. She just avoids you."

"Why did Lizzie pull away from me that way yesterday, then? There was nothing wrong with that hug."

"I talked with Lizzie about that and told her I thought she misread your intent. She wasn't comfortable, probably because you *were* a little drunk. That's all."

"Maybe, but you didn't see Maggie when I brought her home from school after she hit that boy. She was pleading with me not to tell you, and Peg, this is really hard. I hate to have to tell you this, but, she was blatantly coming on to me. I had to physically push her away from me. She started to attack me then, and I had to restrain her."

"What do you mean, *exactly?*"

And I'd thought things were getting better.

"It happened really fast, so I'm not completely clear. In the car, she was begging me not to tell you about her being suspended again, and she started saying she'd do anything, if I just wouldn't tell you. So I lectured her about saying that, how dangerous it could be, that someone could expect her to follow through on those kinds of promises. And I told her I had to tell you she was suspended."

"Go on."

I don't really want to hear this, but I need to know what happened and try to put it together with the girl I thought I knew, before I found out how much she's been hiding and lying.

"She went into the house without a fuss, but once we were inside, she threw herself up against me, her front against mine. I told her to stop it, but she started touching me." Richard's blushing. It's clear this is extremely uncomfortable for him.

"Peg, there's no way that girl's a virgin. I'm sorry, but it's just not possible. I pushed her away and she got angry. She came back and pounded at my chest with her fists, so I grabbed her and managed to turn her around so she couldn't hit me, and kept her in a bear hug to walk her to her room. Once she was inside, I let her go and stepped back into the doorway quickly, and told her to stay put."

"Did she stay in her room then?"

"She was still screaming at me, threatening to tell you all kinds of lies, then she looked inside her shirt and started insisting I'd grabbed her—her 'boob'. I was telling her she was mistaken, or if she wasn't, that it had been an accident, when she whipped her shirt off and pointed to it, screaming for me to look at what I'd done."

"Did you look?" And neither of them told me about this?

"I, I did. I was shocked. And I saw red fingerprints above her bra. I didn't mean to grab her there, but I must have. It was an accident. Please believe me."

"What happened after you saw the marks?"

"I apologized, and asked her to please put her shirt back on, that she could talk to you about it when you got home. I told her she was to stay in her room, that I'd be downstairs working."

"She didn't say anything to me. And neither did you."

"Later I went back up and talked to her through her door. I told her you had to know she was suspended, but she could tell you why. And I apologized again if I hurt her, and told her I'd wait and let her tell about what had happened between us, too."

"She didn't."

"I know. And the way she cried when she told you about the trouble at school, I thought she felt bad about all of it and that maybe she'd learned her lesson. So I didn't say anything. I thought it was over and done with and maybe things would get better between us."

"But now you want to send her away? Why?" I brace myself for worse news.

"She stayed in her room most of the time she was suspended, so I thought things *were* getting better, but then, just before you came home the last day, she threatened me. She said she'd tell you everything that had happened, only she'd say *I* came after *her*. She said she had bruises and she had taken pictures of them and if I ever made her angry, she would show them to Lizzie and you, and make up all kinds of stories about me."

"You weren't afraid to go against her about the camping."

"I was! But she's a kid. Whatever she's done, however she acted with me, whatever threats she made, she's still your little girl. I love you, so I have to try and protect her. I really think it was a mistake to let her go, even if his family is there. It scared the hell out me to tell you so, but I had to. A few drinks helped."

"Actually, his stepmother was awfully young."

"Do you know where they're camping?"

"Lakeshore State Campground."

"Do you want to go down there to check it out?"

That was my first thought, but I'm surprised he's suggested it. "You're not afraid of the scene she'll make? Or what she's going to say about you?"

"No. I've told you the truth. I should have when it happened. It's been hell, wondering when everything would explode. I'm relieved to have it out. You do believe me, don't you?"

"She hasn't said anything, and she would have if it hadn't been her fault." I hate this. I don't want it to be true, but why would he make it up? "Yes, I believe you. I just don't understand what's going on with Maggie. I hope she hasn't gotten into drugs."

"You know she's been drinking."

"I know. And Lizzie told me it *wasn't* just the one time." I sigh. "I'm getting a new student Tuesday, a girl Maggie's age, whose life fell apart, because she had the wrong companions."

"I'm sorry, sweet pea." He pulls me into a hug. "So do you want to go check out the campground?"

"I guess we should. We'll have time to get there and back before Lizzie gets home from Serena's."

40: Maggie

I wake up next to Jimi on the couch. He's staring at an evangelist. Spooky kid. He's gotta be at least two. They're supposed to be pudgy, noisy, and hyper. He's skinny, quiet, and doesn't move much. It's so wrong that they left him with a stranger all night.

It's already noon. Haven't slept this much in ages. I look for food in the kitchen. Ate the end of the soup last night and, aside from mustard, ketchup, and two cans of cola, there's nothing else. I pour a can of cola into two glasses and take them out to the living room. Give one to Jimi.

"Sorry kid, this is all I could find for breakfast."

He holds the glass and drinks out of it without spilling. Maybe he's not retarded, after all. Haven't changed his diaper. He's gotta need a new one after the whole night, but he's not fussing. I pick him up.

"Come on, Jimi. You gotta need a change."

He lies still on the table and stares at me. The diaper's soaked. His bottom's in awful shape. There aren't any of those little wipes they use on baby's butts.

A bath would help. Not in that tub, though. I carry him naked to the kitchen and sit him on the shelf with his feet in the sink. While I get out a couple dishtowels and a washcloth, he pees and it arches toward the drain. Glad it didn't reach the clean dishes.

"Good aim."

He just stares at me. He stays put while the sink fills up. I watch the temperature and put a little dish soap in the water to make it sudsy. He stares at his feet as they disappear in bubbles.

"You're gonna get a bath, you know, b-a-th?" I sound it out slowly.

"Ba," he says.

"Great. You *can* talk. Ba. You're gonna get a ba."

He touches the suds and sucks in his breath like he's never seen a bubble before. When the sink's half full, I turn off the faucet and try to lower him into the water. He doesn't bend his legs, so it doesn't work. He squirms and squeaks like a mouse caught in a trap. So I hold him half standing, with my left arm, while I bring the soapy washcloth up to his butt and wash it gently. I'm afraid of hurting him, it's so raw. Keep telling him it's okay. It must feel good—he gets quiet and holds still.

Finally, he sits in the water. I put some suds on his head and work up a lather, being careful not to get any in his eyes—don't want to set him off again. His hair was all crusty with something. It's soft once it's clean. I wash the rest of him, finishing with his face. Layers of dried-on food come off his cheeks. When he's all clean, I set him back on the counter and let the water out of the sink. He squeals again and pulls his feet up out of the water.

"It's okay. You're okay. You're safe."

He must think he'd disappear like the water. That would scare me, too. When the sink's empty, I rinse out the suds and sit him down in it. I use a glass to rinse him off, body first, then his head. He screams when the water comes down over his face and I gotta hang onto him so he doesn't fall. When he's all rinsed, he smells a lot better. I dry him off with the dish towels. He seems more like a normal little kid now. He's even starting to look at me, and I'm making faces to make him laugh.

I carry Jimi back into the dining room and put a clean diaper on him. His butt's still red, but it doesn't look quite as sore, and there aren't any chunks of poop on it anymore. That's gotta feel better. I set him on the couch and look for some clean clothes for him. There's a pink T-shirt that must be Crystal's on the dining room table. Everything else is dirty. Everything in my room is filthy, except for my own things. Maybe Jimi's clean clothes are up on the third floor. Charlie said not to go up there, but he shouldn't mind if I just get clothes for the baby. I start up the stairs, but the door at the top's padlocked, so I go back and put the pink T-shirt on him.

I'm carrying him back to the couch when there's a loud rapping on the front door and someone shouts, "Hey, Charlie!"

I call out, "Charlie's not here."

"When's he gonna be back?"

"Not sure."

"He's supposed to meet me here. Lemme in."

I look at all the locks and think about Crystal's warning.

"You can wait out there," I call through the door.

I sit on the couch watching cartoons with Jimi. My stomach growls. Weird that Jimi's not fussing for food. The locks on the front door click open. Charlie comes in with a skinny guy I haven't seen before.

"Where the fuck is Crystal?" Charlie demands.

"I dunno. She went out last night and left me to watch Jimi."

"She fucking left you to watch things?" He seems angry with me. I get angry back.

"She just shoved Jimi at me and left. I think it *sucks* the way you all call him a 'thing'. He's a little kid. He's actually a pretty *good* little kid, and he's nice to hold now I've cleaned him up."

Charlie looks confused. "She just asked you to watch the kid?"

"Jimi. He has a name."

"She didn't tell you anything else?"

"She said to keep the door locked and not open it. That guy's the only one who came around, and I made him wait outside."

"Okay. Uh, thanks for looking after the kid and things. You know, things, like not letting anyone into the house."

"Oh." I'm so stupid. Things meant the house, not the baby. "Since you've been nice enough to let me stay, I cleaned up the kitchen."

"Cool. Thanks."

Then he takes the skinny guy upstairs for a few minutes. Crystal gets home right when they come down and the skinny guy takes off. Charlie holds up his hand like he's gonna slap her, then he stops.

"I should. I really should. Don't ever take off like that again and leave a stranger here alone with the kid."

So he does care about the baby some. Jimi must be his.

"I told her not to let anyone in. I get sick of taking care of things for you while you go out fucking other chicks."

"And what were you doing last night?"

"I was just partying with Tina and Amber."

"Like I believe that."

Crystal starts coming on to him and the two of them head upstairs, still leaving me with the baby.

I start to play peek-a-boo with him. He likes it. I try to think of other things two-year-olds like. I go into the dining room to look for toys in all the stuff on the floor. Jimi follows me, crawling really fast. First time I've seen him move on his own. He goes past me into the kitchen and pulls open a cupboard. He crawls into it, then starts screaming. I pull him out butt first. He's hanging onto an empty cracker box. He keeps screaming.

"What the fuck are you doing to him?" Crystal demands as she whirls into the room and grabs him away from me. All she has on is a big T-shirt. She glares at me.

"He's hungry."

"Shit. I forgot. We're out of food again." She goes to the stairs and screams, "Charlie, we need food." She puts Jimi on the floor and heads upstairs. He starts to crawl up after her and she snarls at him. "*No!*"

He plops back onto his butt and watches her go up the stairs. I go to my room. He's not my kid—it's not up to me to watch him—but I find myself listening in case he tries to come up the steps.

I haven't had a shower since Friday morning. That's only skipping one day. We've done that camping, but I feel really grubby, especially after cleaning the kitchen last night. Bathtub's too nasty to use, so I just rinse my pits and put on some deodorant. Rinse my face, too, which makes me feel a lot better. Brush my hair and almost feel good.

Crystal and Charlie stop on their way downstairs. "We're gonna get something to eat," Charlie says. "Come with us."

Sounds like an order. I'm not sure I wanna go with them, but some food would be good, and so would some fresh air.

"Okay. I'll be right down."

I throw my hairbrush and Mom's journal into the daypack. Just in case, I put in a change of clothes, too. My clothes from yesterday are still wet, except my fleece and the poncho. Put both of them into the pack, too. My money's still in my socks and pockets.

Crystal must have had clothes for Jimi up in their room. He's dressed like a regular little kid now—even has sneakers, one of those cute little hats with the brim all the way around, and a little rain jacket.

"Thanks for cleaning him up," says Crystal. "He'll be filthy again in an hour, but he smells sweet now."

She sounds more like a mother now.

"Is it okay to leave my pack here?" I ask.

"Sure," says Charlie. "I always lock the place."

We wait on the sidewalk while he uses different keys on the locks, then we head down to the river. It's still cloudy but not raining steady anymore. I check street signs. The house is on Calder Street and we cross Second. Joe's place was on Third. Maybe I'll come back that way later, see if it's still there. If I asked to walk that way now, they'd ask why. Mom's diary is none of their business.

It doesn't take long to get to the festival. We get funnel cakes first. Charlie buys for everyone. Jimi gets one all for himself and eats the whole thing! We get Mexican after that. I buy my own.

We're in the kiddie part getting Jimi's face painted when a guy with a skateboard comes up and starts talking to Charlie.

"They've got a bunch of movies at Whitaker Center," he says. "Free. Independent stuff. Most of it's not worth seeing, but they're showing one on Gator Rogowski this afternoon."

"Who the fuck is that?" Crystal demands.

"My hero when I was a kid. Awesome boarder."

"So, what, he dies or something?"

"Come watch the movie and see."

We head to the Center. They're showing short flicks. They're not too bad. Crystal gets up with Jimi a couple times 'cuz he's starting to get squirmy—glad to see him acting like a regular kid. She holds him by the hand and he walks some, too. Kind of wobbly, but walking.

People keep coming up to Charlie. He seems to know everyone. Some of them sit with us for the boarder movie. It's a Sundance film. We rent a lot of those at home, at least we used to. It's not just about skateboarding. The dude's in prison for rape and murder. There's a reception after the movie. They give out awards and we score some free food. There's an old feature film showing at midnight.

Charlie says we'll come back after we make a grocery run.

41: Peg

Richard drives. I take my novel and pretend to read, but I'm going over and over everything he told me. If I hadn't seen Maggie that day she got drunk at the creek, there's no way I'd believe him, even with the things Lizzie's told me this week, but the fact that Maggie didn't say anything tells me she's at fault somehow.

But so am I.

"I left the girls alone too much when we were dating."

"You thought you could trust them."

"I should have paid more attention. The way she was developing, I should have realized Maggie needed a new swim suit, and that she'd get teased. But that crowd at the creek! And she took Lizzie with her."

"That's why I had to tell you. I'm afraid she's influencing Lizzie."

"Someone down there must have taken advantage of her. That's the only reason I can see her changing this much."

"If she got drunk regularly, it was probably more than once."

I know he's right. And if that happened, it would explain all of the behavior changes. I know. This is my fault. It's not too late, though. I can talk with her and help her understand that whatever's happened, she doesn't have to let it change who she is.

We check every site at the campground. There's no little red car. No Maggie. We get out and walk down to the beach. They're not there. Back at the campground, I get her picture out of my wallet and ask around. No one's seen her. There's a retired couple who've been camping almost a week. There's been no little red car, and the only tent campers are the ones here right now.

If Maggie didn't go camping, where is she?

On our way back, we ride in silence until we get to the outskirts of Buffalo. At least he's not rubbing it in that he *did* know my daughter better than I did myself. I'm not sure how to start looking. I rack my memory for details.

"Sarah Smith. That's the stepmother's name."

"Smith? Did you get a phone number?" he asks.

"No, I didn't think to ask if they had a cell phone with them."

"Any chance Maggie left a number in her room?"

"I'll look when we get home."

This big of a lie overrides her right to privacy. Richard's knuckles are white as he grips the steering wheel. He's as concerned as I am. Back at the house, we go straight to the girls' room and I search Maggie's drawer in the desk. No phone numbers. Nothing personal. I know she keeps her diary in her pillow case. It's time I read it, but it's gone, too. I look in the closet for it, but almost everything is Lizzie's. No diary and no phone numbers.

"I'd better call the police."

"And tell them what?" Richard demands. "You don't have a phone number or address and you're not sure the stepmother was for real. The police will think you've been negligent. You could lose your teaching license and then where would we be? Besides, if you call them in, she'll lie about me, too."

I think about what happened when my new student got involved with the police and court system. Richard's right. I don't want to call them unless it's absolutely necessary.

"But I can't do nothing."

"She'll probably come home from whatever party she's at about the same time she's expected. Spend the time figuring out what you'll say to her now you know what's been going on, and that she wasn't where she said she was going."

He's right. She'll probably be on time or close to it.

Lizzie's friend drops her off just before she has to go babysit.

"Lizzie, do you know where Maggie went this weekend?" I ask.

"They told you they were going down to Lakeshore."

"Richard and I drove down there today. They aren't there. Maggie didn't tell you what she's *really* doing?"

"Why'd you do that? They probably decided to go to a different campground, that's all. I gotta go or I'll be late."

"Did you eat?"

"I'll eat with the kids or have some of their leftovers."

I tell Richard I want to wait up for Lizzie and talk some more about Maggie when she gets home. He doesn't argue with me this time. He goes downstairs to do some work. I try to read. There's nothing else I can do right now, anyway.

42: Maggie

One of the guys we've been sitting with has a car. He gives us a ride to a big supermarket. I offer to buy some groceries.

"Cool, pick up diapers. We'll get the rest," says Charlie. "You take the kid."

They all go in while I get Jimi out of the car—ticks me off how they keep dumping him on me. I complain to Jimi as I carry him into the store on my hip. He doesn't understand the words, but my tone makes him get this worried look on his face. Kids that little aren't supposed to look like that, so I shut up.

I pull out a cart, put him into the kiddie seat, strap the safety belt around his waist, and head for the baby aisle. I see the same kind of diapers that were at the house and put a bag in the cart. I get some baby wipes, too. Charlie walks by and says to get crackers, without stopping or looking at us. He's weird. I get graham crackers with cinnamon on them and some saltines, too.

Jimi keeps bouncing in the cart through the checkout. Crystal's right behind us with a bunch of milk, cereal, and cheese. I take Jimi out to the car and put a seat belt on him. There isn't any car seat.

The driver comes out first and opens the trunk for the diapers and my grocery bag. Crystal and Charlie come out with her bags.

"WIC," she says.

Then Charlie opens his coat and sticks steaks and other stuff into her bags. The driver slams the trunk and glances at the store. We get into the car and drive away. I look back—nobody's there. No one caught them. Us.

"You do that all the time?" asks the driver.

"Sure," brags Crystal.

"Unless we gotta go to that little store on Second Street. They watch everyone too close," Charlie adds.

When I was five, I stuck a pack of gum into one of Mom's grocery bags. She found it when she was putting everything away, looked on the receipt, didn't find it, and nailed me for it. She made me take it back and give it to the storeowner. I never even considered shoplifting again. It was too scary when I was little, and it would be too embarrassing now to have my mother walk me back into a store like that. And she would, too. She'd be disappointed in me right now—just going along with this—but I'm hungry, and my money won't last very long.

They smoke a joint while the steak cooks. Charlie offers it to me.

"No, thanks," I say.

"Why not?"

"She'd sleep through the movie," says Crystal.

I take her excuse. "Yeah, I'm a lightweight."

We drive back to the theater. I have trouble paying attention to the movie. Keep wondering if Mom realizes I'm gone yet. It's Sunday night. Lizzie was gonna babysit sometime this weekend, but she might keep the money in her wallet for a day or two. Guess it doesn't really matter. That's all the past—gotta plan my future.

I won't stay with Charlie and Crystal for long. Don't wanna live like them. But Charlie said he knows someone who might have ID, but who? I ask him after the movie.

"Oh, that's Matt," he says. "Saw him tonight, but I forgot to ask him about it. I can hook up with him tomorrow, see if he's got something that'll work for you."

The driver parks across from the house. Jimi's still sound asleep. He slept through most of the movie, too.

"Okay if I crash at your place tonight?" the driver asks. "It's too late for me to go home."

"Sure. You can sleep with her," Charlie answers. He nods at me.

My stuff is up in that room, and it's the only place I've got to stay tonight. I follow them all into the house, not sure what I'm gonna do. Charlie locks the locks as the rest of us file up the stairs.

"Hold Jimi a minute so I can take a leak, would you?" asks Crystal.

She leaves the door ajar while she uses the toilet. Jimi's a warm lump in my arms. When she comes out, I pass him back to her.

"Thanks. 'Night," she says as she heads up to the third floor.

I close the bathroom door and squat over the toilet. Rinse off my hands and face. There's a grungy mirror above the sink. The lighting gives me huge shadows under my eyes. I look scared. I don't even know this guy's name. Woulda been nice if he'd asked *me* if he could stay. He's in the hallway when I come out.

"I'll be right back," he says as he heads into the bathroom.

I'm unzipping my sleeping bag when he comes up behind me, puts his hands on my hips, and kisses the back of my neck gently. I cringe.

"You okay?" he asks.

My stomach's in knots. I don't have any words.

"You don't have to do anything," he says.

I start shaking and tears pour down my face.

"Hey, hey, that's okay."

He turns me around and pulls me into a gentle hug. He rubs down my spine, over and over, telling me it's okay, 'til I quit crying.

"Sorry," I say. "I just wasn't expecting this. We didn't even talk or anything."

"It's okay. I just need a place to crash. I mean, if you wanted to, that would be great, but really, it's okay if we don't do anything."

Breath rushes out of me and the tears start up again.

"Come on. We can leave our clothes on and cuddle up to keep each other warm. Can you handle that?"

"Yeah, sure," I snuffle. "Thanks."

"Come on, let's lie down and get some rest."

We cuddle up like two spoons. He's behind me, with his arms around me, but it's okay. It feels like he's protecting me, not like he's trapping me.

"What's your name?" I whisper.

"C.J."

"You live with your uncle?"

"Yeah. I help him with his restaurant."

"Where are your parents?"

"My dad died when I was ten, cancer, which wasn't fair. He was a real health nut. My mom remarried when I was sixteen. I can't get used to seeing them together, so I asked if I could live with my uncle, and everyone agreed. So I came down here to live."

"How old are you?"

"Eighteen. How old are you?"

"Fifteen tomorrow. Today, actually. It's after midnight."

"Happy birthday. No wonder you got scared. You're just a kid."

"I'm not that much of a kid."

"I bet you're still a virgin."

The shaking starts again. I can't control it.

He keeps holding me and petting my arm. I start to hyperventilate and break away to sit up—take a gulp of air and hold my breath.

"You okay?" He sounds scared for me.

"Um-hm," I answer, still holding my breath. I let it out slowly. The shaking's easing off now, too.

"What happened to you?" he asks, stroking my back.

"My stepfather. He—you know."

C.J. swears quietly.

I start rocking back and forth from the waist up. He holds onto me and pets me and tells me it'll be okay, it's not my fault, over and over again, 'til I fall asleep.

43: Peg

I wake up on the way to the door. Someone's rapping on it loudly. My heart is pounding as I open it. Lizzie is there with Mr. Peterson. She's on the verge of tears. He looks grim.

"Lizzie? What's going on?" I ask.

She starts to respond, then hangs her head.

"If you don't tell her, I will." Mr. Peterson is furious.

"Lizzie?"

She hunches her shoulders and keeps her head down.

Mr. Peterson explains, "While my wife was talking to Lizzie and paying her, I took out the garbage, and I found this in our trash."

He holds up a beer bottle. It's Richard's brand.

"Lizzie, explain yourself," I demand.

"I wondered what all the fuss was about, so I took one of Richard's beers with me. I didn't even drink half of it. It tasted awful."

I'm stunned.

"We wanted to make sure you were aware," says Mr. Peterson. "We won't be having Lizzie watch our children now."

"I wouldn't think so. Thank you for letting me know why. Lizzie, go to your room and get ready for bed. I'll come talk to you in a few minutes."

When they've both gone, I close the front door and lean against it. First Maggie, now this! And Richard. We have to stop keeping alcohol in the house. I never did before and he doesn't need to be drinking all the time, either. I go to the girls' room.

"What were you thinking?"

"I dunno." She sighs. "It was stupid. But the kids at school always talk about partying. I just wondered what the big deal was."

"I've let you try a little."

"On New Year's Eve. Barely enough to taste it. Besides, that wasn't beer and 'most everyone drinks beer. Richard drinks it all the time and doesn't even get drunk unless he has a ton. You drink, too."

"Richard and I are adults. You know the difference. I am not going to argue that point. Last night, the smoke smell, did you try that, too?"

"Yeah. Cigarettes are really nasty. Worse than the beer, even."

"Well, at least you didn't like them. Are you going to try anything else, Lizzie?"

"No, I won't. I promise."

"You didn't take your responsibility seriously, either."

"About the kids, you mean? I waited 'til they were asleep."

"You were still responsible for their safety. You didn't know how it would affect you, whether you'd be able to respond to a sick child or an emergency properly."

"I didn't think of that. I guess I should have but I only had a couple swallows."

"I believe you, but you're lucky nothing went wrong."

"I lost a really easy way to make money."

"That's not your only consequence. You are grounded until the end of school and I'm not sure what I'll let you do over the summer."

"Yes, ma'm. What about our project? We still have to finish that."

"If you need to work together, it will be in my classroom after school." I pause to let this sink in. She hasn't asked about Mexico. She probably realizes it's out of the question now.

"I was waiting to talk with you, anyway. What has Maggie said to you about Richard?"

"He creeps her out, that's all."

"Richard says they got into a fight the day she got suspended, and he had to physically restrain her."

"She didn't tell me about that."

"Well, I guess I'll have to wait until she gets home." I look at our surroundings. "This room is a mess."

"I know. I haven't put anything away this weekend. It's been nice not having to keep everything out of Maggie's way."

"I want it cleaned up before she comes home tomorrow."

"Yes, ma'm."

I tuck her in, give her a kiss, and turn off the light.

I can't believe this. What has happened to my family?

Monday, May 29, 2000

44: Maggie

Sometime in the night, we've shifted positions.

C.J.'s still got his arms around me, but he's rolled partway onto his back. My head is on his right arm, and his left is holding me against the side of his chest. His eyes open as I start to edge the left one off me. He lifts it quickly.

"You okay?" he asks.

"Yeah. But I gotta pee."

He gives a little laugh. He's glad I'm feeling better.

Someone cares.

I come right back and plop down beside him. "We shoulda got some cleaner for that bathroom."

"No kidding." He grins. "Crystal and Charlie are slobs."

"How do you know 'em?"

"I buy my weed from Charlie."

"He's a dealer?" I squeak.

"You didn't know?"

The locks, the people coming and going. I should have known.

"I am such a dunce," I say. "Do you smoke much?"

"Not really, and only my days off. I've gotta work today."

"I don't really like it."

"Then don't smoke."

He goes to the bathroom and I get my brush out. My hair's really oily—gotta wash it soon.

I like C.J., but there's something bugging me.

When he comes back, I ask him, "Did you take anything from the grocery store yesterday?"

"No."

"Did you know they were gonna?"

"No, that's the first and last time I give them a ride to a store. My uncle would fire me if he knew about that. I've never shoplifted."

"But you know them well enough to stay over."

"Anyone can, as long as Charlie trusts them. I'm eighteen. I live with my aunt and uncle, but they don't keep tabs on me. I just didn't want to disturb my uncle coming in so late, and I thought it would be nice to sleep with you."

"Sorry about that."

"Actually, it *was* nice. Not exactly what I had in mind, but nice."

"So, you don't mind?"

"Not getting laid? Nah. It's not a big deal. I don't have a girlfriend, so I like to have some fun when I have a chance. But only if that's what the girl wants, too."

"Hooking up just for fun."

"Yeah. And *you* are not ready for that."

"What makes you so sure?"

"You saying you want to?"

"Maybe . . ."

He pulls me to him and starts kissing my face—my forehead, my temple, down the side of my jaw, and onto my neck. All those times necking with John on the couch when Mom was out with Richard I never got this hot—not this quick. His kisses are coming back up. The corner of my mouth, and then his lips are on mine. His tongue is testing my mouth. My lips open and our tongues feel each other. Then I'm sucking on his tongue and he groans.

He pulls back and looks at me, then says, "I really want you, but are you sure you want to do this?"

"I wanna do it right. I don't want him to be the only one."

C.J. pauses and looks at me curiously. "But would it be right?"

I'm not sure and he knows it. He drops his hands off me.

"Maggie. You're hot. Totally. But I don't want to make things worse. You're a good person. I watched you with Jimi yesterday. He got more attention from you in a few hours than he usually gets in a week—or a month. What that pervert did to you wasn't your fault. You need a chance to get over that before you hook up with anyone."

I'm relieved and ticked off at the same time. "I'm not a kid, you know."

"No, you're not a kid," he agrees. Then he throws one hand against his heart and the other across his forehead and gasps, "You're a wounded young woman."

I laugh. "Okay, I'm wounded. Maybe sex with you would heal me."

"Maybe. But it might make matters worse." He gets all serious. "I'm not going have a relationship with a fifteen-year-old runaway. It would be a onetime thing for me, and I don't think you could handle that. You need loving, not a casual hook up."

He's right. I woulda done more with John if that was right for me.

"Fine, then," I say primly. "Thank you for your kindness. Have a good day at work." I hold out my hand for him to shake.

He laughs as he takes it and gives me a kiss on the cheek, too.

"Happy birthday, Maggie."

45: Maggie Reads Peg's Journal

We're the only ones up. C.J. leaves for work. I eat toasted oats, wash my dishes and what's left from last night. Then I go upstairs and zip myself into my sleeping bag with Mom's journal.

I miss Mom and Lizzie. Some birthday. Find the spot I left off. It's the end of May and Mom's period is way late.

May 29, 1972

Pregnant.

What am I supposed to do about that? Maybe I'm not. I've skipped a month before. But I can't stand it here anyway, and I don't want anyone to start wondering. I feel fatter already. Maybe it's just bloating because I'm late. God, I hope I'm not pregnant. But if I am, I'm pretty sure people will be able to tell by the end of school. Another month? Yeah, it'll be obvious by then. I think.

There is no way I will ever give this town another scandal.

I have to leave. But if I go away, give it up, then come home, everyone will count months and know why. So there won't be any coming back. That probably means I won't ever finish high school, so there's no reason to worry about leaving before finals. I'll go to Harrisburg. Joe's really nice, and he won't look down on me for being pregnant. He'll understand. Maybe he'll help me again.

Still blaming herself for getting raped.

I'm glad Richard used a condom. Said he didn't want to catch anything from me. Didn't want to leave evidence is more like it.

Over the next few days, Mom sounds more and more desperate. She talks about running away. Her period still hasn't started.

She must be planning on having the baby, but what happened to it? How could Mom keep all these secrets from us?

She had five hundred in the bank that she got out to take with her. More than me. Jan gave her a ride to the bus station in Erie. Mom was wearing a hippie skirt and lacey T-shirt with no bra. Wish I had a picture of that! Mom had a blanket, not a sleeping bag, and she remembered a towel. Otherwise, we prepared pretty much the same. But her parents didn't see her leave. Can't believe she didn't get suspicious when I had that big pack stuffed for a few days.

She figured her parents were so into each other, they wouldn't even notice she was gone for a week. Wonder if Mom and Lizzie've figured out I'm not coming back. They'll definitely notice I'm not there.

Some older guy at the bus station, Nick, pretended to be Joe so Jan would leave her. He was going to Harrisburg, too, and even bought Mom's ticket. He gets Mom to choose a new name – Pyra.

June 3, 1972

We had sex in the alley behind the bus station! I thought we were just going to make out some, but then I realized I wanted it, and it's not like I'm a virgin anymore. There's no reason to stop. It made me feel really powerful and at the same time so ... submissive, I guess ... like willing to do anything. I guess that's what happened at the frat house, but I was too messed up to know what was going on. Now that I've had sex on purpose, I like it. Being close to Nick makes me ache for him. The sex makes me feel as if I belong to him. I want to do it again. If that makes me a slut, I don't care. I'm Nick's slut.

I close the journal. It's way too personal, not stuff anyone should know about their mother. She only did that 'cuz of what happened at the frat house! I could have been like that with C.J. But he knew how messed up I'm feeling and wouldn't let me make it worse. I'm so lucky to have ended up with C.J., not someone like Nick. He's gotta be bad news.

I need to find out what happens with him, and whether she has a baby or not. I open it back up.

She's not writing every day anymore. Skim through the next months. She totally gives herself over to Nick. He gets her smoking pot and taking 'ludes, which I think means Quaaludes.

I check the front page again. Yes, this is my mother's journal. She doesn't even drink much. She'd flip if she knew I've tried pot. Charlie's a drug dealer, but I'm movin' out, soon as I get some ID.

46:Peg

When I wake up, Richard has bacon cooking. It's past noon! I go rinse off my face, then walk out to the kitchen. He's making eggs, too. He's a good cook when it's something he wants to do.

"Let's not let Maggie ruin the day until she gets home," he says. "If Lizzie's not busy, maybe the three of us can watch a movie together."

"You didn't wake up when she came home last night, did you?"

"No. You fell asleep on the couch and I covered you up. I figured you'd wake up when she came in. You didn't?"

"Oh, I woke up all right. Mr. Peterson brought her home. She's fired. She took one of your beers down there to try it out."

"Oh, no. Was she drunk?"

"No, and she claims she threw most of it away, but she shouldn't have had it at all, let alone while she was babysitting."

"Of course not. That's why I suggested having Maggie go live with her friend, though. Before she leads Lizzie any farther astray."

"Well, we were drinking last night, too."

"We're adults."

"It's not a good example. I never kept alcohol in the house."

"We're adults. We're allowed to drink."

"It's how much and how often."

"I know I had too much Friday night. But that's not a usual thing with me, and you know it. Why are we arguing about this anyway? It's the girls who are giving you trouble, not me."

"I'm sorry. Do you think we could get an old refrigerator so you could keep your beer downstairs? So it's not so accessible?"

"Sure, that's reasonable. I'm the only one who drinks it. I still want my privacy, though. You can't keep pop or anything else in it."

"No, just your beer. Maybe we can get one of those little ones."

That might limit how much he keeps on hand, too.

The eggs are done. He cooked enough for Lizzie, too.

I knock on her door. She's got the covers over her head. I pull them down gently.

"Richard made breakfast."

"Okay," she says, sniffing. "Bacon! I'll be there in a minute."

Lizzie joins us in jeans and a sweatshirt. She's getting like Maggie with the big clothes. We don't discuss last night's events while we eat.

"When's Maggie supposed to get home?" Lizzie asks as she finishes and clears her dishes.

"Four."

"I'll clean up the room before then."

"You'll have to share a room when you go to college, you know."

"Yeah. When I go to Mexico, too."

"Mexico is probably not going to happen."

"You can't do that! Not for one little mistake! Mom!"

"What's this about Mexico?" Richard asks.

"Her Spanish class is going to Mexico for a few weeks this summer. Someone dropped out, so Lizzie had a chance to take that girl's place."

"It's not fair! This is the only thing I've done wrong. I've been good all year, and I have straight A's!"

"I thought you were worried about money," Richard says.

"She's been babysitting to save up for the ticket."

Lizzie composes herself and tries again. "Mom, please don't say no yet. Please, at least go to that planning meeting. Please?"

"I don't know if I could trust you."

"Please. Go to the meeting. It's not a vacation trip, I'll be learning a lot and it's all chaperoned. Please, Mom. You can ground me the whole rest of the summer, just please don't say I can't go to Mexico."

It probably would be a good learning experience, and I don't want to stop trusting her altogether because of one mistake, or because of anything Maggie's done.

"I'll go to the meeting to listen. But you'll have to convince me you can find a new way to pay for your ticket."

Lizzie knows when to quit.

"Okay," she says, and heads to her room.

"Isn't that a decision we should make together?" Richard asks.

"I guess so, though if she earns the money herself, it doesn't impact our finances."

"It does if she gets into trouble down there and we have to bail her out . . . but she's your daughter. You do what you think is right. I'm going to take a drive. Maybe I can find an inexpensive refrigerator for the basement."

As Richard leaves, I clear the table and get out the makings for Maggie's birthday cake. Both of the girls like my carrot cake. I make it from scratch, and shredding carrots feels therapeutic. Once it's in the oven and I've cleaned up the kitchen, I settle on the couch to read my book. A little later I hear Lizzie swear. Then it gets very quiet.

Neither of them used to swear, at least not in my hearing.

I decide to ignore it. So much for a pleasant holiday weekend. Once the cake is out, I focus on the story. It's my way of escaping.

47: Maggie Reads Peg's Journal

Crystal and Jimi come down from the third floor. Hear her using the bathroom. I pretend to be asleep, in case she looks into this room. Soon as they get downstairs, the TV goes on.

Don't feel like talking to anyone. Thought reading the journal would make me feel closer to Mom and Lizzie, but it's like someone I never knew. Mom never told us any of this. She let us believe that she's always been the way she is now. I sink into her words.

She writes about how hard it's raining, and how the river keeps rising. She thinks about "swirling away in the water." That was the Quaaludes, or maybe she was depressed. At least her period finally starts. Then they have to evacuate for Hurricane Agnes—the river already over the banks in places.

As bad as things are for me right now, they're not as bad as they were for Mom when she tells Nick she's not on the pill. She finally finds out what condoms are, and he's not happy about using them. At least I knew what one was. I'd never actually seen one, though, until Richard.

I don't wanna think about that.

There's one page, no date, just one sentence.

Nick hurt me, but it was my fault for being stupid.

Shit. Blaming herself again.

Then he starts "sharing" her. I so can't believe this is my mother. But then, I couldn't believe how she let Richard talk her into selling our house, either. The next entry's worse.

August 23, 1972

Nick moved me in with the other whores across the street. He shoved me into a room where they were all sitting around watching TV and I was crying and promising to do whatever he wanted if he'd please take me back and he said he had a new girl moving in and I was not to speak to her or he'd make me wish he'd killed me. I kept begging him not to give me away to a pimp, but he laughed at me and left.

My stomach aches. Mom was so used by that guy. This probably was his plan from the moment he saw her at that bus station.

I'd stop there, but there's only two more entries.

August 25, 1972

What's wrong with being a prostitute? It's the world's oldest profession, and with Quaaludes, I like it. I like being a whore. The next time Nick's with me, I need to show him how much I love him for showing me who I really am.

That had to have been for Nick to see. He musta been checking her diary and she didn't want him to know she was planning her escape.

August 29, 1972

On my way West.
I will NEVER let myself be used like that again.
I'm not Pyra anymore.

That sounds like Mom.

Maybe none of it is real. Maybe the whole journal is a story she was writing. But it sounds real. If all this happened to her, would she believe me about Richard?

Except he's her husband, and she's been going along with all his other crap. If she did believe it, he'd twist it around to blame me.

She'd believe him.

48: Peg

Lizzie's not making a sound. Richard's still gone. I'm whipping right through the novel. I take a break to stretch and get some pop. There isn't any in the refrigerator.

I wonder if Richard has any in the basement? He keeps the tequila down there. I'm not sure if he has any mixers. I start to go look for pop, but stop part way down the stairs. I can see where he's got his computer and file cabinets set up. The tequila's out in the open. I know he drinks it straight. I shouldn't invade his space. He doesn't even want me to *clean* his office area. He said he wants one part of his house that's still his own. I can understand that.

I go back to the kitchen and close the door.

The cake's cool. I open a can of cream cheese frosting. The girls like that as much or better than my homemade. Once the cake is frosted, I dig out the decorations and candles. Now it looks like a birthday. I used to get balloons filled with helium and put them in the birthday girl's room while she was still sleeping, but they outgrew that years ago.

It's almost four. I hope Maggie gets back on time. Maybe they did just go to a different campground. I better go see if Lizzie got the room straightened up.

49: Maggie

Musta dozed off after I finished Mom's journal. The sun's out now—won't flood this time. I dig out clean undies, a shirt, and socks.

Keep a hundred dollars in my socks, fifty in each one. Doesn't bulge under my arches anymore. My cash is going awfully fast. There's only one fifty-seven and change left for my pockets. Need that ID soon. Downstairs, Crystal and Jimi are on the couch, of course. He's got milk dried on his face. It's almost four o'clock.

Crystal leers at me. "Thought you were gonna sleep all day. C.J. keep you up all night?"

"Actually, I was reading."

What we did or did not do is none of her business. I walk right past her into the kitchen and help myself to cheese and crackers. The dirty dishes are piling up. These people are pigs. I definitely need to find another place to stay, but not 'til I connect with this Matt guy for ID. The front door slams, then I hear Charlie's voice. He must have gotten up and gone out while I was sleeping.

"Where's Maggie?" he says.

He meets me in the dining room.

"Hey Maggie, this is Matt. He's got some ID that might work."

Matt looks like a skeleton with skin. His eyes are almost black. He pulls out a license and holds it up, looking from it to me and back again. "Looks like you, just shorter hair."

He hands it to me. Shauna McLaughlin. The hair cut's wrong and the picture's not much like me, but it's a real license. Height and weight are close enough. Hair color and eyes match. People always complain about their license photos. It's good enough to pass.

"Where'd you get it?" I ask.

"If you'll notice, the address is in Pittsburgh."

"But did she lose it here?"

"If you don't want it, I have another buyer waiting. I was just doing Charlie a favor by giving you the first opportunity."

I don't wanna lose out. This may be the best I'll get. It says she's eighteen. I can do eighteen with ID backing me up.

"How much do you want for it?"

"I also have her social security card. Both for two hundred."

I don't say anything, but I start to hand it back to him.

"If it makes you feel better, I trade with a guy I know in Pittsburgh."

"That's more than I thought it would be."

"For you, for Charlie, I'll make it one seventy-five, but that's the best I can do. The social security card is worth that much by itself."

I look over at Charlie.

"Let her have them for one fifty," he says.

Matt pauses, then agrees. "You owe me, though, Charlie."

I empty my pockets and count out the money. Have seven dollars left, plus the hundred in my socks. Way more than I planned on paying, but the social security card should make it a lot easier to get work.

Matt takes the money and hands me the license and card with a flourish. I put them in my left back pocket, not with my money. Don't wanna accidentally drop them when I go to pay for something.

"Just don't use it anywhere near Pittsburgh," Matt warns me.

I have ID! It's time to move on, find a better place to stay.

They head for the front door and I'm right behind them, headed for the stairs to get my stuff and leave, when everything goes wrong. As Charlie opens the door, two guys in ski masks shove their way into the house. They're waving huge guns around and shouting at everyone.

"Down on the floor! Hands behind your heads!"

I lie on my belly on the floor. All I see are shoes. Nikes under black polish. A scuff mark on one, blue.

"Keep that kid down on the floor!"

The smaller one gives his gun to his partner and starts checking us, one by one. He makes Charlie stand up first. Charlie's way bigger, but there's a gun on him the whole time, so he just puts his hands in the air and doesn't say a word. The little guy doesn't find much money, but he dangles Charlie's keys in front of him like they're the big prize. Then he has Charlie get back onto the floor and checks Matt the same way. Matt's got wads of cash stashed all over and a gun tucked into the back of his pants. The little guy takes it all, and cell phones, too.

Crystal's next. She has a hard time hanging onto Jimi while she's being searched. She's only got some change.

Then it's my turn.

I hold my arms up and let the guy pat me down and check pockets. I don't care, as long as he doesn't have me take off my socks and shoes. He takes the seven bucks, then pulls out the license and social security card. He drops them, then pushes me back onto the floor.

The carpet stinks. It probably *was* food Jimi was eating off of it when I got here Saturday. That was day before yesterday?

"Everybody, get your hands back behind your heads." The little guy turns to his partner, "I'll go get his stash. Shoot anyone who moves."

Crystal holds onto Jimi as tight as she can and still lie on her belly. She can't put her hands behind her head, but the gunman doesn't seem to care. He's watching Charlie and Matt more closely. Seems like I've been staring at that blue spot on those stupid shoes forever.

Then Jimi wriggles free from Crystal and she starts to go after him. A gunshot blasts. The bullet hits the wall above the couch. Don't know if it was a warning, or if the guy's a rotten shot, but Jimi crawls behind the couch and everyone else hugs the floor.

"Next time it won't be the wall."

His voice is squeaky high, like a cartoon character I used to watch. Try to remember which one, but can't quite grasp it. Doesn't fit this situation. Thinking about it helps me not panic. Then his partner comes downstairs with a garbage bag and two stuffed pillowcases.

"What was the shot?" he asks.

"The kid got loose and she started to get up. I shot the wall and they held still." The big guy is still squeaking. Could be his regular voice, or maybe 'cuz he's nervous.

"Shoulda shot her. Where's the kid?"

"Behind the couch. What's with the pillow cases?" The squeak slips a little. I think he's trying to disguise his voice.

"The bag wasn't enough. He had all kinds of shit up there. Way more than we expected." The little guy takes his gun back, then turns to us and says, "We should probably shoot every one of you in the head, but I'm feeling really lucky right now, so we won't. But don't anyone move for five full minutes after we leave. You, girl in the sweatshirt."

He's talking to me. I lift my head to look up.

"You have a watch. Tell these people when it's five minutes."

"Okay."

"What time is it now?"

Can't believe how calm I'm staying—put my cheap watch under my face and check the time. My voice doesn't even waver. "4:05."

"Hear that? Don't move until 4:10."

They leave and the locks click. They're using Charlie's keys. I think we can still get out. After one minute Charlie gets up. Matt follows.

"You see his fucking shoes?" asks Charlie.

"Yeah, dumb fuck. Like we wouldn't recognize them."

"He's been wearing those shoes the whole time I've known him, for crying out loud. What a moron. As if that stupid voice would fool us."

"Who do you think the little guy was?" Charlie asks Matt.

"I don't know. Doesn't he have a brother?"

"He joined the military. But he's got a fucking cousin who's short."

"I know the guy. It was probably him."

"Fucking stupid assholes. They think I'm just gonna let them walk away with my shit?"

Charlie takes off up the stairs. Matt's right behind him.

I grab my new ID cards off the floor before Matt notices them. He lost the money—he might want them back. Head upstairs for my other stuff. Soon as that five minutes is up, I'm out of this house for good.

"Fuck!" Charlie screams from the third floor. "Fucking assholes! They got it all!"

Things are crashing up there. Charlie keeps on ranting.

I've got my pack on my back, but he's coming down the stairs two at a time, so I stay out of sight.

"Matt, we've gotta get those fucking guns back."

"Absolutely. The buyers expect the deal to close on schedule."

Hear the locks on the front door. Check my watch. If they get shot, those guys will come in and finish us off, too.

I go to the stairs and call down, "It's only been three minutes."

Matt turns and stares up at me. I wish I'd kept my mouth shut. He points a bony finger and speaks in a terribly clear tone.

"You were not here. You did not see anything. You heard nothing. Do you understand?"

"Yes. Yes, I understand."

"It would be best if you found another city."

"No problem. I'll be gone today."

They open the door. Charlie takes a quick look each way. Of course the robbers are long gone. He and Matt head away from the river. They don't even close the door—there's nothing to protect anymore.

I go downstairs. Crystal's pulling Jimi out from behind the couch.

"Is he okay?" I ask.

She nods. She's crying.

"What are you gonna do?"

"Stay here, I guess. Don't have anywhere else to go."

"What about your family?"

"Fat chance they'd help. Been on my own since I was thirteen."

"Isn't there a shelter or something?"

"They always want you to get straight. I can't do that. All Charlie wants is fucking."

"That doesn't bother you?"

Crystal shrugs. "It's better than hooking."

"Wouldn't it be better for Jimi if you went to a shelter?"

"They'd take him away from me. He's all I've got."

"Well, I'm out of here," I say.

"You better leave the city. You don't wanna mess with Matt."

"Yeah. I got that. Good luck. Take care of Jimi."

"I know I'm a lousy mother, but I love him."

Jimi's clinging to her neck, watching me. "Bye-bye," he says.

"He must really like you. He hardly ever talks to anyone but me."

She doesn't need to know he talked to me before. I tighten the straps on the pack and head out—my mile-eater stride, like Mom's.

Some birthday. But it isn't my birthday anymore.
I check Shauna's license. My new birthday's the end of summer.
Fifteen today, nineteen in August—feel older than that already.

50: Peg

Lizzie has the door closed, so I knock. Instead of yelling for me to come in, she opens it a few inches and whispers, "Is Richard here?"

"No, he went for a drive and he hasn't come back yet."

She pulls me into the room and closes the door. She's put a few things away, but the room is still a mess.

"Lizzie, you need to finish before Maggie comes home. Even if she's in trouble with me, you still need to be considerate."

"She's not coming home."

"Don't say that," I respond sharply. Last night that was my first thought, but if she didn't go camping, she'll still be home on time.

"She left a note in my money box. She's not coming home."

"She took your money? That's why you swore?"

"Yeah. Sorry, but she took all of it."

"That was hours ago!" I snap. "Why didn't you tell me right away?"

"I wasn't sure what to do," says Lizzie. "The note's to me, not you, and she left her diary for *me* to read."

"She wanted you to read her diary?" That doesn't make sense.

"Well, she didn't exactly say so, but the note kinda suggests it."

"Let me see the note."

She hands it to me. I read it to myself.

Dear Lizzie, I'm sorry I'm taking your money. I'll pay you back. But I'm running away and I need it. I'm leaving you my diary, but don't let Mom see it. Don't ever be home alone with Richard. You're right. He's more than creepy. I love you and Mom—Maggie.

"No," I moan. My knees start to fold.

I grab the chair and sink onto it. Richard was right, she's setting him up as a villain. I wish he had said something sooner. I could have talked to her. I could have stopped her. I should have known when I saw that enormous backpack. I should have stopped her.

"Mom, I know she said not to show you, but I think you really need to read her diary. Not the beginning. Start here. Like a month ago."

Screaming won't help. I take the diary.

51:Peg Reads Maggie's Diary

I need to start at the beginning, to understand why my Maggie changed so much. Something must have happened at the creek. That has to be the explanation. She was never a manipulative child. But if Maggie's run away, finding her quickly is the priority. Lizzie's right, any clues to where she's going will be in the last entries. Understanding can wait.

April 30, 2000

Mom went back to work. I stayed in bed. Could hear Richard walking around the house. Once he opened my door. Pretended to be asleep so I wouldn't hafta talk to him. I hate him.

May 1, 2000

Happened in the shower—know I locked the door. Was almost done when he pulled open the curtain & stared at me. Said now he's seen me, I don't need to come on to him anymore, then he smiled & flipped his finger under my nipple. Then he left.

This entry is before she got suspended, before the incident Richard told me about. When she was sick. Was she plotting against him even then? Or did she go back and write this later?

Lizzie sighs. I look up as a tear runs down her cheek. She believes this! How could Maggie pull her into this! I go sit next to Lizzie on her bed and hold her.

"Honey, Maggie would have told us if that happened. You know that. She didn't say anything to you, did she?"

"No," she says, blinking to stop more tears from falling.

Grabbed a towel & locked the door, then leaned against it to get dressed. Listened for him before I dashed to my room. Put on my Bills sweatshirt & got up on my bunk. Sat in the corner, ready to kick him in the teeth, but he didn't come in, then Mom & Lizzie got home, & I heard him say "I love you" to Mom. She wouldn't believe me. Too weird. Besides, she's in love with him.

Asked Lizzie to stay home with me tomorrow. She told Mom her throat was scratchy, so Mom's letting her stay home in case she's got strep, too.

"Is that true?" I ask.

Lizzie nods.

"What did she say to get you to stay home?

"She just said he was giving her the creeps."

My Maggie would have met me at the door and blasted him. She would at least have told Lizzie that day. This is pure manipulation.

"Her note said not to show me the diary, Lizzie. If it were true, she'd want me to know, but she didn't. She's trying to get you to join her against Richard."

Within my anger there's a glimmer of hope. Maybe she hasn't really run away. She may want me to think he's driven her away, so I'll leave him. She may be home soon, or she may want me to find her. I ignore Lizzie's protests and read for a clue.

May 5, 2000

Bet he did it to scare me into staying out of trouble, creep! He was drunk. Might not remember—or maybe he's embarrassed. He hardly came out of the basement this weekend.

"You *know* Maggie would never make those excuses if he'd really done that."

"Keep reading, Mom." Lizzie pulls back and watches me read the next entry.

I got suspended again. Was walking down the hall when a hand bumped the same place he touched me in the shower. Punched the kid, then realized it was an accident. They sent me home with Richard, even though anyone could smell the tequila over the mouthwash. Tried to go to my room. He grabbed my shoulder & pinned me against the wall.

There's no date on the entry, but this is the day Richard told me about, the day she got suspended. This isn't the way he said it happened, though. My anger against Maggie subsides as I read on, and I find myself chilled.

He called me a teasing little slut. He was really drunk—started messing with my buttons. I pushed his hand away, then he grabbed my boob so hard I yelped. He squeezed harder, told me to keep my mouth shut. Told me I was going to do exactly what he told me to do, & I wouldn't say a word to anyone 'cuz my mother would hate me forever for lying, or for stealing her husband, if she believed me.

Maggie couldn't believe that. But I *don't* believe this. She *must* have made it up to get Lizzie against Richard, too. My hands are icy.

He said I wanted it or I woulda said something the other day. He said Mom wouldn't believe me if I tried to tell now. He's right. So I just did what he told me to do. After, he made me take a shower. I was afraid he'd come in there & start all over, but he didn't. I still don't feel clean. He let me tell Mom about being suspended. She was so disappointed. I cried & told her how sorry I am & that I hadn't meant to do it & I promised I'll never get suspended again & she believed me & gave me a hug. It is so good to have her believe me again. I won't tell her about Richard. She'd think I was lying.

"What on earth has Maggie been reading to come up with this?"

It feels as if there's no blood left in my hands. How can that be when my heart is pounding?

"You think she made it up?" Lizzie is outraged.

"Richard told me a very different story about what happened that day. And Maggie threatened to lie about it."

"That's what *he* said. Who are you gonna believe?"

"Think about it, Lizzie. Maggie lied about the creek, she lied about drinking, and she lied about the boys she hit last year. This is the same thing, only more serious." Lizzie *has* to see this is just another story. It *has* to be a lie, or we may never see Maggie again. "Even if she didn't want to tell me, don't you think she would have told *you* about this right away?"

"Maybe, but she wouldn't run away just to get you mad at Richard."

"She might have, Lizzie. She might think it would make me divorce him and move back home. She may not have run away at all, or not very far." I hope so.

Lizzie holds her mouth the same way my mother used to when she was angry.

Stayed in bed after Mom & Lizzie left today. Hoped he'd forget I was there. But he came. Stinking of tequila. Told me I was saying the right things, but he had to know I wasn't faking it, that I'd really learned my lesson. He made me beg him to punish me for being a slut and a bad daughter. He watched me shower when he was done. Made me turn & show him every part of my body. Only marks are on my boob from yesterday. If he bothers me again, I'll show Mom. I was so glad to see her & Lizzie. I helped without being asked. Then Richard suggested we all play a board game together, as a family, & I smiled & said "Let's" & tried to sound cheerful for the whole game.

This is so warped. Could Maggie actually make it up? This is an awfully elaborate and indirect way for her to make allegations against Richard, and she *has* been on her best behavior lately.

I have to know the truth. Richard admitted there might be bruises, but said he grabbed her from behind, not the way Maggie says. The marks would be different. "Did you see the bruises?" I ask Lizzie.

"No."

So much for empirical evidence.

Either this is all true and Maggie didn't think she could tell me, or she's become a horribly manipulative liar. I need to know which it is, but I've failed as a mother either way. Depression settles on me like a heavy blanket. The next entry only makes it worse.

Richard said I had to be punished again, 'cuz Mom's still worried about me. Told him I'd show her the bruises on my boob. He laughed & said he already explained that I tried to take off & he might have grabbed it by accident. She believes him & knows I'm a liar. He can do whatever he wants.

My tears never stopped, but I quit crying out loud.

It was just my body, not me. When he was done, he washed me in the tub like a little kid, all gentle, but explaining softly that whenever he's got me alone he'll discipline me, if I'm not being good enough to my mother. Said he doesn't want to, but he will. I know he'll always find a reason he has to . . .

"This reads like cheap fiction, Lizzie. She doesn't say exactly what he did, probably because nothing happened."

Manipulative is better than the alternative.

Lizzie hugs her knees and rests her chin on them. She's not talking.

"Has he *ever* done *anything* to you to make you believe this?"

I want her denial.

"The way he kissed me the other day."

"I was right there!" I reply impatiently. "He was drunk, so it was a little sloppy, but there was nothing inappropriate about it."

"I didn't like it."

"You don't like Richard!"

Exasperated, I skim the rest quickly, looking for clues to Maggie's whereabouts.

We can talk about the diary when she's safe at home.

Mother's Day, 2000

Lizzie & me took Mom out for breakfast, just the three of us. Mom said she knows it's been tough on us, having to move & share a room & everything, but she's really glad we're working through it, 'cuz she really loves Richard.

I won't hurt her by telling. I'll just stay in my room as much as I can and make sure I'm never alone with him again and I'll be really good.

This sounds like genuine Maggie. I did tell the girls that, and she *has* been staying in her room all the time, and she *has* been on her best behavior.

I shiver.

My hell.

Was sleeping when he came for me today. Mom and Lizzie went out shopping for shoes. He knew he had me for an hour. I can't live like this.

Lizzie sees the part I'm reading.

"Remember, Mom? Maggie was asleep when we went to buy my shoes, and I *told* you she was acting bizarre the other night. She was afraid of being left home alone with him."

That makes an uncomfortable amount of sense.

May 25, 2000

Someone who doesn't even know me noticed before Mom or Lizzie.

Chip, the quiet guy who sits next to me in third period, stopped me after class Tuesday & asked if I was okay. I totally fell apart. He took me up to the projection booth above the theater. No one was there. Can't believe I pulled down my collar to show him the fingerprints. He asked about a doctor, I told him no. No doctor. No talking to teachers. No making phone calls to anyone. He understood. He's got a friend who ended up in foster care. Safe, but her mother didn't believe her & won't talk to her anymore.

Mom won't believe me. Not after everything I pulled trying to break up their engagement. And I can't live like this—Chip said he'd help me & he really came thru. We're gonna pretend I'm camping with his family for the holiday weekend.

So I'm out of here. This is my last night in this house

I don't know what to believe. Chip certainly didn't look like the kind of boy to party all weekend. But I don't want this to be the truth.

"I *hope* Maggie's lying."

"What if it *is* the truth, Mom?"

What if my husband has terrorized and abused my daughter?

"He'd get the divorce papers in jail." I answer firmly, though my body is shaking visibly.

"What are you gonna do?"

"I don't know, Lizzie. Do you *really* think this happened?"

"I did when I first read it, but you're right it's not like Maggie not to say anything, and I'd kinda expect her to totally claw his face. But she's been acting weird lately, too. And I don't care what you say about what happened in the kitchen, it didn't feel right, Mom."

I try to replay that moment. I'm just not sure.

Lizzie continues, "And he does look at Maggie differently when you're not there. I can't explain it, but it gives me the creeps."

I curl into myself on Lizzie's bed. The shaking is getting worse. What if I've delivered my Maggie to a monster? She'll never come home. I'll never see her again.

"She has to be making it up," I whisper.

"What if she isn't?"

Lizzie's question hangs in the air.

Either way the answer is the same. Maggie needs our help.

52: Maggie

The photographer's still at his booth, but he's got customers. I hang back and wait. He looks over, smiles and gives me a nod to let me know he remembers me and knows I'm there. I breathe easier. I know I need to get out of town before Matt and Charlie catch those guys and start thinking about how much I saw and heard.

Wish I had sunglasses. The worst birthday of my life, and it turns out sunny. That stuff at the house shoulda happened at night, or on a cold, rainy day. Not a beautiful afternoon.

Wonder if the robbers realize Charlie recognized them. Probably not or they woulda killed us—part of me wishes they had.

The photographer finally gets a break from customers.

"Hi," I say. "Looks like you're doing a lot of business."

"Mostly lookers, but enough buyers to make the trip worthwhile."

"How much longer are you gonna stay open?"

"A couple hours, maybe more."

"Are you leaving for home, then?"

"I've slept in my camper the last three nights. I want a hot shower and a real bed tonight. I'll head for home early tomorrow."

A customer interrupts us, then people keep coming. He said he'll be here at least two more hours. I'm hungry. Maybe I can find the restaurant-coffeehouse from Mom's journal, if it's still here.

It only takes a few minutes to hike up to Third. I'm by the Capitol Building. If I were a restaurant owner, I'd wanna be close to it. I decide to walk a few blocks to my left first.

A few minutes later, I'm looking at signs in the window advertising gyros, baklava, and a bunch of other stuff I don't recognize. There's a coffeehouse on the left—with stained glass windows. No dragons, just grapes and stuff, but it's real stained glass. There's a sign on that door asking people to bring their poetry and songs for open mike night. That would take a lot of guts, more than I have. I start to walk away, then C.J. steps out of the coffeehouse.

"Maggie, how'd you find me?"

"I was just looking for someplace to eat."

"What's with the pack? You find another place to stay?"

He has no idea what happened at the house. Should I warn him? Or would it be more dangerous for him to know? It's probably better not to say anything.

"I'm going to check out some other parts of the country."

"So I might not see you again. Come on in, I'll buy you dinner."

He takes my pack and leads me into the coffeehouse. He seats me at a table in the corner and leans my pack against the wall. The place is pretty busy.

"This is Aji's section. He'll be right with you. Order anything on the menu. We serve the same things as in the restaurant—same kitchen, different ambiance."

"Are the prices the same?"

"Yes, but I told you, your dinner's on me."

"Thanks."

"I've gotta get back to work. Talk to me before you leave, though."

"Okay."

The place is full of good smells. It's all Greek food on the menu, but each dish has a description and a number. There's lemon-flavored soup that sounds good, and I've had a gyro before.

"What would you like tonight?" Aji's voice is deep and sweet.

"I'll have the number one soup, a number fourteen gyro and the fresh lemonade."

It's kinda strange to sit alone in a nice restaurant, but being tucked away in a corner helps. C.J.'s busy seating people, checking to make sure customers are satisfied. He flashes me a smile. I start memorizing the information on my ID.

My soup comes first. It's delicious. By the time it's gone, I'm not sure I'll be able to eat the rest of my order. Aji brings out the lemonade and gyro. I just look at it.

C.J. stops by to ask if everything's okay.

"The soup was wonderful. I just need to wait a few minutes before I can eat the rest."

"Okay."

He starts to leave, but I call him back.

"This is weird, but I've gotta ask, is your uncle's name Joe?"

"Yeah. How'd you know?"

"I think my mom met him a long time ago. When she was my age."

"No kidding? I'll tell him. He'll want to meet you."

"Oh, no, that's okay. He probably wouldn't remember her."

"He might."

C.J. goes back to work.

His uncle spent one afternoon with my mother long before I was even born. *She* probably doesn't remember *him*. What am I doing here? I start nibbling at the gyro, worrying about what I'm going to say to C.J.'s uncle. The next thing I know, the gyro's gone, and I've got about an hour to get back to the river. Then C.J. brings out a piece of baklava with a candle flickering on top.

"Happy birthday."

"Thanks, and thanks for not singing."

Only a few people notice the candle. They smile and get on with their meals and conversations. C.J. sits down across from me.

"Uncle Joe will be out in a minute. He wants to meet you."

"I really don't know what to say to him."

"Don't worry about it. So, what did you do for your birthday?"

"Well, I read my Mom's journal."

Aji brings me more lemonade. I pass him my dirty dishes, to be helpful. Klutz that I am, I knock a fork onto the floor. I bend down to get it 'cuz Aji's hands are full. It's right by his shoes.

THE SHOES. He's polished them black for work, and put in skinny laces so people won't usually notice he's not wearing dress shoes. The scuff mark's the same.

I turn towards C.J. as I sit up, and pass Aji the fork without looking at him. He *must* have recognized *me*—I'm still in the same clothes. Can't let him know I've spotted him. He takes the fork and leaves.

C.J. looks concerned. "You're white. Just bending over didn't do that, did it?"

"No." I pause until Aji disappears into the kitchen.

"How well do you know Aji?" I ask.

"He's worked for us about six months now. He's a pretty good guy. He's the one who introduced me to Charlie."

I'm paranoid that someone will hear what I'm saying. I lean forward and whisper with my hand cupped so only C.J.'ll hear.

"He robbed Charlie today."

"How do you know that?"

"I was there. Two of them came in with guns, wearing ski masks."

"Was anyone hurt?"

"No."

"If they wore masks, why do you think it was Aji?"

"He wore the same shoes."

"You're going by his shoes?"

"So's Charlie. And the other guy who was there, Matt."

"Matt?"

"I bought ID from him," I whisper. "They took a load of money off Charlie and Matt, and other stuff, too. They're really ticked off. I'm on my way out of town, to get away from the whole thing. If they come after him here, it could be awful. I think they were gonna get guns."

His uncle startles us by pulling a chair over to the table.

"So, Maggie. C.J. says I knew your mother?"

"You just gave her a motorcycle ride one afternoon."

"When?"

"I think it was spring, the year you had that big flood down here?"

"Agnes? We still measure everything against that storm. I did have a motorcycle back then, but I was engaged. I wasn't giving girls rides."

"I think you were going to see someone in Canada?"

"Oh, I remember. I was going to see George, C.J.'s dad, before my wedding. Your mother got stranded at the college and I gave her a ride home. A nice girl, and pretty—what's her name?"

"Peg."

"That's right. *Peggy Sue* kept running through my head the rest of that trip."

"You really remember her?"

"Sure. She looked a lot like you, especially around the eyes."

He's right. Mom and I have the same shape and color eyes.

"I even looked for her a few years later. Someone pointed out the house and said she didn't live there anymore, so I left."

"I bet she'd like to know that. She came here looking for you and someone told her you were away on your honeymoon."

He nods. "Maria and I went to Europe that summer."

"Did you get divorced? When you went to look for my mom?"

"No." He chuckles as if that would be ridiculous. "Maria was with me. We were on our way to visit my brother. How is your mother?"

"She's fine. Married. My sister's in high school; I just finished my freshman year at Fredonia State." Lies flow right out of me now.

"So you're doing some sightseeing?"

"Yup."

C.J. hasn't said a word. His uncle gets up to leave.

"Good luck, and give your mother our best. Tell her to stop in if she's ever in town. Maria will be sorry she missed you, but she's in Greece a few more days, visiting family. Nice meeting you, Maggie."

"Nice to meet you, too."

He puts the chair back and disappears into the kitchen.

"I manage this side; he does the restaurant side," CJ explains.

"Doesn't he have any kids?"

"Three. Peter's an attorney and George makes stained glass. He did those windows. Anna is married to a naval officer and she teaches. They've lived all over the world. They're in Germany now, with two little kids."

"I forget my mom didn't even have me 'til she was in her thirties. It's weird to realize people her age are grandparents."

"My father was older than Uncle Joe, but they had me late, too. Are you going to eat that baklava now, or should I wrap it?"

I take out the candle and try a small bite. It's incredibly sweet.

"Actually, could you wrap it up? I'm pretty full right now."

"Sure."

"What about Aji?"

"I'll tell him Charlie's after him. If you're right, Aji will leave right away and we won't see him again."

"Thanks. I wouldn't want anything to happen here."

I check my watch. Don't wanna miss that guy. I need the ride.

"I've gotta go."

"Let me wrap that for you."

I put on my gear while I'm waiting. C.J. comes right back with the baklava. I have him stash it in a side pocket of the pack, then he walks me to the door.

"I'll wait a few minutes to talk to Aji. So you're leaving town?"

"Looks like it."

"That wasn't much of a stay."

"Trust me, it feels like a lifetime."

"Have you thought about calling your mom?"

"Can't." I sigh. "I just hope my sister doesn't show her my diary. She'll probably hate me if she reads it."

"You wrote about what he did to you?"

"Some. I left it with my sister in case he tries something with her. But, he probably won't. She's not like me. She's always good."

C.J. shakes his head. "Quit blaming yourself. You really don't think your mother would believe you?"

"I don't know. Maybe, but I don't wanna hurt her. Like you said, I am hot. Maybe I *did* make him think I was coming on to him. Not on purpose, but . . ."

"You're a kid and he's an adult. He had no business doing anything. Especially when you're his wife's daughter."

"Yeah. But he was drunk, at first. That was probably part of it, too."

"Quit making excuses for the scumbag."

"Yeah, well, I gotta get going. Thanks for dinner and everything."

"Remember, we're always here if you need anything."

C.J. gives me a quick hug.

"Thanks," I say, and I leave before I cry.

53: Peg

Lizzie keeps the diary and note in the room she shares with Maggie. Shared? No, Maggie has to be coming home.

I take a steamy shower, trying to get warm and clean. As I scrub my body, I rehearse what I'm going to say when Richard gets home. I can't just ask. He'd never admit it if it were true and I have to know the truth. I wish Maggie would come home right now and say it was all a hoax.

Lizzie knocks on my door as I'm getting dressed. "Mom, he just pulled into the driveway. What are you gonna do?"

"I'm going to find out the truth. Go to your room and stay there."

"Okay. Be careful."

Careful? I hear her door close as the front door opens.

I finish my last buttons and head out to face Richard. I'd rather not have this conversation in the bedroom.

He's in the kitchen when I get to him, rummaging for leftovers.

"Hi, sorry I took so long. I got a newspaper and was checking for used refrigerators. Turns out an old friend of mine had one for sale."

He seems so normal, so reasonable.

"Maggie's not here," I start.

This is even more difficult than I imagined.

He pulls the lid off some leftover potato salad and gets a fork out of the drawer, saying, "I told you the camping was a scam. But I thought she'd be back on time, to protect her cover."

"She called."

He stops with the fork halfway to his mouth. "Where is she?"

"She's in the hospital."

"Are you sure?"

He should be asking if she's hurt, why she's at the hospital. That's what I practiced. This isn't going the way I planned it. I brace myself and forge ahead, looking him straight in the eyes. This is my husband!

"She's claiming you raped her."

He doesn't flinch. He sets the fork down carefully and gets very still. He maintains eye contact. He wouldn't do that if it were true, would he?

"I told you I was afraid she was setting me up." He sighs and shakes his head. "I shouldn't have spoken out against her going camping. I told you she threatened to lie about me. Well, if there's any evidence of sexual activity, it's from the people she spent the weekend with."

He never said this last part when I was practicing the conversation in my head. I fumble for something to say that makes sense.

"She's been at a safe house all weekend," I blurt out.

I find myself hoping this fiction is true, that Maggie went to a safe house for runaways. This is a big city. There has to be at least one place like that.

Richard still looks straight at me. His body seems to be frozen.

"But they didn't take her to the hospital until today?" he asks.

There's something in his voice that I'm ignoring.

I answer, "She didn't tell them until today."

"Did you talk to anyone besides Maggie?"

"No."

"She's probably making it all up and isn't even at the hospital," Richard responds. He eats some of the potato salad, as if glad the issue is over and done.

I'm no good at lying; I give up and tell him, "I just said that because of what she wrote in her diary. She's run away."

"You don't know where she is?"

Relief. That's what I was ignoring. His body mirrors the relief I hear in his voice. Comprehension slices into me like a knife. He's relieved that she hasn't been examined, relieved that she's gone. He's hasn't asked what she wrote in her diary because he *knows* what he did.

I accost him with words torn from my gut. "How could you!"

"You believe her?" Richard sounds amazed.

"Yes. I believe her." How could I have doubted her? How could I have thought she would make up something like this?

He shakes his head as if I've lost my mind. "After all the trouble she's caused, all the lies she's told, you still believe her?"

"Yes!"

I'm shaking with rage and fear. I may never see Maggie again, and it's all my fault. I should never have brought this man into our lives.

"I know you *want* to believe her." He reaches out as if he wants to console me.

I recoil. He won't admit what he's done. Not to me, not to anyone, ever. How could I have thought I was in love with this monster?

"I'm going to the police," I tell him coldly.

His face and voice are instantly hard. "If you do, come back ready to move out." He walks out of the room and goes down to his office.

I get my purse and keys, then get Lizzie with a finger across my lips. I motion for her to bring the diary and note. Neither of us say a word as we slip out of the house and get into the Explorer.

How could I have let this happen to my baby?

What kind of mother am I?

54: Maggie

I hike back to the festival fast as I can.

Some of the stalls are already packed up and gone, leaving big empty spaces, but the photographer's still there. Check out his card while someone buys a photo. His name's Dave and the card gives all his contact info. The customer leaves. Dave comes out in front of his booth and looks around.

"Looks like that's it," he says. "Unless you're buying something?"

"No, I don't have enough money. I do like 'em."

"So what brings you back?"

Suddenly, I'm shy. "I was kind of hoping you might, uh, like some company."

"I can always use some help breaking down," he says.

He starts putting away photos and I end up talking to his back.

"I really need to get out of town," I say. "I was hoping I could ride along with you? If you tell me what to do, I'll help out. It'll be nicer than riding all alone. I've traveled a lot. I'm really good company."

He turns to look at me. "I help you and you help me?"

"Yeah."

"How old are you?"

"Eighteen."

"I don't think so."

I pull out the driver's license.

"Shauna McLaughlin?" he says.

"That's me." I rattle off the address as if I'm bored with it.

"So you want a ride home to Pittsburgh?"

"No, I don't need to stop there. I wanna see some of the country. If you can give me a ride to Illinois, that'll be a good start."

"You say you've traveled a lot?"

"Oh, yeah. I've been all over. I'm kinda heading for California this time, but I figure I'll check things out along the way."

He looks at my license one more time. "Your hair's longer."

"Yeah, that was taken last year. It was a lousy picture to begin with, now it looks even less like me."

"Mine doesn't really look like me, either." He hands it back to me. "What the heck, I could use some good company. Help me pack up."

"Great!"

I help him load the pictures into plastic tubs and we carry them to his camper.

"Just put them up on the bed and shelf."

It takes a few trips to get all the photos. Then we fold up the tables and his chair. We slide the tables into the center aisle of the camper on their sides. The only thing left is the booth itself. It's a three-sided tent with no floor. He's surprised how much help I am taking it apart.

"We camped a lot when I was a kid," I explain. "Our tent had the same kind of framework."

The tent goes on top of the tables. The camper's packed solid now.

"I guess you can't sleep in here when it's packed."

"No, I only sleep in it while I'm actually set up at a show. I'll stay at a motel tonight, then drive straight through on the way home. It's a long day, but I don't mind driving like that."

The camper's too full for my pack with the sleeping bag and frame.

"I guess it'll have to be up front with us," he says.

The only way it'll fit in the cab is squeezed next to the passenger door, with the top and the sleeping bag leaning over the seat. I've gotta sit in the center—shoulder to shoulder and hip to hip with Dave.

"Lucky it's a bench seat," he says. "But you need to lean away from me, so I can shift. The motel will probably have laundry bags. If you split up your stuff, we should be able to get it all into the back. That'll be better tomorrow."

He pats my thigh as he says, "Though if I'm going to be crowded, nice it's someone who's good company."

55: Peg

"What happened?" Lizzie asks as we drive away. "I couldn't hear."

"He didn't admit anything, but he did something to her."

"Where are we going?"

"To the police station."

We sit waiting for at least an hour. We have the note and the diary. Finally Officer Wilson leads us back to his desk

"Okay. Who is the missing person?" he asks.

"My daughter, Maggie May Lewis."

"Maggie a nickname?"

"No, that's her real name."

"Does she have any nicknames?"

I look at Lizzie to double check, then shake my head no.

"Also known as?"

"Maggie May Wilson is on her birth certificate, but she's never used Wilson."

"Mother?"

"Me. Margaret Lewis Crandall. I've always gone by Peg, though."

"She lives with you?"

"Yes."

"And who else?"

"Her sister, Lizzie Lewis, and my husband, Richard Crandall."

"Father?"

"Tom Wilson."

"His address?"

Lizzie interrupts. "He died right before I was born."

I let the lie pass. There's been no contact since the divorce. He could be anywhere, and he might as well be dead to us.

"Maggie's age?"

"Fifteen today."

Date of birth comes next, then he asks for height and weight. I look to Lizzie, who shrugs. "A little taller than you, Mom."

"About 5'5", 115 to 120?"

Maggie has no scars, tattoos, or other marks, unknown blood type, last seen by her dentist back home. I give the dentist's name.

"Picture?"

I give him my wallet photo. "That's this year's school picture."

"She still looks the same?"

"Yes."

"Which high school?"

"West."

"Last seen?"

"Friday, around six, right after dinner."

"Where?"

"Home."

"Did you see her leave?"

"Yes, she left with a boy from school and his stepmother. At least she claimed to be his stepmother. She looked awfully young."

"Names?"

"The boy is Chip, and she introduced herself as Sarah Smith."

"Their address and phone number?"

"I don't know. The whole family was going camping, no one would have been there anyway."

"What kind of vehicle were they driving?"

"I'm not sure. It was a little red car. Four doors, I think."

I feel exposed as a sloppy, inadequate mother.

The officer asks Lizzie if she remembers anything more.

"They were going camping at Lakeshore State Park, near Dunkirk."

"But my husband and I checked. They didn't go there."

"When were they due back?"

"They promised to get her back by four today."

"Well, she's only a few hours late. You may have gotten the name of the campground wrong, or they may have changed plans."

"No. It's her birthday. I made a cake."

"Maybe they forgot you were planning dinner and stopped to eat on the way home, or had car trouble."

He's placating me. I've been pigeonholed as a mother who knows she's been careless and is now overcompensating with anxiety.

"No, she left a note," says Lizzie. "She ran away."

Why didn't I just say that in the first place? My brain's not working properly. Lizzie hands him the note. He scans it while she leafs through the diary.

"Here," she says, holding the diary open and handing it to him. "This is last week. This is why she left. My mom's husband raped her."

Officer Wilson sits up straighter and lifts his eyes from the note. Lizzie points to the entries she had me read. He skims them quickly.

"This doesn't actually say he raped her, but it's pretty clear that she's accusing him of sexual abuse. Do you believe he did this?"

"Yes. I didn't believe it, so I told him she was at the hospital, that she was accusing him of rape. He denied it, reminded me of lies she's told, problems she's had with boys the last year or so, and he said if there was any evidence of sexual activity, it had nothing to do with him. Then when I told him I'd made it up, she wasn't at the hospital, he was relieved."

"He was relieved that she wasn't at the hospital?"

"He was relieved there wouldn't be any hard evidence against him."

"You're sure of that?" His eyes bore into mine.

I meet his gaze steadily. "Yes. I'm sure. I know it wouldn't hold up in court or anything, but yes, I know he was relieved it would be his word against hers. He doesn't think anyone will believe her."

"But you do?"

I nod.

"How about you?" he asks Lizzie.

"Yes. I've seen him watching Maggie. It's creepy."

"And she was supposed to be back today?"

"Yes, but she wrote the note explaining she was running away."

Lizzie is impatient for them to start looking for Maggie. I know how she feels. He's doing something on his computer, but I can't see what from this side of the desk. I just want them to start looking for Maggie.

"Where is your husband now?"

"Home."

"He knows you were coming here, and why?"

"Yes. He said I should come back prepared to move out if I was going to tell her story."

"Are you moving out, then?"

"I hadn't really thought ahead that far. I just want to find Maggie. But I can't imagine staying in that house another night."

"She definitely knew this boy she left with?" asks Officer Wilson.

"Yes. He's someone she knows from school."

"So it's clear she's a runaway, that she left of her own volition."

I agree.

"Any ideas where she's headed?"

"Maybe she's still with that boy? I don't really know. He's the only friend she's made here."

"Okay." He stands up and walks over to a printer as it spits out three pages. He glances at them quickly, then hands them to me. "Check that I got all the information right."

I skim over the details we've discussed and return the papers.

"That looks right," I say. "I should have gotten more information about the boy and his family."

"He's in her third period class," Lizzie says. "It's in the diary."

"That helps. I'll leave a note for the day shift," says Officer Wilson. "They should be able to find him."

"We know what he looks like."

"Good point," he says. "I'll tell whoever's assigned the case to have you meet them at the school. Make sure you get a number to them when you've settled in a motel. Is there anything else you can tell me?"

"No."

"Okay. I'll get this going, then. Wait here." He comes back a few minutes later with three cans of pop. "Okay. First step's done. I just got her information onto NCIC."

"What's that?"

"The National Crime Information Center. She's in as a runaway. Every police station in the country will have the information in minutes, if they don't already."

"It sounds too easy."

"It's easy to get the information out. But for a cop to spot her among all the young people they see every day? Especially when a runaway doesn't want to be found? Especially with no idea where she's headed, don't hold your breath for NCIC to work. Sorry."

"What else can I do?"

"Here's the phone number for the Center for Missing and Exploited Children. You can call from here and use the data I just typed up. While you make that call, I'm calling CPS."

As a teacher, I realize he means Child Protective Services. Teachers and police are mandated reporters, required to report the alleged sexual abuse. He has to call them.

"Until we talk to Maggie," he says, "we don't have enough to press criminal charges, but CPS may be able to help you and Lizzie vacate the house safely and get an Order of Protection from Family Court."

Lizzie's stomach growls loudly and we laugh uncomfortably.

"Did you two eat dinner?" asks Officer Wilson. We shake our heads. "Neither did I. You like pepperoni pizza?"

"Sure," says Lizzie.

"I'll order an extra large and tell CPS that you're waiting here until they come talk to you."

By the time we're done with our phone calls, the pizza has arrived.

"I called the hotline, which is in Albany, but I also got a message to the local night shift," says Wilson. "They know Albany will accept a police report, so they'll be over as soon as they can. They said it might be awhile, though. They're at the hospital with a toddler."

I'm surprised when he hands the diary back to Lizzie.

"I really don't have a case until I talk to Maggie, but take good care of it. We may need it if we get enough to charge him with anything."

The pizza is gone before we realize it.

"I'm going to need some boxes to pack things up. Is there a place nearby that would be open?" I ask.

Officer Wilson gives me directions to a twenty-four-hour grocery. Lizzie stays with him. When CPS gets there, they can interview her first. They'll probably want to do it without me right there, anyway.

56: Maggie

It only takes a few minutes to get to the motel. Dave parks around the side and pats my thigh again as he gets out of the truck.

He doesn't notice me flinch.

"You wait here. I made a reservation for one. I don't want them to charge me for an extra person because they see you."

"Okay."

I'll be sleeping in the truck, but I'd like to take a shower. Three days is too long—can't stand my hair, it's so greasy. Feels like I've been camping all weekend. Funny, that's where I was supposed to be—shoulda been home a few hours ago. So now they know for sure.

Wonder if Mom saw the note—shoulda left another one for her with some garbage about hating school. Lizzie probably showed it to her, which means Mom read my diary. So she hates me. Maybe I should call and tell her I made it all up. I don't know.

Dave comes back. "The room's right over there on the ground floor. Don't even need to move the truck. Bring your pack. You can spread things out to rearrange it."

He gets his bag out of the camper and leads the way. The room's clean but small, with one double bed. I set my pack against the wall.

"You go on and use the bathroom first, Shauna."

It's a good thing I'm the only other person in the room, 'cuz I don't know who he's talking to for a moment. Not long enough for him to be suspicious, though.

It's a clean bathroom! I lock the door while I use the toilet.

He has his suitcase open on the bed and some clothes neatly piled next to it when I come out.

"I'm going to take a nice hot shower," he says.

"I'd really like one too, if it's not a problem."

"It's no problem. But unless you want to share, you'll have to wait."

"I'll wait."

"Okay. There's a Chinese restaurant right across the road. Thought you might like to join me for dinner after we clean up."

"Thanks, but I already ate. I saw a store right before we got to the motel. I need a few things. I'll go get them while you're in the shower."

"Make sure you take the room key."

"Okay."

He picks up his pile of clothes, then gets his wallet and truck keys off the dresser and takes them into the bathroom, too. He locks the door. So he doesn't trust me totally, either. It makes sense for him to be careful when he just met me, but it doesn't feel good, either.

I don't really need anything at the store. Just didn't wanna be in his motel room while he's in the shower. I stick the room key in my pocket and make sure the door locks behind me. The store's one of those little places that carries mostly snack food. Don't wanna waste money, but I pick up a two-liter of cola. I check to see if there's anything else I should get. Pick up a phone card, in case I decide to call home, and the feminine hygiene section reminds me I'm due any day so I pick up that stuff. I've got eighty dollars and twenty-eight cents left when I'm done.

Dave's already out of the shower and dressed in clean jeans and a fresh shirt. He's also shaved, and it makes him look a lot younger. I'd been guessing he was close to Mom's age, but he's more like thirty.

"Shower's all yours," he says.

I put the two-liter on the table. "Help yourself, if you want some."

"Thanks. I'm going to get the Chinese as takeout. They close at ten and it's already nine thirty. Sure you don't want anything?"

He hands me the menu. I'm a little hungry, after all.

"I'd like the pork fried rice," I say. "Could you split one with me?"

"Sure thing. I love the stuff."

I pull out three dollars and put it on the table. "My share."

"No need for you to do that."

I shrug and leave the money, then take my pack into the bathroom. I listen for him to leave, then check that the door is locked and doesn't have that little hole Richard used to open the one at his house. I take a hot shower, lathering my hair twice and scrubbing myself from forehead to toe with the washcloth. Shave my legs, too. Clean is so nice. There are still three dry towels. One goes on my head, another takes care of the rest of me. I think about stealing the dry one, 'cuz I forgot to bring a towel. But Dave might get stuck paying for it, if they keep track. I put on clean clothes and comb out my hair. He's coming into the room with a bucket of ice as I come out of the bathroom. He seems startled when he sees me.

"You look about fifteen right now."

"I showed you my ID."

"Yeah, well, food's on the table and I got ice for the cola."

"Great. I'll figure out how to repack everything after we eat."

"Okay."

Dave opens the takeout boxes, then pulls a half-empty bottle of rum out of his suitcase.

"Would you like some?" he asks.

"Just a little. I'm a lightweight."

Don't want it, but don't want him to wonder about my age again.

"I got spring rolls. I don't need all of them. Please have some."

"Thanks. I love spring rolls."

I end up eating half the spring rolls and trying his beef and broccoli, as well as eating more than half of the pork fried rice. After all I ate at C.J.'s, it's amazing. Must be nerves. I try to take little sips of my drink, but I'm thirsty, too. I pour myself a second glass and keep it in my hand, so he can't add any rum.

"Sorry I ate so much of your food," I apologize.

"I had plenty. They gave me two fortune cookies. Take your pick."

I take one and break it open.

He does the same. He reads his out loud. "Good things will come to you. That's always nice to hear. What's yours?"

"You will have great success later in life."

"Sounds good for you, too. Do you know what you want to do?"

"I haven't made up my mind. That's part of why I'm traveling."

"You sounded like it was really important for you to leave right away. Are you in trouble?" he asks.

"No, but I saw something I shouldn't have, so I need to leave."

"No one knows you came here with me, do they?"

"No. And no one's looking for me. They just said to leave town."

"The police?"

"No."

"Okay. You don't want to go home to Pittsburgh?"

"No."

"Problems with your family?'

"That's why I'm not living with them."

"Well, you're eighteen. They can't bother you now."

"Nope."

I get up and clear the trash off the table. There aren't any leftovers. He finishes off the cola, with a good helping of rum.

"There's a plastic bag for laundry on one of those hangers." He points. "Go ahead and use it for some of your stuff. Divided it'll fit in the back."

I put my pack on the bed and start pulling things out to reorganize.

"I need to take a dump," he announces, as if I really need to know.

On his way past the bed he stops behind me. He runs his hands down my sides and pulls me up against him. I freeze.

He speaks softly. "I'll be ready for that 'good company' when I come out." Then he goes into the bathroom and shuts the door.

I try to shrug off the sense of his touch while I put everything back into the pack. My shampoo's in the shower—gotta leave it. I roll my sleeping bag back up, tie it on top, then swing the pack onto my back. I'm getting good at that.

I hike rapidly up the road, away from downtown—can't go back there. There's a highway ahead, but it's too late to hitch. Besides, he might come looking for me. I stop at another motel. It's after eleven. The clerk's a gray-haired lady.

"Excuse me, ma'am, but I need a room?"

She looks at my pack and sleeping bag. At least I'm clean.

"I've got one room left. Don't expect anyone else will stop this late. You can have it for thirty-five bucks. Just don't tell anyone you got it that cheap."

"Thank you ma'am."

"But I need to see your identification. We don't rent to minors."

I show her Shauna's license.

"You're from Pittsburgh?"

"Yes ma'am."

She hands me some paperwork that asks for my name and address. I remember to put down Shauna's. I leave the phone number blank and give it back to her.

"What's your phone number?"

"I don't have one right now."

"Do you have a car?"

"No."

"How'd you get here?"

"I had a ride from Pittsburgh. They let me off up by the highway. They're going home to Scranton."

"Where are you headed?"

"Rehoboth Beach."

"We used to go to Rehoboth when the kids were little. How do you plan to get there?"

"I figured on catching a bus from here."

I hadn't really thought about it, but it makes sense. Except it means going back downtown to the bus station.

"You can catch the city bus down at the corner. It'll take you to the bus depot. It runs all day."

"Thanks."

I give her the thirty-five dollars and she gives me a key.

"Out and around the back."

"Thank you."

"Make sure you're quiet. I have a lot of customers who leave early to miss rush hour. There's a continental breakfast five to nine. Checkout's at noon."

"Okay. Good night."

Once I'm safe in the room, with deadbolt and knob locked, I put the pack and sleeping bag down, pull my shoes off with my toes, then climb into the sheets with my clothes on. Traffic on the highway hums me to sleep.

57: Peg

They're stocking the store, so I have my pick of boxes. I get some lawn bags, too. I think we'll be able to get everything into the Explorer with the back seat down. I was annoyed when Richard didn't want us to "clutter" his house with our things. Now I'm glad. I want to get it all out tonight. It may be difficult to do later.

As I drive back to the police station, it hits me that I'm supposed to go to work in the morning. I need to call the automated sub-finder. But when I get there, two social workers are talking to Lizzie and the man comes over to me.

"I'm Mr. Hanford. Can I speak to you separately? Then we can be done with this more quickly."

I go over the situation with him, then ask him what he thinks.

"Well, as night crew, we only do the initial assessment, to determine whether the children are safe right now. As long as you don't return to the house, it would appear Lizzie is safe tonight. Maggie may not be, but none of us have control over that at this point. You've done everything you could, as soon as you were aware there was a problem, so I don't think you'll be held accountable for any of this."

"What will happen to Richard?"

"We'll need a statement from Maggie. It depends how strong that is, but even if there isn't enough for a criminal case, there may be enough for family court action. Runaways usually stay with friends a few nights, then come home on their own," he offers. "Even when they have good cause to run away."

"I'm hoping she's staying with this boy who picked her up, but her diary sounds like she was planning to leave town."

"I hope not. That lowers the odds of finding her."

"I know."

I want to focus on something I can control. "You said Lizzie was safe as long as I don't return to the house. But we need our things. I'd like to go ahead and get them tonight and be done with it."

"We need to talk to him as the alleged perpetrator. Normally, we'd leave that for day shift, since the kids aren't with him. But if we don't get any more calls, we can go over with you and talk to him while you get your things packed and ready to go. Wilson already suggested that."

"Thank you. I was a little scared about going back there."

"He said they can send a police escort with us. It's a slow night."

"Are they going to talk to Richard?"

"No. He said they'll want to talk to Maggie first, as long as you're sure she left with friends and it's not an abduction."

"They have to find her first." Maybe that means they'll look harder.

Officer Wilson comes back with Lizzie and the other social worker. He gives me his card and reminds me to call when we get to a motel. Then we leave. The social workers and a police car follow the Explorer through deserted streets. The police don't use the siren or lights.

"Lizzie, you wait in the car," I say when we get to Richard's house.

The social workers meet me at the door and I let myself in with my key. The police wait in their vehicle. As soon as I step through the door, I hear Richard snoring loudly. Mr. Hanford follows me down the hall. Richard's passed out across our bed. There's an empty bottle of tequila on the floor.

"Do you want me to wake him up?" I whisper to the caseworker.

"I doubt that would be very productive. We'll sit in the dining room and finish writing out your statements and work on some other reports while you pack things up," offers Mr. Hanford quietly. "Then, if he wakes up, we'll talk to him. I'll let the police know what's happening."

I check the kitchen first. Tears well up when I see Maggie's cake, but I don't let myself cry, not yet. It's untouched. Richard doesn't eat much when he's drinking. Empty beer cans litter the shelf and table.

"No wonder he's passed out," comments Mr. Hanford's partner.

"This is Maggie's birthday cake," I explain as I cover it.

"Let me take that out to your car for you," she says.

Lizzie comes back with her, both of them carrying boxes.

"Do you want me to start on our room?" Lizzie whispers.

"No, let's work together."

There isn't much to pack in the kitchen—my blender, a few special coffee mugs, including one with kittens on it that's been Maggie's since she was five, and a few other things. We put it all into one box.

The dining room, where the caseworkers are quietly writing, has nothing of ours except a large mirror that was my mother's. I take it down off the wall and carry it to the car while Lizzie takes the box from the kitchen. The police car is gone.

The only thing in the living room is a gift bag with birthday presents for Maggie. I put it beside the door and we move on to the girls' room. I'm amazed at how well Lizzie is holding up. It's past midnight. We work quickly, but are slowed by the need to be quiet. We get Maggie's things, too, of course. Finally, there's nothing left in their room but the furniture. That's all Richard's.

I'm glad I kept the Explorer. There's still plenty of room. Richard didn't like me parking it in front of his house. It's old and has lots of mystery dings and scratches. Maggie came up with that phrase.

I know there's nothing in the backyard. All my gardening things are in the storage unit. I was going to get them out next weekend. I check the garage and the hall closet. There are a few items in each, including my Haviland. Lizzie empties the girls' bathroom.

I let the social workers know that only my things in the master bedroom, bath, and closet remain. Lizzie goes to wait in the car; I go alone into the bedroom. Richard's still snoring loudly. I tiptoe through to the bathroom in the dark, gently close the door, and turn on the light. The closet is off the bathroom. There are two boxes and two bags full when I'm done with those areas. I turn off the light and take one at a time out to the car, then return to the bedroom to empty the dresser into bags. The drawers have to be moved slowly. I fill two more trash bags with clothing.

As I take the last one to the car, I whisper to the caseworkers. "Just one more trip."

I slip into the bedroom and quietly turn the blinds to let in a little more light before clearing my bedside table and the top of my dresser. Item by item I load a box, careful not to make a sound, then when I lift it, things shift and click against each other. Richard snorts. I freeze until he resumes his regular snore. Mr. Hanford meets me in the hallway and takes the box. He carries it out to the car while his partner collects their things and I pad silently through the house for one last check. Nothing. I shut the door quietly behind us and lock it. I start to take my key off the ring, but Mr. Hanford stops me.

"You don't know if you'll need that again."

I keep it. Mr. Hanford walks me to the Explorer.

"Thank you," I tell him.

"Do you know where you're going to stay?"

"No. A motel somewhere."

"Here's my card. Call as soon as you have a room."

Lizzie is in the passenger seat, asleep, holding Maggie's cake in her lap. I try to take it and put it in the back, but her grip on it tightens. She shifts slightly and mumbles, but she's still asleep. I leave it and check her seat belt. The social workers wait until I start the car, then drive away.

The Explorer is stuffed with our belongings. At the first traffic light, I realize I forgot the girls' bikes. They're in the backyard. I can go through the gate to get them. I'll have to wake up Lizzie to put them on top of the Explorer. There are bungee cords in the garage. It's a good thing I kept the key. I head back.

Parked in the same spot on the street in front of the house, I take Lizzie's sleeping bag out of the back and spread it across the top of the roof to protect the car, though the Explorer's old enough, I shouldn't bother. The light outside the garage goes on as I walk past. It startles me at first, then I remember it's on a motion sensor. There are no windows here. Richard wouldn't realize it was on, even if he were up. The gate creaks as I go into the back yard. I prop it open with a brick, so it won't make noise again until I'm done. The window next to the bed where Richard is sleeping is open a few inches. He's still snoring, but it's intermittent.

Maggie's bike is first. The rear wheel ticks quietly as I push it to the car. I take off the front wheel and squeeze it into the back where the sleeping bag had been. I wake Lizzie to help put the rest on the roof. When we're done, she sits down in the street and leans against the back of the car, she's so tired.

Richard's not snoring anymore, so I grab the seat of Lizzie's bike and lift the rear wheel off the ground. The front one doesn't make a sound. I slide the brick out of the way as I go through the gate. It swings shut behind me, but doesn't latch. I set the rear of the bike down and turn to pull on the gate.

"What took you so long?"

My body jerks back from Richard's voice reflexively. The bike starts to fall. I grab it, keeping it between us as I turn to face him. He's right there, rubbing his head sleepily. I'm glad the bike is between us, but he's between me and the car.

"They were busy. I thought it was going to take forever."

"You didn't tell the police that nonsense she said about me, did you?" He takes a step forward as he asks, but looks over his shoulder at the street. "No, they'd be here, wouldn't they."

The Explorer's in the shadows. He doesn't notice Maggie's bike on the roof.

"It's the middle of the night." He sounds confused.

He doesn't realize we've emptied the house. My mind races to come up with an explanation.

"We came back earlier. You were asleep."

"Why are you out here with Lizzie's bike?"

"She's really upset. I can't make her stay, not until Maggie comes home and we can talk everything out."

"So she's been taken in by her sister's lies?"

I don't want to antagonize him. He reeks from the alcohol. He's probably still half drunk.

"She doesn't know what to think."

"I'll go talk to her. Is she in her room?"

"She's at a friend's house. I'm dropping her bike off tomorrow."

"It would be good to have the place to ourselves for a few days."

"Yes. We do need time to talk and work things out."

He nods and reaches out. I force myself not to flinch as he pats my shoulder.

"I know. You still think of Maggie as your innocent little girl. I know it's got to be hard to believe she'd lie like this, to make trouble between us. I thought she was finally starting to like me."

"I really need to get this bike loaded, if I'm going to get any sleep tonight."

"I'll help you," he says, reaching for it.

I can't let him see Lizzie or the Explorer loaded with all our things.

"I've got it," I tell him, "but can you get the bungee cords for me?"

"Sure. They're in the garage," he says agreeably.

As Richard heads for the house, I wheel the bike out to the car.

Lizzie startles me by whispering. "What if he sees our stuff is gone?" She's crouched in the shadow behind the car.

"We'll have to leave the bikes. I need to get Maggie's off the roof."

The lights go on in the living room as Richard enters the house, then the light in the girls' room.

"Quick, get in the car!" I whisper urgently.

By the time I get in, Lizzie's putting on her seat belt. I latch mine as I turn the ignition, then hit power lock and pull away slowly. Maybe Maggie's bike will stay on the roof if I'm careful. Richard's running down the street towards us as I get to the first corner. I take it slowly, and by some miracle, the bike stays on the roof. But Lizzie screams that he's come around the corner and is going to catch up to us. I accelerate as smoothly as I can, but the bike and sleeping bag slide off the back.

"He tripped over the bike!" Lizzie reports gleefully.

Free of restraint, I speed down the street.

I should be feeling depressed, angry, and anxious, but a sudden sense of lightness overpowers all of that. I realize that I'm relieved to be leaving him.

"Where are we going?" Lizzie asks.

"We'll drop this stuff off at storage first. Then I'll have to sit down and think things through."

"You sound like yourself, Mom."

"Well, I feel like myself."

Myself . . . who am I? I am a well-educated, competent person with excellent analytical skills. So, how did I let this man into our lives? How did I let him manipulate me into selling our home, uprooting us? And how could I have missed what he was doing to Maggie?

A wave of depression hits me. I should have protected my Maggie. Now she's gone, and I may never see her again.

Tuesday, May 30, 2000

58: Peg

The storage unit is closed until six. We have more than an hour to wait, so we drive around until we find a twenty-four-hour pancake house, then go in and order breakfast.

Lizzie senses my mood and tries to reassure me.

"It's not all your fault, you know. Maggie's been weird for awhile, it wasn't just the stuff with Richard."

"Teenagers are supposed to be weird. I should have paid attention. I should have talked with her, listened to her more."

"We used to talk, but we haven't been lately." Lizzie sighs. "I knew something was wrong, but sharing a room was such a pain, I mostly stayed away."

"I let you," I say.

"You know how Maggie asked me to stay home with her when she was sick, 'cuz Richard gave her the creeps?" Lizzie whispers.

"You couldn't have known it was more than that."

"But when she was suspended, she kept asking me how my throat felt, did I think I'd caught strep. I didn't think about it. I shoulda known she wanted me to stay home, that something was wrong."

"It's not your fault. We both have to stop blaming ourselves."

"What are we gonna do, Mom?"

I force myself to think ahead.

"Oh no! The first thing I'm going to do is use that payphone out front and call sub-finder, so I don't have to work today. I was going to do it from the police station, but I forgot. Then we are going to eat, empty the car into storage, find a motel, call the police station and talk to the day shift person who's going to follow up on Maggie. Then I'll meet them at West High to look for Chip."

"Where am I gonna be while you go to the high school?"

"Asleep at the motel?"

"I'd rather go with you."

"We'll see how you feel then. Now I have to go make that call."

"I'll skim through the diary again to see if there's any clue where she might go."

Lizzie pulls out the diary while I go make my call.

One advantage of this city school is that they have an automated sub-finder. It can be called any time, day, night, weekend, or holiday. It only takes a couple minutes.

"I didn't find anything," Lizzie says as she puts the diary back into her pack.

"Maybe Chip will help us when he realizes I believe her."

"If he's at school."

"I hope he didn't go with her, though at least she wouldn't be out there alone."

The waitress brings our omelets and juice. We both clean our plates. That pizza was a long time ago, and we've been up all night.

Lizzie yawns, then asks, "What if Chip doesn't know where she is?"

"I don't know, honey."

"It didn't sound like the police would be able to do much."

"No, it didn't, but Chip may know exactly where she went. Let's go. The storage area should be open by the time we get there."

We arrive as they open. We leave the bags with our clothes in the car, and the bathroom items, too. Everything else gets packed into our storage room. I find our empty suitcases and toss them into the car.

"Lizzie, do we have any other recent pictures of Maggie?"

"No, Mom. She's been dodging the camera for a couple years."

"I know, but aren't there any others?"

Lizzie shrugs. "I don't think so, at least not any that would help."

"I have a large copy her school photo on my desk at work. I'll get it later."

We unload the rest quickly, sharing a grimace when we store the front wheel of Maggie's bike. We work well together. The girls and I always were a team. I'd forgotten how good that felt.

How did I ever let myself feel so separate from them? There's a knot of panic pushing up against my ribs. What if we never find Maggie? I can't let Lizzie know the depth and breadth of my fear.

I'm glad the lease for this storage is in my name only. I change my entry code on the way out, so Richard won't have access anymore. We check into a cheap independent motel. They have a lot of vacancies, so they cut us a break and don't charge us for last night.

I'm glad I kept all my own charge cards and bank accounts. Richard didn't like it, but he'd had credit problems. I wanted to keep my good rating. At least I did something right.

We get a nonsmoking room that actually smells clean. Lizzie takes the first shower. I call our principal and catch him just before he goes out to watch students arriving for school.

"I wanted to let you know I called in for a sub at the last minute. I'm not sure they'll get someone out there on time."

"Are you sick?"

"No. I'm having family problems. My older daughter ran away. Lizzie and I were at the police station all night."

"Are your lesson plans ready for the sub?"

"Yes. I came in on Saturday and finished them. They're on my desk, with plans for the rest of the year, and Betty has my emergency plans on file, too."

"I'll make sure someone's in there first period to cover until the sub arrives. Can you be called at home if there are any questions?"

"No!" I don't really want to tell him more. I barely know him. But I can't have them call at home, either. "Lizzie and I are at a motel by the Thruway, and we'll be sleeping or out looking for Maggie all day."

"Oh."

At least he doesn't ask anything else.

"I'll come by later and see how the sub is doing," I assure him. "I need to pick up a picture of Maggie that I have on my desk, anyway."

"I'll be here until five. Stop in and let me know how you're doing. I hope you find your daughter."

"Thanks."

That's the most I've talked to him since I interviewed for the job.

Lizzie is out of the shower, getting dressed, when I call the police station. I explain that Officer Wilson told me to call. They put me through to an Officer Arden. She sounds annoyed.

"I've just gotten the file on your daughter. Wilson left a note saying I should have you go to the school with me to talk to this boy she went away with for the weekend. Is his last name Smith, too?"

"I'm not sure."

"Is Chip his real name or a nickname?"

"A nickname, for microchip, I don't know his real name."

"There are thousands of kids in that school."

"We can identify him. That's why Officer Wilson . . . "

She cuts me off before I can say anything else. "So she took off with this kid you don't know, for the weekend, *with* your permission?"

"Yes, but," I start, then she cuts me off again.

"But she left you a note saying she was running away."

"Yes."

"And Wilson's note here says the girl's accusing her stepfather of sexual abuse. So that's her excuse for running away."

"Reason, not excuse."

"I take it you believe her."

"Yes."

"You always choose that kind of guy?"

"Are you meeting me at the school or not?"

"I have three other new cases. I'll probably get over there before three. Give me your cell number, and be sure you call if the kid gets in touch with you. They usually do."

"I don't have a cell phone."

"You should. How do you expect your kids to stay in touch?"

I give her the motel number.

"I take it that didn't go well?" asks Lizzie.

"No, it did not. She thinks Maggie will come back on her own." I blink away tears. "Why didn't I get more information about that boy?"

"We need to focus on finding Maggie, Mom. No guilt trips."

"Right. Well, if I can't depend on the police, I'll go to the school myself. It's eight now. Third period should start in about an hour or so, don't you think? I'll get a shower. You get some rest."

I take a long hot shower, trying to feel clean. That woman talked to me like white trash, or a negligent mother. Lizzie's right, though, we need to focus on finding Maggie instead of blaming ourselves. The hot water soothes my neck and shoulders. I almost fall asleep standing up.

When I come out, Lizzie is sound asleep on one side of the bed, still holding the diary loosely. I quietly rummage through my dresser bag for clothes. I put on some jeans and one of the less wrinkled shirts. I sit on the floor with an open suitcase and start folding clothing into it.

My journals are in that bag, too. I don't want Lizzie to see them, so I stack them in my suitcase under the clothing. The first one is missing. It must still be in the drawer. Well, I'm definitely not going to go back to the house for it now.

It's almost nine. I should let Lizzie sleep, but I'm afraid to be apart, so I wake her up. She splashes water on her face and is ready to go.

We get to the high school just before third period.

When I explain the situation to the principal, she politely refuses to allow me to speak to any student. She will not check my credentials with the principal of the middle school.

"You need to let the professionals handle this," she insists.

The bell rings as we leave her office. Lizzie pulls me aside.

"Wait here, while I go talk to the guidance secretary, Mom."

She pulls Maggie's school ID tag from her pack as she goes through the door. "Um, can you please tell me where Maggie Lewis goes third period? She, like, grabbed my backpack and ID by mistake, and like, my backpack has all my homework and books in it? Including the notes for a speech I need to give in third today? So, like, I really need to find her and swap back? Like, right away?"

The secretary goes to the computer with Maggie's ID while she chastises Lizzie, "You should be wearing your lanyard, not leaving it on your backpack. She's in Mrs. Weissman's third period."

"What room number?"

"That's 235," the woman says, "Will you return this to her?"

"Sure. Thanks."

In the hallway, she puts on Maggie's ID and tells me to put on my own from the Middle School.

"They'll never look twice, as long as you're wearing something around your neck."

She's right. We make our way through the crowded halls to room 235, where Mrs. Weissman is standing outside of her door, monitoring the hallway during the passing period. I explain that I am Maggie's mother, trying to locate the boy I believe helped her run away. Lizzie goes on into the room while I'm talking and spots him. She comes back to the doorway and points him out to Mrs. Weissman.

"Chip Taylor? I'm shocked. He hardly ever says a word in class. He's the last one I'd expect to help anyone run away." Mrs. Weissman calls him to the door.

He sees us when he's crossing the room, and hesitates.

"Chip, you need to get over here, *now*," Mrs. Weissman says.

The other students notice, but the bell rings and she tells them, "Business as usual. Do the activity on the board. I'll be collecting them in five minutes."

She steps outside with us, but keeps the door open a few inches, so she can still monitor her class. "Chip, you clearly know Maggie's mother and sister."

"Yes, ma'am."

"Maggie has run away. If you know anything, you need to help them find her by telling them now."

"I can't help you."

"How was the camping trip?" I ask him.

He's fumbling. He didn't expect us to find him so soon.

Lizzie breaks in. "We know why she ran away."

He blushes, but doesn't say anything.

"My mom and I moved out last night, after I found Maggie's diary."

"You moved out?" he asks.

He's focusing on Lizzie. I keep quiet.

"Totally. Except our bikes." She grins. "Maggie's fell off the roof of the car and tripped him when he was chasing us. *And* we told the cops everything."

Mrs. Weissman motions to me that she's going back into her room. I ask Chip to please help us find Maggie.

"You mean you believe her?"

"Yes."

"We didn't think you would. She's been in so much trouble."

"Well, I wasn't sure at first, but I am now. Do you know where she's staying?"

"We took her to the bus station, the big one downtown."

"When?"

"Right after we left your house. She was in a hurry. She had to get her ticket and she said her bus was leaving soon. Maybe seven thirty?"

"Did she tell you where she was going?"

"Pittsburgh."

"Did she say why?"

"She said she'd been there a few times with you. We figured it was easier to hide in a city than a small town."

"If Maggie calls you, tell her to not to go back to Richard's house," Lizzie says. "Let her know we went to the police and they'll know where we are."

I hand him Officer Wilson's card and he copies the information into his notebook. He scribbles something else, tears off a piece of paper, and offers it to me.

"I gave Maggie my email. Maybe she'll get in touch that way. If she does, I'll forward it to you."

My hopes soar. "Did she give you an email address?"

"No, she said she didn't have one anymore."

"Yeah, Mom," says Lizzie. "Our old emails were connected to the server, so we lost them when we moved. School blocks email and your your computer is broken, so neither of us has gotten around to setting up new ones."

"Maybe she'll go to a library and set up an account so she can email Chip." I turn to him. "Did she say anything else that might help us find her? Pittsburgh's a big place."

"I'm sorry. I think she's planning it as she goes. She might have kept going."

"She took my babysitting money. That was almost two hundred," says Lizzie. "How far would that get her?"

"Not too far." I hope.

"Uh, if she has two hundred you know about, then she has more than four hundred. I gave her one and she sold her CDs."

My stomach feels like there's a rock in it, and it's hard to breathe. I realize Maggie has really hit the road.

The police won't find her.

59: Maggie

It's past ten when I wake up. So much for the free breakfast.

I call Greyhound. There's a bus to Rehoboth this afternoon. The ticket's forty-nine dollars and I've only got forty-two and some change left. Gotta make some money today—maybe C.J. and his uncle can use some help. Gotta go downtown anyway. I'll stop and ask before I go to the bus station. Just in case, I get out my good clothes and hang them in the bathroom while I shower. The steam takes out some of the wrinkles. I put on jeans and a T-shirt, but fold my work clothes carefully on top of everything else in the pack—strap it all down and drop the key off in the lobby. There's a different woman working there now.

"Guess I missed the breakfast."

"Guess you did."

I'm halfway to the door when she tells me to wait a minute. I turn around. She disappears into the back room and comes out with some pre-packaged Danish and a carton of milk.

"Here. Looks like you could use it."

"Thanks."

60: Peg

Chip goes back to class. We leave before the principal catches us in the building. The pressure in my stomach keeps expanding. It's pressing up through my throat into my head.

"What next?" Lizzie asks me in the car.

Her question is muffled. My ears are throbbing. We may never see Maggie again. Lizzie expects me to have the answers. There's never been anything I couldn't fix, but Maggie could be anywhere by now. But no, I can't think like that or I'll fall apart, and then who'll look for Maggie, who'll take care of Lizzie?

"Mom? What now?"

Action. That will hold us together. We'll track down information ourselves and give it to the police. Maybe then they'll be able to find her. My mind starts working, organizing what needs to be done.

I exhale and the pressure subsides to a tolerable level.

I answer Lizzie, "First, we need to find out what buses left Friday night around seven thirty."

"She bought a ticket to Pittsburgh."

"Maybe, and maybe she just told him that."

"We could check the schedule online."

"Good idea. I'll take you back to the motel to sleep, then go to school, check the bus schedule, get that photo, and check on my sub."

"Can we get food before you drop me off? We ate breakfast awfully early."

"Sure. I should probably eat something, too."

We're passing a mall, so I pull into the parking lot. On our way to the food court, we pass at least three cell phone stores.

Lizzie gets some Chinese. I have two cups of coffee and pick at my food. The rock's still taking up most of the room in my stomach.

"We need to have a number where we can be reached. It's time to put aside my dislike of cell phones and get one."

Lizzie of course agrees.

I pick one of the kiosks at random. The salesman shows us a huge confusing array of charges and plans and phones that can think for you.

"What I need is a phone, nothing fancy, just a phone that can be called from anywhere, and I need to make calls from anywhere."

"Anywhere in the world? Or anywhere in the country?"

"The country. I think that'll be good enough." I don't think Maggie would leave the states. At least not right away.

I finally choose a plan that covers the entire country, and agree to pay for free nights and weekends. Then he says he can give us a second phone for a small additional cost. "Family plan," he says. "You do have to share the minutes, though."

"Can we call each other?"

"Absolutely."

"Okay. I'll take two. Set me up."

"Two?" asks Lizzie.

"Yes. I won't worry so much when we have to be apart."

It's after eleven when we finally walk away with our new cell phones. Lizzie's half asleep before we get to the motel. I listen while she locks the door with the chain and the deadbolt. I arrive at my classroom during the period before lunch.

"Ms. Lewis!"

The class erupts with a dozen questions.

"I'm not staying. I'm not sick. There are some personal things I have to take care of today. I just stopped in to use my computer. Please get back to your work."

The sub gets them back on task, following my plans. He's good.

Greyhound's website requires a destination to find a schedule, but I get the phone number of the Buffalo terminal. I leave the room to call the bus station on my new cell phone in the empty hallway.

"I'm looking for my daughter who's run away. She apparently left town on a bus Friday evening, sometime around seven thirty."

I hope that's right. As I suspected, nothing for Pittsburgh.

"There's only the 273 for Syracuse. It leaves a little before eight."

"Syracuse? Does it make any connections in the Adirondacks?"

"The 255 goes to Saranac Lake, but it leaves in the morning. You'd have to wait overnight in Rochester or Syracuse and let it catch up to you if you left on the 273."

"What other connections are there in Syracuse?"

"Well, that bus gets into Syracuse at 11:10 p.m. Two buses leave at 11:30. The 273 goes on through Utica and Albany to New York City and the 9002 goes to Baltimore and Washington D.C."

"I hope she didn't go to New York or Washington."

"Well, the 273 only stops in Utica and Albany, but the 9002 stops in a lot of smaller places. Maybe she went to one of them."

"Where? Where does it stop?"

"Cortland and Binghamton, New York; Scranton, Wilkes-Barre, Hazleton, Pottsville, Pine Grove, Harrisburg, and York, Pennsylvania; then Baltimore and D.C."

Wilkes-Barre, Hazleton. I haven't heard those names in years. The missing journal . . . maybe Maggie found it. "That might be it!"

"You should bring a photo down here. A young girl by herself, someone might remember her. If not an agent, then one of our benchwarmers."

"Benchwarmers?"

"Homeless people. They can't live here, but if they don't cause any trouble, we don't either. Most are gone now it's warm, but there are a couple of regulars. The best time to come would be evening, since that's when she left."

"I'll come by tonight, then. Thank you."

Harrisburg. Please let that be it! At least there's a chance of finding her if we have the right area. The bell rings and students flood into the hallway. I evade a deluge of questions by reminding them they need to get to lunch. The sub is waiting for me in the room.

"Is everything okay?" he asks.

"Not really. My daughter's missing."

"That must be awful. I can fill in as long as necessary. I like your classes, but can you wait here a few minutes while I grab some food? Then I can take a quick look at your plans and ask any questions."

"Sure."

"Can I get you anything?"

"No thanks, I already ate."

Alone in my classroom the depression overwhelms me. The bulletin boards of student work, all the displays I prepared so carefully. . . none of it means anything. I want to drop everything and go look for Maggie myself, but that's not sensible. That would leave us without income, as well as homeless. I sink into my chair.

I'm staring blankly out the window when Evan comes in the open door.

"Peg, what's going on? You're not sick?"

"No. Maggie ran away," I blurt out.

"Oh, no. Did she leave a note or anything?"

"Yes. She made serious accusations against Richard."

"Ouch. How'd he take that?"

My voice sounds strangled as I tell him, "I ended up going to the police and giving them the information."

"You think it's true, then?"

He sounds surprised, but not shocked. That makes the answer easier.

"I hate to admit it, but yes, I do."

"Do you have any leads?"

"She got on Greyhound Friday. I'm hoping that she's headed for Harrisburg."

"Why there?"

"A journal I wrote at her age is missing. I ran away to Harrisburg."

"Really! You never impressed me as being that wild."

"I let my parents think I was dead for ten years."

"You're kidding." He looks stunned. "Things were that bad?"

"Looking back? No. Nothing like Maggie's running from."

"Would she go to your parents?"

"No, they passed away. There's no extended family at all."

"I'm sorry. Will the police look for Maggie in Harrisburg?"

"Even if they believe my hunch is right, I remember hiding from the police, and the cop I talked to this morning thinks Maggie will come back on her own."

"But you're afraid she'll be gone for ten years."

"Or forever. My parents were in the same house with the same phone number. She won't know where we are if she does decide to come back."

"So what are you going to do?"

"I want to tell that sub to take over for the rest of the year and go find her myself. Is that crazy?"

"Can you afford to do that?"

I pause to make sure I'm being realistic.

It's only a few weeks' pay, and I'll probably want to look for a new job anyway. No reason to stay in the city now. When I speak, it's with my old confidence.

"Yes, I can. I have the money from the house. I kept my money and credit separate, so there's no problem with access. It may mean having to downscale once I find her, but I can leave and go look for her."

"Then do it."

"That's what I needed to hear."

"Lizzie can stay with us."

I'm amazed by his generosity.

"Thank you, but Lizzie and I need each other right now."

The sub comes back with his lunch. He says he'll be happy to take the class for the remainder of the year. I call the principal, who asks me to bring the sub up to speed, then come to the office to fill out some paperwork.

"You won't be coming back next year, will you?" asks Evan.

"I doubt it. Even if they renew my contract, there's nothing to keep me here."

"I'll take care of all your things," the sub promises. "If you make a quick list of what's your personal property, I'll box it up separate at the end of the year."

"I'll take it to my house, if you're not back by then," Evan says.

He gives me his home address and phone number. I give him the cell number, with tears in my eyes. They are so kind.

61: Maggie

The city bus doesn't give change. I'm gonna put an extra dollar in when the man behind me says he'll cover the difference.

"I can give you a dollar for four quarters," I offer.

"Keep it," he says.

"Thanks."

I take a seat near the front while he puts in the rest of his own fare. When he ignores me and moves to the middle of the bus, I relax and watch for the Capitol building. That's where I get off, just past noon. I walk up the street and look in the restaurant window. It's packed with people in suits. So is the coffeehouse. I stand by the *Please Wait to be Seated* sign 'til C.J. comes over.

"I thought you'd left town," he says.

"My ride fell through. Had to stay in a motel last night."

"I'd like to visit, but we're working shorthanded. Aji took off when I told him Charlie was looking for him."

"I'd like to work—need more money for a bus ticket and stuff."

"Have you ever waited on tables?"

"No."

"I don't have time to train you during lunch, but if we could get you washing dishes, the regular dishwasher could help out the waitresses by keeping their station supplied. You want to try it? It's dirty work."

"I'm washable."

"You're hired, then."

"Thanks."

He takes me back to the kitchen. I put my pack in a little closet with other people's personal stuff and he hands me over to the guy who's doing dishes.

"Got you some help," he says. "Maggie—Will. She's never worked in a kitchen. Show her how to do the dishes, then you can keep the waitress station supplied."

"I'll put on a clean apron and bus tables for them, too," Will says.

"Thanks. They'll appreciate the help."

Then C.J.'s gone. My stomach's in a knot. I've never done anything except babysitting. Dishwashing sounded easy, but there's this huge sink and a big metal box and dishes all over the place. Will sticks an apron over my head.

"Wrap those strings around you, then tie it in front."

He's changing his own apron while he talks. He's done before me and starts explaining stuff and pointing at things.

"Okay. Quick lesson. I bring the dishes back in these bins and stack them over here. Glasses and liquids in one, everything else in another. You take the garbage out and throw it in this can. If it gets too full, there's another over by the wall—got it so far?"

I nod and he continues, "Keep three racks going all the time: egg crate for the glasses, flat rack for cups and bowls, slotted rack over the sink for plates and saucers. Silverware goes in one of these baskets."

It's pretty easy to follow this, 'cuz there are already partially filled racks set up and he's loading dishes as he says it. I start helping.

When the dishwasher's done, he shows me how to push the clean rack out with the dirty one. He stays and watches me a few minutes, then takes out a clean rack of glasses.

I finish one bin and move on to the next. I'm loading plates into a slotted rack when Will brings another bin of glasses.

"They need plates next, so finish that rack first."

Then he's gone with a stack of clean plates. I load more as fast as I can. I can do this.

I get another slotted rack from under the sink and start loading it. A greasy plate slips out of my hand and breaks just as Will comes back.

"Don't worry. Just sweep it up and put it in the garbage," he says as he gets a broom and dustpan from over by the door and takes care of it for me. "I forgot to tell you to watch out for broken glasses in the bins. You can get a nasty cut if you're not careful. Just throw away broken stuff. We get a few every day."

Then he's gone again. I'm focused on the work and don't even see C.J.'s uncle there, until Will brings in another bin of dirty glasses.

"Hey, she's a fast learner," Will declares.

"Keeping up?" Joe asks.

"Almost as good as me," Will says.

I smile and keep working. Sweat is pouring off my face. Will brings in dirty bins faster than I can load them.

Finally, I start to catch up. He's not moving as fast anymore. It's two o'clock. Rush hour's over. C.J. comes back to talk with me.

"Will says you're a great worker."

I don't know what to say, so I just shrug and grin.

"Are you up for working some more tonight?"

"I need the money. I didn't ask what you'd pay."

"Just minimum for dishwashing, but we really need another server."

"A waitress?" I perk right up. Waitresses get tips.

"Yeah. Do you have black pants and a white blouse?"

"Yes, I do."

"How about black shoes?"

"No." My hopes crash—didn't think to pack my good shoes.

"Well, just keep washing for now."

He leaves. A little later, his Uncle Joe comes over to talk to me.

"So, C.J. says you need to make some money?" he asks.

"Yup, I've been spending more than I expected."

"You make more as a waitress, and that's what we need right now. Do you want to learn another job today? Or did we wear you out?"

"I'm fine. But, how about Will?"

"He doesn't like having to deal with the customers. He's happier back here. C.J. says you have clothes you can wear, but you don't have any black shoes?"

"Just my sneakers or sandals. I forgot to pack my heels."

"Heels would kill your feet in an hour. What size do you wear?"

"Nine." I've always been a little embarrassed at the size of my feet.

"Maria wears a nine. There's a pair in the office. Come with me."

The shoes fit. They're soft black leather with a flat rubber sole—like a nurse's shoe, except the color. That reminds me of Aji, and the reason I've gotta leave as soon as I can. Tomorrow afternoon should be good enough. Aji's gone, so no one should care that I'm still here. It's not raining anymore. I can sleep in the park.

"I've never been a waitress before."

"That's okay. Even if you can only handle a few tables, it's better than no one at all. Use the restroom to change, then go up front. C.J.'ll show you what to do."

I change and go out into the coffeehouse. C.J.'s waiting for me by the front door. There's only a few customers right now.

"Thanks for getting your uncle to let me work." I tell him. "Is he gonna be upset when I leave right after you take time training me?"

"No, I told him you need some traveling money and probably won't work more than a day or two. That'll tide us over until we hire someone. I just put the sign in the window."

"Good. Charlie and Matt told me to leave town and they meant it. I'll get the bus to Rehoboth tomorrow afternoon. It leaves at four thirty-five."

"Aji was really scared. You're probably right to leave."

"Think I'll be alright if I wait 'til tomorrow?"

"Probably. Charlie did come by here last night. I told him that Aji quit and left without even waiting for his last pay."

"Good. Since they know he's gone, I should be safe here."

"Did you say you got new ID?"

"Yes, but it says I'm Shauna McLaughlin from Pittsburgh."

"That wouldn't work with Uncle Joe. He already knows your name is Maggie. But he won't bother doing paperwork on you for two days."

C.J. shows me where everything is. Waitressing isn't just writing down the order, then bringing it out from the kitchen. It's way more complicated than that. There's different places to put different kinds of orders, and all kinds of little jobs at the waitress station that hafta be done, too.

"How about the bill?" I ask. "How do I figure the tax and stuff?"

"When the people are done, bring the bill to me first, I'll tally it, then you take it back to them and tell them to pay at the cash register."

"Okay. So what do I do first?"

"Let's walk you through it."

There's a customer waiting to be seated. The lady asks for a table for one. C.J. seats her with a menu.

"This is Maggie, your waitress-in-training," he says.

C.J. walks me through each step, but as soon as she orders, I'm in trouble. I'm supposed to put down the numbers of everything, but she asks for a bowl of lemon soup with a small dinner salad. She doesn't give me the numbers. I look at C.J.

"Just write down what she said, then you can put the correct number on it at the waitress station. There's a menu there," he says.

"Okay." I turn to the lady and ask, "Will that be all?"

"Yes, thank you."

I take the order back to the waitress station. C.J. follows and shows me the menu. I put the numbers on the slip.

"Yellow copy on the salad wheel," I say as I clip the slip of paper to the large metal wheel.

They have a salad maker, so at least I don't hafta do that myself. The pot of soup's at the waitress station. I dish up a bowl and put it on a tray, then go back to the kitchen where the salad is ready. I carry both out on the tray and manage to serve them—no problems. Then I ask C.J. how to keep the orders straight when it gets busy.

"Write the table number at the top of the order. Each row of tables has a letter, and they're numbered from the windows to the back wall. Your customer is at table 4A. She's four from the windows in the row against the wall. You'll have rows A and B."

This'll be easy.

62: Peg

The secretary has me go directly into the principal's office.

"So you and Lizzie will be out the rest of the year?" he asks.

"Yes. Even if we get lucky and find Maggie right away, we're going to need some time together for healing."

"I checked Lizzie's records. She's an excellent student, but grades will be up to her teachers. I cleared your absence with personnel. Under the circumstances, they'll allow the four days this week as sick time, but that's all you've got. The last three weeks, that's fourteen days, will have to be leave without pay. Sorry. That's the best I could do."

"Thank you for getting this week paid."

"Betty has paperwork for you. I'll call Lizzie's teachers while you take care of that."

I get the paperwork from Betty and start filling in boxes and signing page after page. She picks up Maggie's photo.

"She's a nice-looking girl."

"That's her class picture from this fall. It's the best one I've got."

"Let me make some photocopies for you."

She comes back with one copy. She's written "MISSING" across the top. "I wasn't sure if she goes by Lewis."

She hands me the poster and a marker to add Maggie's name and description, then my new cell number for the contact, and a bold note at the bottom: Maggie, please call. Don't go back there. We left. Love you, Mom and Lizzie.

"I'll go make you fifty copies."

"Thank you."

When I'm done with the paperwork, I go to the principal's doorway. He's just getting off the phone.

"I talked to each of Lizzie's teachers. They all said she's got a good grasp of the material. The math and Spanish teacher have their finals prepared and are willing to let you proctor them. They're sending them down as we speak. The others will give her a final grade based on work completed, except her cooking class teacher. She insists on giving her zeros for the remainder of the year, which will give her a D."

"That will have to do. Please thank them for me."

"Already done. Will you be coming back next year?"

"My contract wasn't renewed."

"What! That was an oversight. You should have gotten it last month. We'd like to have you return."

"Thank you, but I'm not sure where we'll be living. When do you need to know?"

"Let us know by July first. It's hard to hire good people later than that."

"Thank you."

"Where should we mail your contract renewal?"

I ask him to hold it at the school.

Betty brings in the stack of posters and a fat envelope.

"Lizzie's math and Spanish tests are in here and some other work," she says, "and there's a return envelope. Try to mail it by June tenth, so they'll have time to get the grades in. You can return her books later this summer. Did you call sub-finder for the remainder of the year?"

"Not yet."

"When you're done in here, come on out and we can take care of that. You want the sub you have in there today?"

"Yes."

"I'll look up his number. Do you have direct deposit?"

"Yes, I do." My own checking account.

"What about your personal belongings?" the principal asks as Betty bustles out the door again. "Policy is for them to be removed at the end of the school year."

"The sub and Evan Williams are going to take care of them."

"We all wish you the best of luck finding your daughter."

"Thank you."

I turn in my keys, then take care of the sub-finder call with Betty.

"I hope you find her," she says, as she helps me carry everything out to the car. She's blinking back tears. I haven't really stopped to have a good cry, but hers are contagious.

"Thank you." I blink and sniffle.

Maggie's picture watches me from the passenger seat as I drive. "We're coming to get you," I tell her.

I have to wake up Lizzie to get into the motel room. "Hi, honey."

She yawns and asks me what I've found out.

"I have to call Officer Arden. Listen, so I don't have to go through it twice, okay? I'm exhausted."

"Okay."

When I tell Officer Arden we've talked to Chip, she's angry.

"What do you think you're doing? You're interfering with a police investigation. I told you I'd get to the school today."

I check the clock and tell her, "School lets out in twenty minutes. Just when were you planning on talking to him? We only had his first name, and where he'd be this morning."

"You may have made it impossible for us to find your daughter."

Suddenly, I've had enough of this woman.

"You listen to me," I tell her in a tone more than matching her own. "Take notes. The boy's name is Chip Taylor. He's in Mrs. Weissman's third period class. He told us Maggie left with at least four hundred dollars. They dropped her off at the bus station downtown, Friday night about seven thirty. She said the bus would leave soon. I checked. There's one bus out of there at that time. It goes to Syracuse and there are connections for New York and D.C. The D.C. bus stops in Harrisburg. I think that's where she went because I'm missing a journal that I wrote when I was young and ran away to Harrisburg."

"So you think she ran away to be like you?"

"No, I think she ran away to get away from my husband's abuse. I'm *hoping* she picked Harrisburg because it's where I went. I don't *know* that she went there. It's just the best guess I've got right now." I give her my new cell number and hang up. I turn to Lizzie. "We are not going to depend on them to find Maggie."

"Are we going to Harrisburg to look for her?" asks Lizzie.

"First we'll go to the bus terminal to see if anyone saw her leave. She may have gone somewhere else. We should be there about seven thirty, so I'm going to rest. I was nodding off on the way back here."

"We'll leave tonight?"

"Yes. When we're done at the bus station, we'll head out and stop at a motel along the way. I can't drive far with just a nap."

"How long will it take?"

"We'll probably get to Harrisburg tomorrow afternoon, if that's the bus she took."

"I hope she's still there."

"If she is, I hope we can find her. It's a big city."

At least the motel has good thick curtains for daytime sleeping. It's like being in a cave. Lizzie lies down and is asleep again in minutes. I set the alarm for seven.

What if I'm wrong about where she's going? What if I'm right? It *is* a big city. How will we find her?

I can't sleep. First I fixate on the past, trying to pinpoint signals I must have missed, then replaying my conversations with Officer Arden and Maggie's departure on Friday. I knew something was wrong. I shouldn't have let her go. But that wouldn't have changed what was happening to her. What if she had told me? Would I have believed her?

Then I start imagining the future: looking for her along the river or even out on City Island, people refusing to talk, people helping.

I imagine finding her, and I imagine the police telling me her body has been found. The only thing I can't grasp is simply never knowing.

The last time I look at the clock, it's almost six.

My mind is still racing when exhaustion takes over. The last thing I remember is an image of Joe. I haven't thought of him in years.

63: Maggie

This is *not* easy. I've been working half as many tables as the other waitress on this side, but I've barely kept up with my orders, even with C.J. tallying up the bills for me. I forgot to put the drinks on one order, dropped a bowl—fortunately *before* I filled it with soup, and made a few customers angry 'cuz I took so long writing down every detail of their orders. It's finally slowed a little. I'm helping Elaine, the other waitress, set up the station when C.J. comes back to check on me.

"How's it going?" he asks.

"I keep mixing up who gets which order."

"You're getting it to the right table," Elaine says.

"That's good enough," says C.J.

"For real?"

"For real."

"You're doing great for your first time," says Elaine. "Hey, when it slows down, one of us usually goes home. If you want to stay until nine, I'd be glad to get out of here. My kid wants me to help her with a project for school. It'd be nice to finish it before midnight. That okay with you, C.J.?"

"Think you can last another two hours?" he asks me.

"I need the money."

"See you tomorrow, Elaine. So how'd you do on tips, Maggie?"

"I haven't counted, but I definitely made enough for my bus ticket."

"Good. Do you know where you're going to stay tonight?"

"Motel, I guess."

Actually, I'll sleep in the park, but he'd probably try to talk me out of it. More customers come in, so that ends the conversation. I stay pretty busy for the next two hours. Finally it's closing. I stay and help tidy up, then sit down and wiggle my feet. Uncle Joe comes up to me.

"So, what do you think?"

"It's hard, but I like it. The people were mostly nice, and I made a lot on tips."

"Good. C.J. says you have a bus to catch tomorrow afternoon. You can work until then. I'll pay you off the books."

He gives me thirty dollars. With my tips, that's great.

"So, get your things. It's time to go home." He sees the confusion on my face. "It would be silly for you to spend money on a motel. We have an extra room."

"Thanks."

"Call home first, though. Let your mother know how you're doing."

"Okay. I can use my calling card."

"Save it. Just don't talk for an hour. Tell her I said hello."

They leave me alone in the office to make the call.

I was supposed to be home last night for my birthday dinner. Mom probably made me a carrot cake, and I didn't show up—wonder if she read the diary. Well, guess I gotta take that chance. It rings an awful long time. I'm ready to hang up when Richard answers.

"Hello? Who's there?"

I bite my lip.

"Who is this?"

"Maggie."

"Maggie?" There's a long pause. "What do you want?"

Not where are you, or how are you, or are you okay, but then, it's Richard.

"I wanna speak to my mom."

"Well, she doesn't want to speak to you. She read those lies you wrote about me. She doesn't want anything else to do with you, ever."

"Let *her* tell me."

"I'll go ask if she'll talk to you, but I don't think she will."

I hear him in the background, asking her if she wants to talk to me. Her voice is muffled, but there's an answer. He comes back.

"She won't come to the phone," he says. "She doesn't want to hear any more lies."

I hang up.

I will not cry. I will *not* cry.

I knew this would happen. It was silly to hope for anything else. I'll come back here and make good tips tomorrow, then go to Rehoboth and get a job waiting tables. I'll be Shauna McLaughlin from tomorrow afternoon 'til the end of my life.

I take a few deep breaths and let them out slowly. Pull my shoulders back and straighten up, then walk out into the restaurant.

"That was quick," says Uncle Joe.

"Didn't wanna run up your phone bill." My face smiles. "I told her I met you. She said to say hi. She might come down this way in a few weeks on her way to visit me at the shore. I said hi back."

It's all acting. My English teacher last year said something about all the world being a stage. Guess this is what he meant.

At least I have a safe place to stay tonight, with good people.

64: Peg

I wake up feeling rested, stretch, then look at the clock. Ten thirty! I leap out of bed and peek around the curtain. It's still dark outside. I have a vague memory of turning off the alarm. I wake up Lizzie.

"What time is it?" she asks.

"Ten thirty."

"We were supposed to go to the bus station before eight!"

"The same people will probably be there now. I really needed the sleep. I hardly ever turn off an alarm without waking up all the way."

Lizzie's already pulling on her shoes. I need a five-minute shower to finish waking up. I pick out old jeans, an old T-shirt, and the hooded sweatshirt I wear when we camp.

"We don't want to be too dressed up to talk with people who loiter around the bus station," I warn Lizzie.

"Hang, Mom. Not loiter."

"Okay, hang. Panhandling."

"Spanging. Long A."

"Spanging?"

"Asking for spare change."

"How do you know this?"

"Some mall rats sit near us at lunch. They're always talking about 'hanging' at the mall and who's good at 'spanging' for some cash."

"Okay. We're going to talk to people who hang at the bus station to spange, to see if any of them remember seeing Maggie."

"If you come off like her mom, they'll figure she's running away from you and won't say anything."

"Well, I can't pass myself off as her sister, now can I?"

"We could invent some kind of cover."

"Or we could just tell the truth. I married a pervert. We've moved out and want to find Maggie to let her know it's safe now."

"I guess that'll work."

It takes us fifteen minutes to pack up and clear out. After dropping off the key, I put some change and a few small bills in my pockets, then stow my purse under other things in the back, out of sight. Lizzie has the posters in her backpack. It's pretty worn.

We drive past the station, then park in the first available space and walk back with some of the posters. I don't even have to tell Lizzie to stay close. And I know this won't be the worst place we follow Maggie.

No one on duty remembers her, but one of the men tries to help us. "Let's see. Okay, see that man over by the pay phones?" he asks.

He's pointing to a man in a ratty old knit cap with gray hair falling in tangles down to his shoulders. His skin is weathered leather. A worn fatigue jacket hangs on his shoulders. He must be very thin under it. His legs are clothed in black slacks with small rips where the fabric has gotten too thin to hide the knobs of his knees. He has a filthy pair of running shoes on. A naked toe pokes out of one.

"He's checking for change in the coin returns," the clerk says. "He's here most of the evening, every night. Maybe he'll help."

We walk toward the phones. The man shuffles away, keeping space between us.

Lizzie starts to go to him, but I put an arm out to stop her.

"He knows he was pointed out. We don't want to scare him off."

He's watching us; he saw me stop Lizzie. He starts to approach us, but not directly. He goes to a machine off to the side and checks it for change.

"Mom, what are you waiting for?"

"Give me a poster. Put some up here but stay in sight."

He's checking the machines in a clockwise direction. I walk slowly to a machine well ahead of him, buy a bag of chips, and leave my change. I wait about ten feet from the machine. He gets to it, finds my money, then looks at me. Our eyes connect briefly, and then he holds his face down and looks at me sideways. He's still looking at me, but now he's trying not to let me see into his eyes.

To show I mean no harm, I stand still with palms open to him, the poster lying on top of my left hand. He finally shuffles my way.

"Thanks," he says, holding up the coins I left in the machine.

I nod and offer the chips. He ignores them and looks at the picture.

"Whadda ya want?" he asks.

"I'm looking for my daughter," I explain, holding it closer to him. "She was dropped off here Friday night to catch a bus."

After a pause, he says, "Nice girl. Gave me salsa chips."

My heart is racing. I try to sound casual.

"Did you see which bus she got on?"

"Didn't see her get on the bus. That's outside."

"Do you *know* which bus she got on?"

"No."

I slump. He keeps watching me.

"You her mother?"

"Yes."

"You gonna take her home?"

"Yes and no. Not the home she left. She was running away from my husband."

"He's bad."

"She told you that?"

He shrugs.

"I left him. Her sister and I moved out. For good. We didn't leave anything behind. Now I'm trying to find her."

"Didn't see what bus she got on."

"Thank you, anyway." I start walking away.

"Hey," he calls.

I turn towards him.

"Pennsylvania."

"She went to Pennsylvania?"

"Didn't see what bus she *got* on. She *said* Pennsylvania."

"You're sure?"

"*Said* she's gonna be like her mom."

"Thank you. Thank you ever so much."

He shrugs and turns away, moving on to the next machine.

Lizzie rushes up to me with her pack slung over her shoulder.

"I heard that. You were right. She *is* going to Harrisburg!"

"I didn't give him any clues, I mean he couldn't have just said that, right? He had to have talked to Maggie?"

She thinks, then nods her head in agreement. "He talked to her."

"Did you put up posters? She may have said more to someone else."

"I was watching you."

We quickly put up MISSING posters on the junk food machines, in bathroom stalls, and in areas where there are other signs posted. I even ask a man to post some in the men's room.

When we get back to the car, I have Lizzie take a look at Officer Wilson's card and program his number into both cell phones.

She calls it and gives him our cell phone numbers, then hands me a phone.

"Thought my partner would get the file," he apologizes. "I talked to Arden when I came in. She was furious about you going to the school without her."

"She wasn't going to get there, not any time soon. She was going to wait for Maggie to come home on her own. I don't think she will."

"We traded cases. I'm back on days tomorrow."

"I left all the information with her. I was calling to give you my cell number and to tell you we talked to a vagrant at the bus station who says Maggie talked to him and said she's going to Pennsylvania."

"Pennsylvania? You never mentioned that as a possibility."

"Lizzie, you made a list of what we know so far, didn't you?"

"Yeah, it's right here in my pack," she says as she gets it out.

"Are you headed back to your motel?" he asks.

"No. We're going after Maggie. You have my cell number."

"Going to Harrisburg is not a good idea," he tells me firmly. "You could scare her off if she's there and you're putting Lizzie at risk, too. The chance of finding Maggie is minimal and the chance of one of you getting hurt is huge. You have no idea the places runaways go."

"Yes, I do know. Been there, done that."

"How long ago? Things have changed. Not for the better."

"Maybe. But we'll deal with it. Lizzie is with me. I won't let her get hurt. Here, she can read you the list."

I hand Lizzie the phone and pull out of the parking lot. The one-way streets confuse me and we end up on the Skyway as she finishes the call and hangs up. The Skyway heads south. We should be going east first. This is the way home. Maybe it's a sign. Maybe I should leave Lizzie with friends, or maybe one of Maggie's friends knows exactly where she's going. We'll go there first.

Lizzie's voice breaks my train of thought. "Do you know where to look for Maggie when we get there?"

"I have to sleep on that."

We drive in silence. In one day, our lives have changed completely. Maggie's been gone four days. How much has her life changed?

I'm tired, so I cut over to I-90 and head south. There won't be any oncoming traffic and we should get to Fredonia in less than an hour.

"Mom!"

My body jerks.

"Keep me awake. We'll have to get off at the next exit."

I've been driving on auto pilot. I'm not sure where we are. Here the Thruway's going through fields and woods in the dark. I hold my eyes open as wide as I can and put my window down. Lizzie turns the radio to a loud rock station and jabbers about the music. I'm relieved when I see the exit for Fredonia. Lizzie doesn't argue when I pull off and go to the first motel with a vacancy sign. We carry our bags into the room.

"Okay if I take a bath and read for awhile, Mom? I slept a lot this afternoon."

"Sure, just let me use the bathroom first."

Even though I'm exhausted, sleep doesn't come immediately. Jan and I used to come up to Fredonia State all the time when I was Maggie's age. Then my life fell apart and I ran away. Whenever my life was a mess, I'd think about how kind Joe was that day he rescued me, and wonder what would have happened if I hadn't met Nick on the bus, if I'd found Joe instead.

Wednesday, May 31, 2000

65: Peg

Lizzie's in the shower when I wake up. I stare at the ceiling listening to the water running, then look at the clock.

It's seven in the morning, about thirty-six hours since I read those pages in Maggie's diary. My marriage is over, I've left my job, we have no home, and I have no idea how I'll find Maggie in Harrisburg. She got there four days ago, *if* she didn't change her plan. She may have decided to go somewhere else or moved on already. But it's the only place I know to start looking. I haven't been there in decades, it's not a small city, and I don't know anyone there, not really. The only person I'd have any hope of locating is Joe, *if* his family still owns that restaurant, and he wouldn't remember me.

Lizzie comes out wrapped in a towel with another on her head.

She interrupts my thoughts by saying, "I wasn't sure if I should wake you up."

"I'll get a shower, then we can try to connect with Maggie's friends at school." And arrange to leave Lizzie with one of *her* old friends.

"Why? Can't we just go? Maggie got there *days* ago! What if she doesn't stay there? We might miss her 'cuz we take too long!"

"What if Maggie told one of her friends exactly where she's going?"

"Just *call* them. Mary and Chandra are the only ones Maggie's talked to since we moved."

"I should leave you with one of your friends, too, where you'd be safe. Officer Wilson was right about that."

"Chip wouldn't have talked to you without me there."

I can't argue. I feel the same urgency she feels. "You're right."

Besides, I don't want to let her out of my sight. On the other hand, I don't want to be obsessive about that, either.

"We get some kind of breakfast here. While I make the calls and shower, you go get us some food."

"Okay. I'll get a good selection of whatever they've got."

"Don't forget to take the room key."

"Got it. *And* my cell phone. I'm keeping it in my pocket, so you don't need to worry about me at all."

"Thanks, hon."

Chandra is getting ready for school. I give her an edited version of events, just that Maggie's run away and we're looking for her. She should call us, not go back to Richard's. I give Chandra my cell phone number and she volunteers to get it out to anyone Maggie might contact.

Chandra is apologetic. "She probably thinks I've forgotten her. The last time I called, I got her stepfather and he said I wasn't to call again until she called me. I didn't want to get her into trouble, so I waited. But she's never called."

The call with Mary is essentially the same.

Maggie is out there alone, thinking no one cares about her at all. We've got to find her. Today. Tomorrow could be too late. Please, let her be in Harrisburg. Let us find her.

Lizzie's back with food when I get out of the shower. I dress quickly. We take twenty minutes to chow down, pack, and check out. We're heading to the highway before eight. When we stop for gas, Lizzie digs out our road atlas. While I fill the tank, she checks alternate routes.

"We shouldn't have come this way. It'll add *hours*."

"I know. I was going to drop you off. What are our options?"

"Through Jamestown is the shortest, but it goes through Allegany State Park. The long way might be faster. It's mostly highway."

I glance at the map. The direct route has winding roads through mountains where we could get stuck for hours behind someone doing forty or less.

"You're right, Lizzie. We'll go south to 80, take that across, then cut down through State College. We should be in Harrisburg by two or three."

66: Maggie

I wake up in another strange room. This one smells good—clean. Then I remember C.J. helping me into the house. I was so tired. I stretch and wiggle my feet. They don't feel too bad. I'm still in my waitress clothes and Maria's shoes are on the floor. My backpack's against the dresser.

C.J. taps on the door and pads into the room in bare feet and gym shorts.

"Good morning," he says through a yawn. "How'd you sleep?"

"I was totally out 'til a few minutes ago. Where's the bathroom?"

"Down the hall. It's the first door on your right. We need to be at the restaurant in an hour or so. Uncle Joe already went in."

"Okay if I take a shower?"

"Yup. Fresh towels are in the cupboard across from the bathroom. If you toss your clothes out into the hallway, I'll throw them into the washer for you."

I keep it short so I don't use too much water, even though my arms are awfully sore, and I hang the towel up neatly when I'm done. When I'm dressed, I follow sounds and smells to the kitchen. The washer is swishing clothes in an alcove and C.J.'s at the stove, stirring eggs. He's still barefoot and barechested, but he's got his work pants on now.

"I hope you like onions in your eggs," he says as he scrapes them into a bowl.

"That's the way my mom makes them."

He takes them over to the table. It's in a breakfast nook, surrounded by a big bay window. The center window's got a stained glass panel—a dragon breathing fire at a wizard in front of him. The wizard's casting a spell on the dragon with a crystal and at the foot of the dragon there are tiny, delicate flowers of all colors.

"That's awesome," I say as we sit down.

"Uncle Joe made it."

"I know. He told my mom about it; it was in her journal."

"My cousin, George, does nice work, but Uncle Joe's dragon is my favorite. When it's sunny, you can see a mirror image of it on the wall."

"It's funny how none of his kids work at the restaurant, just you."

"My dad was the one who liked the restaurant business. When he left, Joe had to help. So he never pushed his kids into it."

"But you like it?"

"Yeah, my dad had his own place. I was always there with him."

"Musta been awful for you when he died."

"Yeah, and I was mad when my mom sold the restaurant, but then I started spending summers down here 'cuz she was working. I loved it."

"And you moved here when she married a guy you don't like."

"He's just not my dad. Don't you have any family to go to?"

"No. It was always just the three of us. We were really tight, then Mom met *him* and everything changed, especially her. We quit doing things together, and when we did, he ended up coming along and it was like them and us. I never really liked him, even before."

We eat quietly a few minutes.

Done, C.J. stands up and asks, "What'd your mom say last night? Is she really coming to visit you?"

I shove food around on my plate. He deserves the truth.

"I didn't get to talk to her. She wouldn't come to the phone."

"Who'd you talk to?"

"*Him.*"

"So, how do you know your mother even knows you called?"

"He asked if she wanted to talk to me—couldn't hear what she said, but he said she didn't wanna hear any more of my lies."

"Do you really think your mother would say that?"

The question squeezes my heart. "She let *him* say it. She didn't grab the phone and say he was lying or anything."

I try to shrug this off like it doesn't matter, but it doesn't work. I can hardly breathe, the pain is so huge. My nose stuffs up and tears start leaking out. I turn towards the window to blink and they run down my face. I snuff and swallow, then take a forkful of eggs. It's like eating cotton. I'm glad C.J. doesn't try to make it better.

The washer stops. "All your stuff okay in the dryer?" he asks.

"Yeah. Thanks." I snuffle.

He gives my hand a light squeeze.

I hear him move the clothes, then he leaves me alone. The food gags me now. I put the rest of it down the disposal and run it, then clear the table, load the dishwasher, and wipe the counters. The pan gets left in the sink, soaking. I breathe. I just hafta remember to keep breathing, that's all. It'll be easier tonight.

Tonight Shauna McLaughlin will be on the bus to Rehoboth, and Maggie May Lewis won't exist anymore. Shauna won't need to hold her breath to keep from crying or shaking. I know she won't.

I get lost in the dragon flowers, then the dryer buzzes. I get my work clothes out before they can wrinkle and take them to the guest room to change. When C.J.'s ready for work, I'm ready to go, too.

"I figure I can work 'til about three thirty. That'll give me time to change, walk to the bus station, and get my ticket to Rehoboth."

"Are you sure you want to leave?"

"I've got to, remember? Besides, I can't use my new ID with Joe, and he wouldn't pay me off the books much longer, would he?"

"No, he'd have to put you on the payroll. You should be able to land a job in Rehoboth, though. There's a lot of little restaurants, and this is their busy season, at least it will be once we're done with the rain. You won't be able to use us for a reference, though. Uncle Joe does all that and he won't recognize your phony name."

"At least I'll know how to wash dishes and wait tables. That's more than I knew yesterday morning."

"Pick a little place. You may make better tips at an expensive, fancy restaurant, but there's a lot more pressure. You're better off starting in a friendly, laid back kind of place."

We don't talk in the car. I breathe in time with the wipers. In and out and in and out, all the way to the restaurant. C.J. parks in the back. It lets up for a few minutes as we get out. I walk around the puddles, careful to keep his aunt's shoes clean and dry. I put my things in the corner of the office.

Six hours and I'll be on my way.

67: Peg

The siren startles me.

We're finally out of the fog, but it's raining. I've been so focused ahead I didn't notice the flashing lights behind me. I pull over.

"The registration and insurance card are in the glove compartment, Lizzie, in the folder with the maintenance book. Get them out, please."

I pull my purse out from behind the seat. When the trooper gets to the window, I have my license ready. Lizzie's pulling out the rest.

"License and registration."

I hand them to him.

"You know why I pulled you over?"

"I was going too fast?"

"You were going seventy-eight miles per hour. The speed limit is sixty-five."

"Seventy-eight!"

"You shouldn't be speeding, especially on these wet roads."

"You're right, officer. I wasn't paying attention to my speed. I'm worried about my other daughter. She's missing and we think she's in Harrisburg. We're trying to get there to look for her."

"Did you report her as missing?"

"Yes. Maggie Lewis. They put her into the computer."

"I'll be right back." He takes the license and registration.

"Will he give you a ticket, or what?" Lizzie asks.

"I'm not sure. Probably."

The officer comes back and hands me my paperwork.

"Your daughter's Maggie May Lewis?" he asks.

"Yes."

"She's on NCIC as a missing child. You think she's in Harrisburg?"

"We were told she got on a bus for there Friday evening."

"She's already a few days ahead of you. Getting into an accident will slow you down a lot more than driving the speed limit."

"I just wasn't paying attention. I know you're right."

"You have a clean license. Under the circumstances, I'll let you off with a warning, but slow down and get there safely."

"Yes, sir. Thank you."

"Good luck finding your daughter."

"Thanks."

He goes back to his vehicle. I can see him writing on a clipboard. I put my license back in my purse and hand the rest to Lizzie.

"Well, that was lucky. I guess I better stick to the speed limit."

"Yup. He was pretty nice, really."

I wait for a break in traffic, then pull out carefully. He's still parked. We pass the Meadville exit a moment later, then I hear the siren again. He comes up fast and drives on by us.

"Who do you think he's after?" asks Lizzie.

"I don't know. I didn't see anyone speeding. It might be an accident. We should get off at the next exit and take a side road for awhile."

Only we don't make it to the next exit. Several cars are stopped ahead of us, blocking both lanes. The trooper's car is parked off the shoulder. There's a semi jackknifed across the road on its side. Two cars have plowed into it. They're crumpled. Another, an SUV the same color as ours, is on its roof in the median strip. The officer who stopped us is helping children out of it.

"Wait in the car, Lizzie."

"I can help."

"No, stay here."

I dig out the blanket I keep in the car and take it to the children. The boy's head is bleeding and he's holding his arm. They're both crying, watching the trooper help their father out of the vehicle.

"He needs that blanket more than the kids," the trooper says.

I wrap it around the injured man. He's in shock, unresponsive.

Traffic on the other side slows down. They move out of the way for a rescue truck. It drives across the median strip and two men get out. They go to the crumpled cars first, then come over to us.

"These the only survivors?" they ask the trooper.

"The truck driver is sitting in my car, and there's a woman in there." He points to the upside down SUV. "I didn't want to move her. Looks like a neck injury. She's unconscious, but breathing."

One of the rescue workers crawls into the car.

The other starts checking the man's vitals while he talks to the trooper. "Can you walk the kids over to our truck?"

The trooper leaves with the children.

The EMT glances at me. I'm staring at the car, willing the mother to climb out of it unharmed.

"Are you injured?" he asks.

"No. I stopped to help. That's my blanket."

"Do you need it back?" he asks.

"No, no, that's fine."

"You're soaked. Get back in your car. Dry off, warm up, and be ready to move."

I nod dumbly and go back to the car where Lizzie is waiting. I stand outside her door and start crying. She puts her window down.

"Are you okay, Mom?"

"We would have been in the middle of this. If he hadn't pulled us over, we'd have been one of those cars."

"Is everyone gonna be okay?"

"No. The people in the cars by the truck didn't make it, and there's a lady trapped in the SUV. They think her neck may be broken."

"Oh."

We look at each other and hold hands. The highway behind us is packed with cars, people wanting to get on their way. We're okay.

I realize I'm still standing in the rain, shivering. It could be the rain or shock, but I'm not going to let myself get any more chilled. I find dry clothes, then change in the car. The windows are steamed up enough to give me some privacy. I'm still cold, so I turn on the engine and run the heater until I'm warm again and Lizzie's begging for relief.

The rain lets up, then starts again.

We watch as the front of the truck is detached from the trailer. Then a huge tow truck pulls it up onto its wheels and out of the way.

Troopers put down orange cones and start guiding cars through the path they've made. We pass close to the crumpled cars.

At the next exit we stop at a pancake house. Neither of us wants to eat, but I need a few minutes to put the accident behind us before I drive on through the rain. I wash my hands thoroughly, though I didn't get any blood on me at all. I'm shivering again.

"Are you cold, too?" I ask Lizzie.

"Yeah."

We sit and order hot chocolate with whipped cream. After a refill, I finally feel warm again.

When we get back onto the highway, I stay in the right lane, doing less than the speed limit because of the rain, and leaving lots of space ahead of me. Lizzie doesn't complain. I figure we'll get to Harrisburg about four.

68: Maggie

"Miss? This tea caddy doesn't have any mint tea. I always drink mint tea with my lunch here."

I take the caddy and promise to be right back with mint tea. Elaine's at the waitress station getting water for one of her tables.

"I know there were two of each kind," I say.

"She pockets the mint every time she comes in, and she's a lousy tipper, too. Just keep on smiling, kid."

"I don't feel much like smiling. It wasn't this hard last night."

"People are in a rush at lunch, and the rain makes them crabby. It'll ease up in another thirty, forty minutes. You'll make it."

I paste on a smile and take out the tea caddy.

"Here you go."

"Thank you."

I give the lady her tea and check out another table. They leave a five dollar tip on a twenty dollar bill. That makes me feel much better. I can do this a few more hours.

Elaine's right. It starts thinning out shortly after one. By two, there's hardly anyone. Probably 'cuz of the rain. Elaine leaves for her break, and so do the two women who've been working the restaurant. C.J. and me will handle both sides while Joe picks up some supplies.

"You probably won't have more than a handful of customers for the next two hours," he says. "Maggie, you have to leave by four?"

"Yup, the bus leaves at four thirty-five."

"C.J., pay her cash when she goes. Maggie, tell your mother to stop in for lunch when she goes to see you at Rehoboth."

"I will." The lie comes automatically, but my stomach's got a sour spot in it.

"C.J., I want you to keep an eye on the fellow in the back corner booth of the restaurant. He's been there for hours. Keeps ordering one little thing at a time, so I can't ask him to leave, really, but he makes me uneasy. He seems to be watching people."

"Okay, Uncle Joe, I'll handle it." When his uncle has left, C.J. turns to me. "I hope it's not Charlie or that other guy you saw, looking for Aji. You better stay over here 'til I know for sure."

"You know Charlie, but what if it's Matt?"

"What's he look like?"

"A skeleton with skin."

"There's only one table busy here. I'll go check on him right now."

C.J.'s still gone when the people are ready to leave, so I use a menu to tally up the check myself, but I'm not sure how much tax to charge. C.J. comes back just in time to show me he has a chart by the register. I add the tax and take care of it myself.

"Thank you for coming," I say.

"You've really got it down," says C.J. "Sorry I left you so long. There were some customers checking out over there."

I quiz C.J. while I clear the last table.

"So how about the guy in the corner? Is it one of them?"

"No, it's an older guy, nothing like a skeleton. He's trying not to be obvious, but every time someone goes through the door, his attention is right there. It's pretty clear he's watching for someone."

"Maybe he was supposed to meet a blind date, and she didn't show, but he's not sure how long to stay waiting and looking for her."

"Maybe. Or maybe she got a look at him and left."

"Is he that ugly?"

"No. It's the sneaky way he's watching people. Though I suppose, if he's waiting for a blind date, he might not want to be obvious about watching for someone."

"Yeah, give the guy a break."

"Anyway, I'll keep track of that side until the girls get back. Think you can handle this side by yourself?"

"I guess so."

"Okay. Just come through the kitchen if you need me."

"I'll work on getting things cleaned up and ready for the dinner crowd. But I really need to leave by four at the latest."

"I know. Elaine said she'd be back a little early."

"Okay. Oh, and remind me to leave your aunt's shoes in the office when I go."

"I will. Did you make enough money today?"

"I have enough for my bus ticket and a few days of food. There's always a bunch of college kids working at the restaurants and shops on the boardwalk during the summer. They must share houses or apartments."

"No more drug dealers."

"I figured that out. I'll pay more attention from now on."

"I'll give you a ride if Uncle Joe gets back, but I can't leave if he's not here."

"It's only a few blocks, and I have my poncho to keep me dry."

C.J. goes to the restaurant side. I keep busy cleaning up and getting things ready for the evening crowd.

69: Peg

I stop for gas at two. The driving hasn't been too bad. There's been light drizzle on and off, but no fog and no downpours. We went directly from I-79 onto I-80, so it's all been limited-access, divided highway. We haven't seen any more accidents. We should be cutting south for Harrisburg soon.

"Which exit do I want to use?" I ask Lizzie. She's good with maps. She's been navigator for our trips since she was little.

"I think we want the exit for Bellefonte. Then we get 144 and take it to 322 and take that across and down to Harrisburg."

"How much farther is that?"

"Let me find the key. Okay. Thirty miles, maybe a little more."

"Is it all two-lane road?"

"No. For maybe twenty-five miles it is, then it looks like it's divided highway the rest of the way."

"How far altogether?"

"Um, a hundred miles. Maybe less."

She shows me the route on the map, then we get back onto the road, munching on chips and drinking pop we picked up at the gas station. I think of the accident and decide it's better to keep both hands on the wheel. I hand Lizzie my cola.

"Put the cap on that, please. I don't need any more right now."

"How long do you think it'll take us?"

"If we're lucky, we'll get into Harrisburg before four. There shouldn't be much traffic going into the city then. Most people should be heading the other direction."

"Where do we go when we get there?"

"I've been thinking about that. We should probably go to the police first and ask where runaways would hang out, then plaster those places with our posters."

"The police will start asking about her, and she might leave before she sees a poster."

"I know. Do you have a better idea?"

"What was in your journal? Maybe she went somewhere you went."

"I haven't looked at that thing in years."

"Well, where *did* you go when you were there?"

"I lived with a bunch of kids. I don't even remember the name of the street. None of them would be there anyway."

"Is there *anyone* you knew who might still be there? Who might be able to help us?"

"There was one boy. His family had a restaurant."

"What was it called?"

"I don't remember. I think it was on Second Street."

"Do you think you'll remember if you see it?"

"Maybe, if they haven't changed it much. If they still have it."

"So let's look for it when we get there. We can go to the police later if we need them."

"Okay. We can eat an early dinner there, if we find it, then go to a motel. Then we can use the phone book to look up the bus depot and any other places we can think of that she might go. We'll put up posters first, before we go to the police."

"Maybe I can talk to a kid who'll know the best places."

We have a plan, of sorts. I feel better having a clear destination, even though Joe probably sold the place long ago.

We're in Bellefonte when my phone rings.

It stops before Lizzie digs it out of my purse. "It says there's a missed call."

"Can you figure out who it's from?"

"Gimme a minute." She fiddles with the buttons and finds the number. Just then, it rings again and she answers it.

"Hello? She's driving. Hang on. Mom, it's Officer Wilson."

I pull over and take the phone.

"Have you found her?" I ask, knowing it's not likely.

"No. But I've got a detailed statement from a young woman who says that he sexually abused her five years ago, when her mother was living with him."

"What?" I exclaim. "How did you find her?"

"Mr. Hanford remembered the house this morning. It was his first sexual abuse case. The girl recanted, so it was unfounded, but he said he always believed her. He went back into work to check on it, then had them call me in, too."

"Do they keep records of that?"

"No, if it's unfounded, it's shredded. Your husband's name didn't come up, but Hanford remembered the girl's name, and she's in the system. Apparently she ended up having her own kids and there've been some minor neglect issues. So he talked to the person working with the girl. The girl had already told *her* worker the story, but that woman didn't think anything could be done at this point."

"Can it?"

"When she heard about your daughter, the girl came in right away. She's pressing criminal charges—she didn't try before because she didn't think anyone would believe her after she'd recanted. With two of them testifying it will be a stronger case than either doing it alone. She brought along notes she wrote about it back when it happened. Dates, times, everything. Her statement's very detailed and graphic. I'm sorry to tell you, but he put her through some pretty sick stuff, and threatened her, too. As soon as I get off the phone, I'm getting a warrant for his arrest and to search the house. With this statement and the fact that your daughter is missing, there shouldn't be any problem getting either. I should have kept the diary, though."

"We'll make sure you get it," I say. Maggie was right to run. I'm glad she's safely away from Richard. If we can just find her.

"Does he have any porn or sex paraphernalia?" Wilson asks.

"No. Nothing like that. At least, not that I know of."

"If we find anything, it can be used as supportive evidence. This girl says he took pictures of her, too."

"Check the basement. He didn't want us down there, and I respected his privacy. I was such an idiot."

"From what this young woman says, he's extremely manipulative. At least you believed your daughter."

"Not really, not until he convinced me he was guilty."

"The other victim says he spent months undermining her mother's confidence in her, building a 'bad girl' persona for her, before he even started in on her. *Her* mother bought his version of things hook, line, and sinker. Kicked the girl out and still doesn't have anything to do with her. *You* faced up to the truth in a few hours, even without your daughter there to convince you."

"I still can't believe I was stupid enough to be manipulated like that in the first place. Let me know what you find, please."

"Sure will."

I give the phone back to Lizzie. "He did the same thing to another girl five years ago. She's pressing charges. With Maggie testifying, too, they'll have a good case." I pull back onto the road. "Do you think Maggie will want to do that?"

"Why wouldn't she?" asks Lizzie.

"Well, they'd probably drag up all the stupid stuff she's done the last couple years to try and make her look like a liar."

"We'll be there for her. She can't let him get away with it."

"It may not be that clear for Maggie."

"She'll do it," Lizzie affirms.

Neither of us is admitting we may never find her.

70: Maggie

I get all the dirty dishes back to Will and make sure all the tables and chairs are nice and clean. Then I prep the tea caddies and wrap sets of silverware in napkins. Will brings out racks of glasses and stacks them up. He helps me make sure everything's stocked and ready for the girls coming on for the evening.

"You're pretty good, for a beginner," he says.

"Why don't you wait tables? The money's better."

"I don't like having to deal with the people. Like that lady they complain about who steals tea bags, or kids who throw food, or people who are having a bad day and take it out on you. I'd rather work behind the scenes. Joe pays me more than most dishwashers get. He knows I do extra whenever I can, and the waitresses give me some of their tip money when I help out a lot."

"Is that a hint?" I smile and start to pull out some of my tip money.

"No, that wasn't a hint. Keep your money. I got that you're on your own. You're gonna need it."

"You sure?"

"Yeah, don't worry about it."

He gives me a grin and takes the last bin of dirty dishes out to the kitchen. I can't help him back there. I've gotta stay clean for the front. I wander around, checking for anything I missed, straightening chairs—part of me wishing I could stay here, but a stronger part saying hurry up and leave.

With no one to talk to, I'm more aware of the tightness in my chest. It's not just from being sad. My body's totally tensed up and I've been breathing shallow all day. Now the peach fuzz on the back of my neck's pushing against my collar.

What if Charlie or Matt is around and sees me on my way to the bus station? Or Aji or the other robber? But I can tell them I'm leaving, that I won't be back. That's all they want. I don't need to be this scared. But I am. It doesn't make sense.

It's three thirty. As soon as Elaine gets here, I'm leaving.

71: Peg

We're about a half hour out of Harrisburg when the phone rings again. We're on divided highway here, so I just pull into the slow lane and keep driving when Lizzie hands it to me.

It's Officer Wilson. "I wanted to let you know. We got the warrant for your husband's arrest, for rape, from the incident five years ago. We won't add anything regarding Maggie until we get a statement from her."

"Did you pick him up?"

"No. We're at the house now, but he's not here. We're starting in the basement. The guys found some boxes he had back in the corner."

"I saw those when I helped him move his office furniture down there, before we moved in. He said those were old taxes and stuff."

"That's what they're labeled."

There's a pause. I'm thinking I should hang up or pull over when I hear a low whistle in the phone. I wait.

"You were right to believe in your daughter. He's got all kinds of porn in these boxes. Some of it's pretty sick. A lot of S and M. This stuff fits right in with the statement we took."

I blink rapidly, trying to see the road ahead. There's an exit. I take it and pull off onto the shoulder.

"Mom, are you okay?"

The voice in the phone echoes, "Are you okay?"

Tears are running down my face, but falling apart now won't help anything. I can't stop the tears, but I can function in spite of them. "Yes. I'm okay. I just have to find Maggie."

"If you do, please bring her back to add to the charges against him."

"That will have to be Maggie's decision." I have to sniff up some tears. "You said Richard wasn't there?"

"No, but we'll get him when he comes home."

72: Maggie

Elaine gets back twenty minutes before four. Tips get stuffed into my pants pockets and the apron, pens, and pads get left at the waitress station. We say goodbye and I go to the office.

I take off Maria's shoes first and leave them by the door. Dump my tips on the desk. Almost fifty in ones and fives and a ton of change. C.J.'ll trade it for bills. He's gonna pay me, too.

I lean my pack up against the desk to open it. Jeans and a T-shirt will be comfier on the bus. Sneakers, too. I change quickly, fold my work clothes neatly and pack them away, then tie up the pack. I re-roll the sleeping bag as tight as I can and strap it to the top. I put the frame on the edge of the desk, bend my knees, put my arms through the straps, and straighten up. Seems heavier. I click the buckle on the waist strap, put the poncho on over all of it, and I'm ready to go.

That tightness in my chest comes back. Maybe it's a muscle thing from carrying the pack. Doesn't feel like that, though. I take a deep breath and let it out slow to relax, then go out into the restaurant. C.J.'s by the cash register up front.

I go straight over and tell him, "Elaine's got the other side—just one couple, drinking tea, holding hands."

"All I've got over here is that guy who's been here all day."

I follow his glance over to the back corner table. The man's leaning on his hand, rubbing his forehead—can't see his face. He's probably feeling bad from being stood up.

C.J. opens the register and takes out five twenties.

"Joe paid me last night. That's too much for today, isn't it?" I ask.

"That's what he said to give you. Don't argue."

I pause a minute, then take it. "Okay. I owe you both, tho'."

"It's karma. Pass it on—help someone else when you can."

"I will. Can you change some of my tip money into bills?"

"Sure."

He takes the coins and counts them into the register, then gives me bills. I still have a pocket full of quarters.

He gives me a hug. "Sorry I can't leave to give you a ride."

"That's okay. I have a half hour. That's plenty of time."

"Be careful."

"I will."

I walk out the front door. The bells jingle like Christmas.

It's raining again—not hard, but enough for me to stop and put up the poncho's hood. It's stuck inside the neck. I stand close to the building, trying to stay dry, while I pick at it. It's not stuck tight, but with the poncho over the sleeping bag and pack, and all the extra weight, it's awkward to get it out from behind my head.

Finally it's free and I pull it over my hair. I'm in an orange tunnel now. I hear the bells again and turn to look—it might be C.J. coming to convince me to stay. But it's not. It's the man from the corner table. He musta given up on his date. He's turning away from me, pulling up the collar of his raincoat. There's no one else on the street. I head for the bus depot. It's not far.

I walk slowly at first, then lengthen into my hiking stride. There's no looking back now. Shauna has a bus to catch.

73: Peg

We stop for gas on the edge of Harrisburg and pick up a map of the city. It's after four when we're done with our pit stop and back in the car. I deal with traffic while Lizzie navigates.

"This turns into Cameron Street, Mom. That will take us right downtown. We should try to find that restaurant on Second Street."

"I don't know if I'll recognize it, if it's there. I don't even remember what it *used* to look like, and it's probably changed anyway." Nothing looks familiar. Why did I think we'd be able to find Maggie here? It's a wild goose chase.

Lizzie's not quitting, though. "If we don't find it, we can head over to the bus depot. It's marked on this map. It's right downtown, too. Near the Capitol Complex."

"That's right! I remember! The restaurant was near the Capitol. And even if it's not there anymore, there will probably be another restaurant, or a store with someone who can tell us where to put posters."

"We've gotta make a right somewhere to get over to Second Street."

"Lizzie, I'm not even sure the restaurant is on Second Street. None of this looks familiar. Where's the Susquehanna?"

"The river's over to the right. You can cut across on Maclay Street."

I make the right.

"There's Seventh. We're going the right way. But there's arrows on the map. Second Street is one way the wrong direction. We have to go down Third or Front Street."

I make the left on Third.

Several blocks later, I see it on our left. Coffeehouse and restaurant, combined, yet separate. The restaurant looks the same. The coffeehouse has stained glass windows now. Joe said he did stained glass. Maybe he *is* still here. I pull over and park.

"Is that it, Mom?"

"I think so. I guess I was wrong. It's on Third Street, not Second."

"Good thing Second Street is one-way the wrong direction."

"Don't get your hopes up, Lizzie. I don't know if Joe will still be here; I don't know if he'll remember me; I don't know if he'll *want* to help; I don't know if he'll know *how* to help."

"Let's find out. Come on."

I get out of the car reluctantly.

That afternoon with Joe could have been yesterday. I've blocked out so much of my life during that time. Those hours helped me survive a dark period of my life. I feel a twinge of sadness, realizing that he probably doesn't even remember me.

But this is the only place I have to start looking for Maggie. I straighten up and walk into the restaurant with my shoulders square and my head high. There's a young man at the register.

Lizzie breaks in before I can say anything. She holds out a poster.

"We're looking for my sister. Have you seen her?"

He looks from Lizzie to me and asks, "Are you Maggie's mother?"

Tears well up into my eyes. He knows Maggie.

I nod. " You've seen her?"

"She left about twenty, twenty-five minutes ago. She's catching a bus for Rehoboth. It leaves in a few minutes."

"How do we get to the bus station from here?"

"Will!" he calls loudly.

A young man in a dirty apron comes out from the back.

"This is Maggie's Mom. Watch the front and tell Uncle Joe I went to help her catch Maggie before she gets on the bus." He turns to me. "Where's your car?"

"Right out front."

We pile into the Explorer. I pull into traffic.

"Are you Joe's son?"

"No, I'm his nephew, C.J. Take the next left, on Market."

I make the left and drive two blocks. I can see a bus ahead.

"Just drive around the block. We'll get her," says Lizzie.

They get out of the car. I take my time driving around the block. When I get back to the station, they're nowhere to be seen. I circle again. This time I see them by the bus, talking to the driver. I don't see Maggie. The third time around, they're standing on the curb. I stop and they get into the car.

"She's not on the bus. No one's seen anyone fitting her description. She left the restaurant about a half hour ago, and she would have walked the same way we just drove. She should be here," says C.J.

The driver gets on the bus and pulls out.

"You're sure she wasn't on it?"

"He let me get on and check for her, Mom. I even made sure the bathroom was empty."

"Then where is she?"

Following C.J.'s directions, we drive every alternate route Maggie might have taken to the bus station. We go back and they check with the ticket lady. She still hasn't seen Maggie. They give her a poster with the cell phone number.

"Maybe she forgot something at the restaurant," Lizzie suggests.

We go back to Third Street.

74: Maggie

I'm behind a dumpster in an alley a few blocks from the restaurant. Richard's got a knife poking my side and my face smashed up against a brick wall.

He turns me to face him. "Get that poncho off, and the pack."

I slide the pack off and lean it against the brick wall, then pull the poncho over my head. He's stepped back so I can't throw it over him. I put it on top of the pack.

He glances out at the street, then comes up close to me, so we're both behind the dumpster. The only windows are way up and have closed blinds. He pokes at my belly with the knife.

"You little whore. So you did that kid *and* his uncle."

"No."

"I heard you, his uncle gave you extra."

"I was waiting on tables."

He slaps me. Hard. He's not scared to leave marks, that's for sure. I taste blood and my ear's ringing. The knife's still poking my gut. If I try to get away, he'll win. I know he's stronger than me.

This time he'll kill me if I try.

"Take your clothes off."

I move as slow as I dare. At least he's taken a step back again. Pull my fleece off and put it on top of the poncho.

"So tidy? Well, I'm being tidy now. Your mother is devastated by your lies. She doesn't want to see you again, ever. I'm going to make sure you always remember you don't want to come home. You will *never* try to contact her again."

The rain's soaked through my shirt—might as well be naked. Start on the first button, then he changes his mind. He points and tells me to get down on my knees.

I obey. I look up and he's opening the front of his raincoat with his free hand. It doesn't matter—one more time. Shauna will never put up with this. I stare right through him.

Suddenly, Richard collapses forward. I push so he doesn't land on me. The back of his head's gushing blood.

Matt leans down to wipe the handle of his gun on Richard's coat, leaving dark liquid smears behind, then he lifts the barrel up towards me. My eyes fly toward Richard's knife, but Matt kicks it aside before I can move. Keeping his eyes and his gun pointed at me, Matt gets the knife and sticks it in the back of his waistband.

His gaze bores into me as he demands, "Where's Aji?"

My heart's pounding. I can't breathe. "I don't know," I wheeze.

"Yeah, right. That's why you're working at the same restaurant."

"They were shorthanded 'cuz he quit. I needed money to leave."

"You're full of shit. You were in on it with him from the start. We're going back to Charlie's house. You'll tell us where they are."

He yanks me up and shoves his gun into the small of my back.

"Walk fast," he demands. "Slow down or call for help, you die."

To avoid the restaurant, we walk towards the river for a block, then up Susquehanna Street. I'm supposed to be on a bus. Wonder if anyone will ever figure out what happened to me—probably not.

Matt bangs on the door. I hear the locks being opened. Charlie slams the door shut behind us and locks up again.

"What's she doing here?" he demands.

"I've been watching the restaurant to see if Aji's stupid enough to go back for his check, like we agreed. Turns out, this bitch is working there. Isn't that a cozy little coincidence? They had her on the inside here, to tell them when to hit you."

"I never saw them before they came in here," I plead.

Matt takes my chin in his hand and bites his words. "Don't lie."

He pulls the gun up above his shoulder. At first it's pointed down at me, then he turns it so it's pointing up in the air. Then he swings.

I dodge the blow, but lose my balance and end up on my knees in front of him, holding myself up with one hand. He kicks me in the gut; my bladder empties onto the floor. I curl up in it, crying.

"What the fuck, Charlie."

Crystal. I can't talk. She looks right at me, then turns to Charlie.

"I'm gonna get the kid and get out of here. I don't know anything."

Charlie looks over at Matt. Matt nods. Crystal disappears.

"You will tell us how to find Aji and our belongings. All you can control now is how much pain you experience before you die."

Matt pauses to let this sink in and I start rocking in my puddle.

It doesn't matter. No one cares. It doesn't matter. Nothing matters. He grabs me by my hair and grinds my face into the floor. The urine gets into my eyes and stings. He jerks my head back up. I gasp for breath and choke on droplets of pee. He slaps me.

"Where's Aji?"

"I don't know."

He sighs, "Charlie, this may take awhile."

Crystal comes back with Jimi.

Charlie unlocks the door to let them out. When it swings open, I scream "HELP!" loud as I can.

Matt's foot hits the side of my head.

75: Peg

C.J. holds the door for us as we enter the restaurant. Joe's standing by the cash register. I wouldn't have recognized him, except for his eyes. Those green eyes are still the same.

"Peg?"

"Yes. Joe."

"It's good to see you." He greets me with a hug. "And this must be Maggie's sister?"

"Yup, I'm Lizzie."

"Did you miss the bus?" asks Joe.

"It left without her. She never got to the station. We were hoping she forgot something and came back."

"No, she didn't. Does she have any friends here?" Joe asks. "Maybe she ran into someone she knows and decided to stay another day."

"She's never been here before," I tell him. "C.J., has she made any other friends?"

"Not really. She stayed with some people a couple nights, but it didn't work out well. She wouldn't go back there. But she called home last night and talked to her stepfather."

"She talked to Richard?"

"Yes," C.J. replies. He sounds very worried.

"Is that a bad thing?" Joe asks.

"Maggie ran away because of him, Uncle Joe. She lied to you about the call. Actually, he told her that her mother wouldn't talk to her."

"We weren't there. We left Monday night."

"He made her think he was talking with you," C.J. explains.

"Maggie couldn't believe I wouldn't talk to her."

C.J. pauses, then reluctantly answers, "Yeah, she did."

It feels like my heart is in pieces and bleeding. So Maggie thinks I've rejected her. She might do anything.

"Did she have any plans?" I ask C.J.

"Yes, she was going to Rehoboth and planned to get more restaurant work. She learned fast here the last couple of days."

"So you don't think she was going to do anything . . . stupid?" I can't say the other s-word.

"No, she wouldn't do anything like that," C.J. reassures me. "I'm worried about her stepfather, though. Does he have Caller ID?"

"He does," Lizzie answers. She sounds frightened.

"I don't understand. Why is that a problem?" I ask.

"He knows where she was calling from, Mom. If he knew last night, he could have been here this morning."

Joe interrupts, "Caller ID would just show the phone number."

"All he'd hafta do is a reverse search online," Lizzie explains. "You have the name of the restaurant and the address in the phone book, don't you?"

"Yes. It's a business. People need to know where we are."

"He can get the address from the number?" I ask.

"Of course," Lizzie says.

C.J. nods his support. "He could have had the restaurant name and address minutes after he got off the phone."

I pull out my cell phone and find Officer Wilson's number. He doesn't answer. I leave a voice message: It's urgent that he calls me back right away.

"Richard knows that I went to the police to report Maggie as a runaway," I explain. "When he saw all of our things gone, he probably figured we told them what she said in her diary and that the only reason they didn't come arrest him was because they hadn't talked to Maggie."

"Have they issued a warrant against him?" Joe asks.

"Yes. Another girl came forward. They have a warrant for his arrest because of that, and they already searched the house. I need to know if they've got him in custody."

The bell rings and customers come in. Joe seats them and one of the waitresses takes over. He disappears. C.J. brings us a pot of tea. I stare at my new cell phone, willing it to ring. C.J. excuses himself to check on the coffeehouse.

Lizzie and I sip tea in silence. It's still raining outside. Waves of anxiety keep flowing through me. It's almost five.

"I can't stand just waiting here, Mom. I think we should be out looking for her ourselves, not just sitting and waiting for the police."

"We already drove every route she could have taken."

"*She* wasn't driving, Mom. There could be shortcuts that we should check."

When he comes back from the coffeehouse, I call C.J. over.

"C.J., are there any shortcuts Maggie might have taken to the bus depot, places we didn't check with the car?"

"I suppose she could have cut across the Capitol Complex, but I doubt if she would. She doesn't know her way around that well. Most likely, she'd just take Third down to Walnut or Market, but it probably wouldn't hurt to walk it. Let me check with Uncle Joe, he's back in the office."

76: Maggie

I smell cat pee. No, it's mine. I'm wet. I remember and hold still.

Everything hurts.

I keep my eyes closed. If I'm awake they'll hurt me again.

A wave of nausea rises up from my middle. I puke. My eyes open against my will. It's all down the front of me—stinks. I'm duct-taped to one of the dining room chairs. My head's the only thing that can move and puking made it lift off my chest. Dizzy—feel like I'm gonna barf again. My head's too heavy—let it drop and close my eyes. Stomach settles some, too.

"Matt, she puked all over herself."

I hear Matt come in from the kitchen.

"What the fuck did you puke for, bitch?"

He kicks the leg of the chair. Pain sears up my spine into the base of my skull.

"Open your eyes, bitch."

I follow orders.

"You're so nasty, I don't want to use my hands on you now."

Matt grabs the only lamp in the room, yanks its cord out of the wall, then out of the lamp. He tosses the useless light fixture into the corner. It lands with a soft thud on a pile of dirty clothes and trash. He doubles the cord in half and wraps the ends around his hand. He comes over to me. Seeing him move towards me makes me dizzy. I've gotta close my eyes again.

"I know you're awake, bitch. Where's Aji?"

"I don't know," I whisper.

Life has already left my voice. I hear the cord cutting through the air. When it hits, I puke again. Then everything goes blissfully black.

77: Peg

Joe comes out with C.J. "Peg, we were talking. There was a man in that corner booth all day. He seemed to be looking for someone."

"Did he see Maggie?"

C.J. answers, "Maggie came through here for her pay. The guy got up and left right after she did. Do you have a picture of your husband?"

"No, but I'll ask the New York police to fax his license photo to the police here. You and your uncle can look at that, if they ever call back."

"I have a friend in the police department here," says Joe. "I'll call him. He'll make sure they start looking for her right away."

"Do we hafta wait for police, or can C.J. and I start looking?" Lizzie asks. "I can't stand just sitting here. We could put up posters."

"We can walk towards the bus station, if it's okay?" C.J. asks.

"Go ahead. Just stay together and be careful!"

Joe calls the police department and explains the situation quickly to his friend. He hands the phone to me.

"Peg, this is Patrick Murphy. Who's your contact in Buffalo?"

"Officer Wilson." I pull out his card and give Murphy contact info.

"What is your husband's name?"

"Richard Crandall."

"And your daughter's?"

"Maggie May Lewis."

"Do you have a picture of your daughter?"

"Yes. We have about twenty posters. And she's on NCIC."

"I'll request your husband's license, then we'll come over there."

As I hang up that phone, the cell finally rings. It's Wilson.

"Have you arrested my husband yet?"

"No, he hasn't been back to the house."

"He may have known how to find Maggie, and she's disappeared. I just talked with Patrick Murphy, with the Harrisburg police. He'll be calling you for information on Richard."

"There's a call coming in right now."

I put down the cell. I feel as if I'm being strangled. "Now we wait."

"Patrick understands that time is important here," Joe reassures me as he warms my tea. "He'll be over as fast as is humanly possible."

78: Maggie

I'm awake again—won't open my eyes. Feel nauseous. Try to relax my stomach so I don't vomit again. Let go of all the pain.

I hear them talking, I think.

"She's not waking up, Matt. You shouldn't a kicked her in the head that hard."

"That really doesn't make a lot of difference, now does it? We're gonna kill her, anyway."

"But she can't tell us anything, this way."

"Leave her alone for awhile. She may come to. If she doesn't, we can dump her in the river after dark."

Can I get awake enough to fight them off?

Not now. Feel myself fading out again.

79: Peg

"I'm sorry we're interrupting your business," I apologize to Joe.

"Don't worry about it. I have good people working for me. They can handle the place without C.J. *or* me."

I've been watching the waitresses work. They are efficient. One I haven't seen before comes up to us.

"Joe, is C.J. over here?"

"No, he and Maggie's sister went to look for her. This is Peg, her mother. Peg, this is Elaine."

"I hope you find her okay," Elaine offers. "Maggie's a great kid. She learns really fast and she's a hard worker."

"Thanks."

Joe asks, "Why do you need C.J.?"

"That girl he knows, the one with a kid? She's asking for him. She looks like she's in trouble."

"Send her over here. I know the one you mean, Crystal, isn't it?"

Elaine brings over the girl. A toddler is on her hip. He's dirty; she's jittery. Joe speaks to her softly.

"Do you need some help, Crystal?"

"Yeah, I was hoping C.J. might be able to loan me enough money for a bus ticket. I decided to go home."

"Home?"

"Well, things are just too intense here, you know?"

At that point, C.J. bursts in the door. Lizzie's not with him. My heart stops.

"Where's Lizzie?"

"She's taking the police to the alley where we found Maggie's pack and poncho. They were behind a dumpster. Your husband's there, too. They're calling an ambulance for him. Someone smashed in the back of his head."

"Did he tell you where Maggie is?"

"No, he's unconscious. Crystal, what are you doing here?"

What little color the girl had in her face has vanished, leaving it ghastly white.

Joe tells C.J., "Crystal came by to borrow some money to go home."

C.J. turns back to Crystal. "You'd never go home. What happened?"

Crystal starts crying. "They've got her."

"Who?" C.J. demands. "Charlie and Matt?"

Crystal nods miserably.

"Where?"

"At the house. They think she helped Aji set them up."

Joe and I follow C.J. outside. There are two police cars a couple blocks down, and Lizzie's walking up the street with a tall man in a sport coat.

"Patrick!" calls Joe. "We know where she is! Hurry!"

"She's in a house on Calder Street," C.J. calls. "I don't know the number, but I can show you. She's in danger *now*."

The man in the sport coat must be Murphy. He runs straight to his car without asking questions. C.J.'s there getting into the passenger seat. Then they pull out and head down the street quickly. Murphy must know Joe and C.J. very well to be this responsive.

Joe, Lizzie, and I cross and get into the Explorer.

I put on my four-way flashers and take the first left behind Murphy. I come around the corner just in time to see him make another left. One of the black and whites comes up behind us, siren and lights going. They pass and keep going, making the turn ahead of me.

"Patrick must have called for backup. I don't know the whole story, but one of our waiters quit the other day. C.J. told me Aji had a drug dealer after him. I didn't know Maggie had anything to do with any of that. I'm sorry, Peg."

"It's not your fault, Joe."

We speed up the street behind the black and white. Then, sirens and lights off, they turn left on Calder. I pull in behind Murphy's car. The black and whites turn into a tiny side street and stop. Murphy and one of the officers go up to the door of the corner house with C.J. Patrick motions for us to stay in the car. I grip the steering wheel with all my might. It's the only way I can stop myself from running out after them.

Another officer disappears down the little side street. I assume he's going to cover the back, though as I remember these row houses, there may not be any other exit. We watch as Murphy knocks on the front door. No one opens it.

C.J. calls out, "Hey, Charlie. I got some information for you."

Murphy and the uniformed officer are standing on either side of the door, flat against the side of the house, their weapons drawn and ready. There must be some kind of answer from inside, because C.J. calls out again, not as loud this time.

"Open the door, man, I don't want to be shouting this all over the street. It's about Aji."

As the door opens, the uniformed officer pulls C.J. behind him. Murphy gets a foot in the door before it can be slammed shut, then they disappear inside the house. There are shouts, two shots, then it's quiet. C.J. is still against the side of the house. Joe reaches over to hold my shoulder. My knuckles on the steering wheel are white.

Finally, the uniformed officer comes out behind a young man in handcuffs.

"C.J., you fucking narc. What the fuck are you doing with these fucking pigs?"

"Maggie didn't have anything to do with Aji or you getting robbed, Charlie." C.J. turns to the officer. "Is she okay?"

"We've called an ambulance," answers the cop.

I'm out of the car instantly, Joe right behind me.

"Ma'am, you can't go in there." A young cop blocks my way.

I glare at him as I say, "She's my daughter." The words are ragged, ripped out of my mouth. He'd have to use physical restraint to stop me. He doesn't try.

The house is a nasty, filthy, stinking firetrap.

I find them instinctively. Patrick Murphy is gently unwrapping duct tape from my baby's ankles.

80: Maggie

I wake up again—no, not really awake. I think I hear Mom's voice—she's crying. Maybe I'm dead. Don't hear Charlie or Matt. I peek out of my eyelashes to see if they're gone. First thing I see is Matt's feet. He's lying on his back on the floor.

"Maggie?"

I open my eyes more. It really is Mom, and she *is* crying.

There's a big redheaded man undoing the tape around my right arm. Joe's working on my left. There's still tape around my chest. I'm pretty dizzy—I might fall over without the tape. I need to tell them that, but when I try to talk it comes out all garbled up.

"Oh, God, please let her be alright." Mom's praying.

I smile a little to let her know I hear her, then go back to sleep.

81: Peg

Emergency medical personnel arrive. They glance at the body on the floor, then devote their attention to Maggie.

"She opened her eyes for a moment," I tell them desperately.

Joe puts his arm around me. C.J.'s keeping Lizzie outside.

"Are you related?"

"I'm her mother."

"Any allergies?"

"No."

While I'm being quizzed, his partner checks Maggie's vital signs and talks into a small microphone on his collar.

"Patient is a teenaged female, unconscious, apparent victim of a beating. Reportedly in and out of consciousness. Pulse rapid and weak, breath shallow and rapid, skin cool and pale. Apparently vomited at least once. Loss of bladder control evident. Bruising starting on face."

He runs his hands over her arms and legs. When he touches the side of her head, she rolls it away from him. He looks closer, then pulls each eye open and looks at it with a penlight.

"No apparent fractures. There's swelling over the right ear, appears to be tender, and pupils respond to light unevenly."

He presses gently on her abdomen and she moans. Her eyes flutter open, then shut again.

"Tenderness in lower abdomen."

He looks up at me and asks, "What's her name?"

"Maggie." I feel as if someone's squeezing my throat.

"Maggie," he calls loudly.

She doesn't respond. They move her onto a stretcher carefully.

"Maggie," he calls as they tuck the blanket around her, leaving one arm out. This time her eyes flutter open briefly, then close again.

I move forward and grab her hand as they start to lift her.

"Maggie, it's Mom. I'm here. Please, open your eyes."

Her eyelids tremble. "Try again," the EMT tells me.

"Maggie, it's okay, I'm here. Open your eyes, honey."

They open briefly, then close without her making contact.

"Can I ride with her?" I ask.

"As long as you stay out of our way. We need to get an IV going."

"Give me your keys," says Joe. "I'll drive Lizzie to the hospital."

82: Peg

In the ambulance, they get an IV into Maggie's arm.

She mumbles incoherently. They keep talking to the hospital as the driver takes off, lights and siren going.

"Her vitals are improving," the EMT reassures me.

A gurney is waiting for her. As they transfer her onto it, a doctor comes out and starts checking her.

"Take her for CT scans," he tells the man with the gurney, handing him a piece of paper. "Head and abdomen."

"Good luck," the EMT says, squeezing my shoulder.

I start to follow her, but a nurse directs me to go to registration.

"Then come back here," she says, "and I'll show you where they've got her."

Joe and Lizzie arrive at this point. Lizzie has my purse. I take care of registration. The woman says she's hurrying, but it feels as if she's moving in slow motion. At last I sign papers and she says I'm done.

Lizzie has to stay in the waiting room with Joe, but the nurse is true to her word and takes me to Maggie. She's just going into the machine when I catch up to her. Registration didn't really take long, after all.

They let me watch through a window.

The doctor introduces himself. He's a trauma specialist who just happened to be here for another patient.

"I'll be following through with your daughter's care," he says, then he points to the CT results. "The abdomen looks good, so far. So the concussion is our main concern right now. This is hemorrhaging just above her right ear."

"How bad is it?" I whisper.

"It's relatively small. We have to wait and see, but the fact her vital signs are all improving is good. She'll have to be admitted, of course, and monitored."

"I'll stay with her."

"Good. Keep talking to her. I'll feel better once she's connected with us again. I'm ordering a catheter and some blood work. Did I see your husband and daughter out in the waiting room?"

"Friend and daughter. Can her sister stay?"

"We don't generally let minors stay with the patients, but there's a day lounge upstairs where she could wait close to you."

While they draw blood for more tests, I check on Lizzie. Joe offers to take her to his house, but she rebels.

"No. I'm not leaving until I know Maggie's going to be okay."

I'm not going to argue with her. I know how she feels.

"I have to get back to the restaurant," says Joe. "C.J.'s still giving Murphy his statement and we were already short staffed tonight. Do you mind if I use your car? I'll come back when I've closed up, and see if Lizzie's ready to leave then."

"That would be great."

"I'll bring some food for you both."

"Thanks, but you don't need to do that. I'm not really hungry."

"You will be in a few hours," he says.

He gives us each a hug and leaves.

"I'm thirsty," Lizzie says.

I give her some money, but before she finds out where to get snacks, they come tell us they're ready to take Maggie up to her room.

"May I see her first?" Lizzie asks politely.

The doctor agrees to let her see Maggie. The IV must be helping. She's not as pale as she was before. Lizzie rubs her free arm.

"Hey, Maggie. It's me, Lizzie. Wake up!"

Maggie's eyelids lift enough for us to see part of her irises and the start of a smile pulls at her lips.

"Dun teh," she mutters, then closes her eyes and mouth again.

"You know," the doctor says, "maybe Lizzie can help get her fully awake. I'll make a note on the chart that she's allowed to be in the room with you."

"Thanks!" she says.

They put Maggie into a semi-private room. The other bed is empty. She's got the IV in her arm and the nurse puts an ice pack on her face.

"This will help minimize the bruising," she explains. "We'll keep it on twenty minutes at a time as often as she'll tolerate it. And go ahead and keep trying to get her to wake up enough to talk with you lucidly. Let me know as soon as she does, so I can call the doctor. He wants to talk to her, for further assessment. After that, we'll have to wake her once an hour all night."

"Where can I get some pop?" Lizzie asks.

"The cafeteria's the best place," the nurse says, then tells her how to find it.

While Lizzie's gone, I keep talking to Maggie, calling her by name, telling her I'm here and that she's safe. Then I realize Richard may be in this hospital. I push the call button for the nurse.

"My husband was injured tonight. Can you tell me if he was brought here? Richard Crandall?"

"Of course. You must be worried sick with both of them hurt."

I shake my head violently. "He's the reason Maggie is here, why she ran away. I'm not worried about him that way."

"Oh. I'll check admissions."

She comes back in a few minutes and tells me he's in intensive care, in critical condition. For now, he's no threat to Maggie.

Lizzie comes back with two large cups of cola and some chips.

"I know Joe's bringing something over later, but I was starting to get hungry."

She goes back to Maggie's side and starts chattering to her about everything that's happened since we found the diary. Maggie moves a bit, as if to get more comfortable.

Finally she opens her eyes and focuses on Lizzie.

"You're really here?" she rasps.

"Yes, we're here," I say as I summon the nurse again.

As soon as she sees that Maggie's alert, she goes to call the doctor.

"My mouth's dry," Maggie whispers.

"The doctor will be here in a minute. I'm not sure I should give you any water."

The doctor has Lizzie go out in the hall, but lets me stay and hold Maggie's hand as he reexamines her. Her right ear and the left side of her face are swollen and changing color. She has welts on her arms and her abdomen is tender.

"Can you lift your head?" he asks her.

She barely moves it, then lets it sink back into the pillow and closes her eyes for a moment.

"Dizzy?" he asks.

"Feel like throwing up," she replies.

"That's the concussion. Can you tell me what you remember?"

"Matt kicked me in the stomach and made me pee." She pauses and closes her eyes again. It's clear that talking is an effort. "Not much after that. Heard Mom and Lizzie, maybe."

"I want you to rest now. Go ahead and go to sleep. It's okay, in fact your brain needs the chance to do its own repair work. But the nurse will be waking you up every hour, to make sure you're just sleeping."

Maggie's already drifting off.

"Can she have any water?" I ask.

"Not until the nausea's passed and we're sure the abdomen's okay. The IV will keep her hydrated and we'll add something for the nausea to it. If she complains about dry mouth, the nurse can swab it."

"What about her abdomen? Do you think there's damage inside?"

"The first blood levels and urinalysis look okay," he says. "We'll repeat those in a few hours. The head injury's still the primary concern, and she's showing improvement. That she recognized you is great. The main thing she needs is rest. She'll be here for several days, though, so we can monitor everything and make sure the progress continues."

"The police will probably want to talk to her."

"Not until I give the okay," he says. "She's not to be stressed until she's well enough to get up and walk to the bathroom, and then I'll make them keep it short."

"I won't quiz her, but what if she wants to talk about it?"

"Let her, unless you see her getting upset."

"You're sure it's okay for her to sleep?"

"Yes," the doctor insists. "She needs the rest. The nurse will wake her once an hour. As long as she makes sense then, you don't need to worry. I'm ordering an MRI for her head tomorrow morning. Sooner, if there's any sign she's getting worse. We may do the abdomen, too, if necessary."

Lizzie comes back and sits with me, watching Maggie sleep. The nurse has come in twice when C.J. and Joe return. Lizzie agrees to go with them for the night when the nurse tells us the second round of lab tests look good.

"Murphy talked to the doctor before he took me back to work," says C.J. "He found out Maggie woke up but can't be interviewed for at least a couple of days, but he wanted to talk with you. He hasn't been here yet?"

"No."

"Must have gotten tied up with other stuff."

They've been gone about an hour when Murphy arrives.

I've been dozing off and on in the chair, my head on the foot of Maggie's bed. I'm not sure how long he's been standing in the doorway when I lift my face and see him.

"Did I wake you?" he apologizes.

"I don't think so. I haven't really been sleeping."

"How's she doing?"

"They're pretty sure there's no serious injury to the abdomen now, so it's mainly the concussion, and she's been making sense every time the nurse wakes her up. The last time she grumbled the same way she does when she doesn't want to get up for school."

"I'm glad to hear that. Her face is pretty swollen."

"It'll be bruised for quite a while." I'm relieved to be focusing on something so minor. "Nothing's broken, though."

"The kid we have in custody says it was his buddy who brought her back to the house and did most of the damage, but he didn't know about your husband. We can't press charges against *him* until we talk to Maggie or get the paperwork on the New York charges, but he's not going anywhere."

"The nurse said he's in critical condition."

"He was hit hard, right at the base of his skull."

I hope he dies, but I can't say it that way, not out loud. So I say, "It'll be easier for Maggie if he doesn't make it."

"Yeah. How are you doing?"

"Drowning in guilt." I grimace. "I'm not *really* a stupid woman. I don't know how I let him fool me so completely."

"Hey, when it comes to relationships, we're all vulnerable."

"Have you been married to someone who molested your children?"

"No."

"Didn't think so."

He gives me a chagrined smile. "But I was engaged to a woman who had another fiance in Baltimore. She had me convinced her job took her down there all the time. I didn't have a clue until she decided he was the one she was going to marry."

"Sounds like you got lucky."

"Yeah, but it took awhile for me to see it that way."

The nurse comes in and gently shakes Maggie's shoulder, "Wake up for me, Maggie."

Maggie groans and opens one eye, "I'm still okay."

"Can you move your head any yet?"

Maggie lifts her head an inch off the pillow and plops it back down. "No," she says, "still makes me sick."

"Okay. Don't bother trying until I ask you again." The nurse makes notes on Maggie's chart, then tells me, "She's doing fine. The nausea will probably last a day or two, at least. I'm glad her father's been able to join you."

She leaves the room before I can correct her.

"My father?" Maggie asks, peeking at us through her eyelashes.

"No, this is Patrick Murphy. He's the police officer in charge of your rescue."

"You took the tape off. Thanks," she says, then goes back to sleep.

"I should go and let you get some sleep, too," he says.

"I've been thinking about that empty bed, but I'm not sure how the nurses would feel about my using it."

"I'd ask them for a blanket, then rest on top of it. If you're asleep when they find you, they won't bother waking you up."

"I may do that."

"Here's my card. Will you please call me as soon as Maggie can talk about what happened? I think the dead kid clubbed your husband—the gun he was using had some blood on the grip—but we need a statement from Maggie. We need to know why she was in that alley with your husband."

When he leaves, I ask for a blanket and stretch out on the other bed.

Saturday, June 3, 2000

83: Peg

All day Thursday and Friday, I watched Maggie sleep, and I read her diary from the beginning. I realized how much we lost when I started dating. Some of it would have happened anyway, because children are supposed to grow away from their parents, but I should have made sure I was still listening. I should have made sure we still had time together by ourselves. We missed the same things . . camping, road trips, and cuddling up for movies on the big couch I bought when she was a baby.

Lizzie stayed with us during the days and went home with Joe and C.J. each night. She brought me a change of clothing Thursday and the night staff let me use a shower.

By Thursday evening, Maggie's nausea had eased enough to sip water and suck on Popsicles. Friday morning, they removed the catheter and she made it to the bathroom, but ended up vomiting before she went back to bed. When she tried again in the evening, the trip went fine.

Saturday morning, she is already awake when I open my eyes.

"Hey, Mom."

"Hey, yourself. Feeling better?"

"Much. Except I'm hungry."

"The doctor should make his rounds soon. We'll ask him if you can have some food, but I'll warn you, it'll just be clear liquids."

"Jello's all I wanna try right now, anyway."

Suddenly, I start crying. "I was so scared I'd lost you."

"Me, too. It felt so awful, thinking you hated me."

"I could never hate you."

"I know that now."

I lean over to give her a gentle hug and she holds me tight.

Then she says, "I read your journal, Mom. It ended with you leaving for California. Did you really go there? What about your parents?"

My stomach clenches. How much did I put in that journal? But Maggie's waiting for my answer.

"I didn't call them. The farther I got away, the more they seemed like part of a different lifetime. That's why I was so afraid we'd never find you."

"I know what you mean. It was just a few days, but I've changed a lot, Mom."

I look at her carefully. The entire right side of her face and her right ear are shades of deep red, blue, and purple. They've told me there's no structural damage, but still, it hurts to look at her, and I know that's not what she means. She's never going to be my innocent little girl again.

"I read your diary, Maggie."

"Yeah, when I left it for Lizzie, I kinda knew you'd read it, even tho' I told myself I didn't want you to. I was afraid you'd blame me."

"No. It's not your fault. Don't *ever* think that."

"C.J. caught me making excuses. Richard was drunk, at first."

"That's no excuse."

"I know. And he wasn't always drunk."

"Your diary didn't say exactly what happened."

"I'm not ready to talk about that, Mom."

"You don't have to tell me anything you don't want to."

"Did they find him? I think you said something about it, but I was still pretty fuzzy."

"Yes, he's in ICU here. They're still not sure if he'll make it."

"He made me go into that alley," she says in nearly a whisper.

It's time to prepare her.

"There's a policeman," I say. "He's a friend of Joe's. Murphy's his name. He's going to talk to you later, about what happened to you at that house and with Richard, too."

"The guy with red hair? The one who took the duct tape off?"

"Yes."

"Did you tell him about Richard?"

"Yes. And we told the police in New York when I reported you missing."

"So they'll want me to press charges, too?"

"You don't have to. Another girl came forward. He did the same thing to her five years ago."

"He did it to someone else?"

"Yes. She and her mother were living with him. I didn't even know he'd had someone live with him before . . . I'm so sorry, Maggie."

"I love you, Mom."

"I love you, too."

The nurse interrupts our tearful embrace.

"Well, it's good to see you're back with us completely. How's your head? Any dizziness or nausea?"

"Nope. A little bit of a headache, but I don't feel sick anymore."

"And how's your stomach?"

"Starting to get hungry."

The nurse laughs. "I take it that means you're not having abdominal pain?"

"Nope. Not much. Kinda like my face—aching, but not broken."

"Good. I'll make a note of that on your chart and call the doctor to let him know. He'll be through in a little bit."

"Can I eat?"

"He'll probably order clear fluids, but he'll want to examine you himself first."

"Okay, but can I have another Popsicle to hold me?"

"Sure."

C.J. arrives with Lizzie. They're delighted to see Maggie sitting up. C.J. gives her a cautious hug before he leaves for the restaurant.

"It's cool you're finally feeling better," says Lizzie. "I wasn't even sure you understood everything when I was talking to you yesterday."

"Yeah, I remember all that."

"You want to play cards or something?"

"Yeah, do you have any?"

"Here," I say, pulling out my wallet. "Go get some at the gift shop."

The doctor arrives while Lizzie's gone and examines Maggie. She doesn't seem to be in as much pain.

"You're looking good, young lady," he says when he's finished. "Your reflexes are fine, your pupils are balanced and reacting properly, there's minimal tenderness in your abdomen, and your last blood levels were normal. I've ordered repeat MRIs, blood work, and urinalysis, just to be safe. I want to be sure the hemorrhage is resolving and nothing new is wrong, but I expect everything to come back fine."

"So when can I leave?"

"I want to make sure you can keep food down. Clear fluids today, and if that goes well, a bland diet tomorrow. Any nausea or vomiting, and I want to know about it. Understood?"

Maggie responds, "Yes, sir."

"So if everything's going well, which I expect it will be, you can go home Monday." He turns to speak to me. "She's going for testing. It'll take most of the morning. I hear you haven't left the hospital. Take a break."

"I'll be fine, Mom," Maggie insists before I can object.

I'm not comfortable leaving her side, but she'll be safe here in the hospital. Just to be sure, I ask the nurse to check on Richard's status. He's still critical.

I hope he dies, so we can put all of this behind us right now.

84: Peg

Lizzie and I go to the restaurant while they're busy testing Maggie. For the first time in days, I have an appetite. When we're done eating, C.J. takes Lizzie for a tour of the kitchen. I'm sitting by myself, enjoying the peaceful, friendly atmosphere and drinking a cup of tea when Joe comes over.

"How's Maggie doing?" he asks.

"The doctor's running all the tests again, but he thinks she's doing fine. They expect to let her out Monday."

"Maria gets back from Greece Monday morning. Where will you go when Maggie's released from the hospital?"

"As long as the doctor says it's okay, we're going to our favorite camping spot for a couple weeks and just enjoy being together."

"Good. Do you think you'll go back to your old home then?"

"Our house was sold, but we could find another. We do have friends there. But part of me wants to start fresh somewhere new. I'm putting all those decisions on the back burner while we camp. I'm hoping some of the answers will fall into place on their own."

"It works that way sometimes. But before you go, I know Maria will want to meet you all. I told her about everything that's happened. The family's bringing food to celebrate her homecoming Monday. Will you join us?"

"I'll ask Maggie. I'm not sure how she'll feel about meeting a bunch of people. Her face is still a mess."

"I hope you'll at least stop long enough to meet Maria."

"Hey Mom," Lizzie interrupts. "Will's been showing me how he does dishes. Can I stay here and help? It's getting pretty boring at the hospital. I'm sick of reading and I finished my stuff for school."

"I know. I mailed it out this morning."

"She's welcome to stay," Joe says. "She's been a wonderful guest at the house, very helpful and polite."

"Okay."

"Thanks, Mom. See ya later."

Lizzie gives me a quick peck on the cheek and disappears into the back. When I get to the hospital, Murphy's in with Maggie.

"Hi, Mom."

"I tried to wait," he apologizes, "But Maggie insisted on going ahead without you. She hasn't signed anything, though."

"I wanted to get it over with so I can go back to sleep." Maggie looks beat. "I'm really tired."

"I guess it's okay. Are you done?"

"Yep." She yawns and snuggles down into the bed to sleep.

I go out into the hall with Murphy.

"Did the doctor know you were talking to her?" I demand.

"The nurse checked and he said five minutes. It didn't even take that long." His tone is polite and apologetic.

"She's been through so much," I try to explain my rudeness.

"I know. I just needed the essentials. The dead kid, Matt, is the one who clubbed your husband, and like the other kid said, Matt did most of the damage to Maggie. At least as far as her memory goes."

"I'm glad she can't remember everything they did to her."

"I'll write up her statement and bring it back Monday. You can read it over with her before she signs."

"She may be getting out Monday."

"The nurse said that was a possibility. I actually have the day off, so I'd just as soon get here early and be done."

"Okay. We'll head back to New York then, so I guess it's better you talked to her today."

"Oh," he says. He almost sounds disappointed. "Well, I've got your cell phone number. I'm sure you'll want to know what happens with your husband."

"I don't even think of him as my husband now," I snap. How can he think I'd care what happens to Richard?

"I didn't mean like that! I meant so you'll know if Maggie's going to have to go through a trial against him or not."

"Oh, of course," I say, "but I'm not going to push her to testify against him. There's another girl bringing charges in New York. She's older, and it's not so recent for her. They may not need Maggie."

"It would make it easier for the other girl, and we will be pressing charges for what he did here."

"I suppose." I sigh. "It'll be up to Maggie, but I hate the idea of her being put through anything else."

"Of course, but it may be better for her in the long run."

When I don't respond, he gives me his business card and takes his leave. I spend the afternoon pretending to read while Maggie sleeps, wondering what's best for her now.

Sunday, June 4, 2000

85: Peg

I have Maggie to myself again Sunday morning. I ask her how she feels about the prospect of testifying against Richard.

"He didn't do much here, and I'm definitely gonna testify against Charlie. But it'll be hard to tell the stuff that happened at his house. Did you ever press charges against the guys who raped you?"

I'm drawing a blank. "What do you mean?"

"Did you ever press charges against those fraternity guys?"

"That was my own stupidity."

What on earth did I write in that journal? I need to get it out of Maggie's things and read it myself. I should burn them all.

"Mom," she addresses me as if I'm brain dead. She must be feeling better. "You were raped. You only drank part of a beer the whole night, then when you were leaving, some guy gave you a cola and the next thing you knew it was the next morning. It's totally clear you were drugged. You never figured that out?"

"That's what I wrote? I only had part of a beer?"

"Yeah. Don't you remember?"

"Not really. I tried to forget that night. I blamed myself for going to that party and assumed I was drunk." The importance of the difference hits me full force. Stunned, I whisper, "I let that change my whole life."

"I know," Maggie responds. "Not only did you run away, but you slept around 'cuz you felt guilty you weren't a virgin anymore."

I'm not comfortable that Maggie knows about that, but I tell her, "You know, you don't have to do that. Not being a virgin doesn't mean you have to 'do it'. It's okay to tell a boy you don't want to go that far."

"I know, Mom. I already figured that out with C.J."

"C.J.?" I'm not sure I'm ready to hear this.

"Yeah. I slept with him the first night we met, but we didn't like—you know. I'm not gonna hook up with anybody 'til it's right."

"Okay." I reply haltingly. We used to be able to talk about anything, but it was never like this. I'm not sure what to say.

Maggie sees my discomfort and pats my hand, "Mom, you read my diary and I read your journal. It would be dumb to keep secrets now."

"I suppose." There's so much I don't want her to know.

"It's cool that I can tell you stuff and know you won't be shocked."

"I'm not so sure about that—you're still my baby, you know."

"Yeah right, Mom." She gives me a smile that says I'm being silly. Then she shifts gears. "But I really wanna know, what happened after you left Harrisburg? Did you go to California?"

"Eventually. I lived there for years, pretending to be someone else."

"Seriously?" she gasps. "Did you have a boyfriend?"

I'm about to edit the truth, then stop. Maybe she can learn from my mistakes. I tell her, "Actually, I went through a lot of relationships."

"Did you ever have a good one?

"Not really."

"Why?"

"Well, until today, I would have said I was just unlucky." I pause, searching for words to express the new self-knowledge. "The truth is, I dated nice guys, but I always picked the jerks. I guess I never felt good enough for the nice ones. I thought I was doing better with Richard. He had me fooled. Sorry."

"It wasn't your fault."

"You know, Maggie, the night nurse suggested you get counseling or go to a support group. Maybe we should go together."

"Maybe, but I'd rather write it first, and let you read that, instead of having to tell you everything, or telling you in front of a group."

"That's okay."

"If he pulls through, I'll hafta write a statement anyway."

"Are you sure you want to testify?"

"Yeah, I guess. He made me feel like I deserved what he was doing. I know it was just a head trip, but I'm afraid I might forget that if he gets away with it. Even if that other girl got him put in jail, that would be for what he did to her, you know?"

The doctor checks on Maggie late that afternoon and tells us it looks like she can leave in the morning. Later, while Joe and C.J. are visiting with Lizzie, a new patient arrives to be Maggie's roommate.

"Peg, why don't you come sleep at our house tonight?" Joe offers. "There's plenty of room."

"I'll be fine, Mom. You can't sleep much in a chair. Get a good rest before we drive back to New York."

I can't think of any reasonable objection.

Richard's condition is improving, but he's still critical and under guard; there's no threat to Maggie. Once he can be moved, he's going to a locked facility.

We make sure Maggie's set for the night, then I follow Joe out of the city to his home across the river. There's some juggling of sleeping arrangements. Lizzie and I share C.J.'s room, because there are twin beds from when Joe's boys lived at home. C.J. takes the frilly room Lizzie's been using. I take a long, hot shower and get ready for bed.

As my head hits the pillow, I realize this was a very good idea.

Monday, June 5, 2000

86: Peg

I go to pick up Maggie by myself. She's already dressed when I get there, but we have to wait for the doctor to sign her out.

"Where's Lizzie?"

"At Joe's. He's picking up Maria at the airport. Lizzie and C.J. are getting the place ready for the welcome home party for her."

"I don't mind meeting Maria, and I want to see Joe and C.J. once more before we leave, but I'm not so sure about everyone else. I look awful."

"We'll just stay a little bit, then head north."

Murphy comes by with Maggie's statement. I read over it with her and witness her signature when she says it's all accurate.

"You should know, Mr. Crandall is conscious," he tells us. "He may recover enough to go to trial after all."

"That's okay," Maggie says. "He'll suffer more this way."

Murphy grins at her feistiness.

"Thanks for signing this statement," he says on his way out the door. "I'll drop it off at the office and see you later."

"What's he mean?" Maggie asks.

"Probably when you come back for the trials."

The doctor comes and does a quick check, then signs the paperwork so she can be released. "You have to ride in the wheelchair to the front door," he warns her. "It's hospital policy."

"Okay. I don't wanna cause any trouble." She smiles crookedly.

I laugh. The sound startles me for a moment, then I realize how good it feels.

We drive to Joe's in comfortable silence. I can't find a place to park on the street, so I pull in behind his car. The plane must have been right on time.

C.J. and Lizzie have made two banners and draped them across the living room. One says 'Welcome Home, Maria', and the other says 'Welcome Back, Maggie'. They're all there, as well as other relatives. There's a table full of food and people hugging and kissing us as if we were part of the family. Maria gives me a hug, too.

"I'm so glad to meet you, Peg. Joe always worried about you."

My eyes start filling up with tears. I hold them back and smile.

"It is so good to know that. Whenever my life was a mess, I'd think of Joe and how kind he was to me that day, and I'd realize there are decent people out there. It helped me through some rough spots."

Maria gets pulled away by a relative who's asking her about family in Greece. Joe comes up to me.

"I heard what you said to Maria."

"Well, you are pretty special."

"I'm not the only one, you know. You are a remarkable woman. You've raised two wonderful young women by yourself. Maggie is resourceful, she works hard, and she's bright. Lizzie's been a delightful guest. She cleaned the entire house for this homecoming party."

"Thank you. For everything."

"Don't worry about it. Come on, eat some of this good Greek food, or my aunt and the other ladies will be offended."

C.J. and the girls have already filled their plates high and moved off with some other young people. I'm not really hungry, but I take a little bit of everything and follow Joe out to a table on the patio.

"Thank you, Joe, for everything."

He shrugs. "Do you like the dolmades? My aunt makes them."

I nibble the stuffed grape leaves. "Yes. They're delicious."

I've just finished eating when Murphy joins us with a full plate.

"Patrick! I wasn't sure you were going to make it," says Joe.

Murphy smiles. "I wouldn't miss Aunt Dimitra's dolmades."

"Did you leave any?" Joe asks.

"A few."

"I think I'll go get some more." I start to get up, but Joe waves for me to sit back down.

"I'll get you more food. You liked the salad as well?"

"Yes, and just a little more moussaka, please."

Murphy pauses, his fork in the air. "Do you mind if I start eating without you?"

"No, please, go ahead." I pause. "I never said thank you. I don't know what would have happened if you hadn't acted so quickly."

"I knew Joe wouldn't panic over nothing. He's been helping homeless kids his whole life. Used to drive his father nuts when we were kids."

"You grew up together?"

"He lived right down the street."

I let him eat a few bites before asking, "What about C.J.?"

"He's a good kid, mostly. He knew better than to hang out with those people. We talked it over."

"I'm glad he was there. Without that connection, we might never have found Maggie. She might be dead."

"Yeah, I guess it turned out for the best. He's like his uncle when it comes to helping people."

"Did you find that girl with the baby?"

"Crystal? No. Joe's register was short that day. No one's seen her since. She probably took the first bus out of town."

Joe comes back and puts a plate full of food in front of me. "So what did she say? Did you ask her?"

"Ask me what?" I look back and forth between the two.

Patrick glares at his friend. "I wasn't' going to say anything today. It's a little soon."

CJ and the girls come out to join us.

"Patrick would like to take you out to dinner," says Joe. "He's a decent enough character, for a bachelor."

"You and the girls." Patrick's face is bright red. "There's no rush. Just sometime."

I push my chair back from the table. "I'm sorry, we're leaving for New York. Today."

Patrick takes a breath and starts to say something, but Lizzie interrupts him.

"We'll be back for the trials, Maggie's definitely testifying, but we need to get going, Mom. She's wiped."

Maggie gives me a tired smile. She's leaning on C.J.

Patrick comes around the table and takes my hand between his. "Maybe when you come back. Maggie has my card."

"Okay." I return his smile, though I doubt I'll want to date for a very long time, even once I've gotten a divorce from Richard.

There's a round of hugs and goodbyes with Joe and his family. I check that C.J. got all of our things from the guestroom.

Finally, we leave. Lizzie lets Maggie have the more comfortable front seat, but she leans forward to chat about C.J. and the extended family they just met.

"That Murphy guy's not bad looking, for an old guy," says Lizzie.

"Thanks." I grimace. He has to be close to my age.

Lizzie doesn't notice my reaction to her comment. She's got her own agenda. "Do you think we can get our old house back?"

"I wouldn't count on it," I reply.

"How about your old job?"

"It's gone, but there are four school districts within a reasonable drive. I could get a job with one of them."

"Do you wanna teach?" asks Maggie. "Your journal said you were going to be a writer."

"I like teaching—high school at least. But one reason I went into it was I thought that I'd write in the summers."

"Instead, you spent all your time with us," says Lizzie.

"I wanted to."

"You should write, too," says Maggie.

"But we've gotta get you a laptop," Lizzie adds. "Then we can still go camping."

We ride in companionable silence for a few minutes, then Lizzie asks, "Are you gonna be okay, Maggie?"

"Yeah."

I glance over and see Maggie smiling at me.

"Mom and I are going to find a support group to deal with everything. Not just what happened to me, but all the stuff she went through back in the day. Right, Mom?"

I grip the steering wheel a little tighter. I haven't been open about that with anyone, but she's right, it needs to be talked out. "As soon as we know where we're staying, that's the top priority."

"Maybe Lizzie should come, too, to learn from our mistakes?"

"Well, some of them, anyway."

"Mom . . ." Maggie warns.

"I've made a lot of mistakes."

Under Maggie's steady glare I capitulate.

"If you're going to learn from *all* of them, we've got a lot of talking to do." I laugh nervously. "We don't have to do that with a bunch of strangers, do we?"

"No, we can start right now," Maggie says. "So, when did you stop running away, Mom?"

"Probably today," I admit.

"Better late than never," chirps Lizzie.

"Tell us all your mistakes," Maggie demands.

Good thing it's a long drive.

.

Resources

The best centralized center for resources I've found is at the Rape, Abuse & Incest National Network (RAINN) website. There are resources for children, women, and men. The links for trafficking are also good for those being exploited for non-sexual purposes.

RAINN

rainn.org

RAINN 24/7 Hotline:

800-656-HOPE (800-656-4673)

Other good resources include:

National Center for Missing & Exploited Children

www.missingkids.org

24-hour call center: 800-843-5678

National Runaway Safeline

www.nationalrunawaysafeline.org/

800-RUNAWAY (800-786-2929)

National Runaway Chat and Info

www.1800runaway.org/

800-RUNAWAY (800-786-2929)

Thank you.

Thank you for reading this book.

Please take a few moments right now, while the story is still resonating, to help others find it.

Amazon's algorithms control book sales – the more reviews and ratings a book gets, the more often it pops up for people to see. The more attention it gets there, the more attention it gets elsewhere and the more likely it will find its way to libraries, too.

So please, review this book on Amazon. You don't have to purchase it there to post a review and/or rate a book. You can copy and paste the same review at Goodreads or other places. A review can be short and simple – "Interesting story." is enough for the review to be counted. Don't forget to give it a star rating.

Review links:

www.amazon.com/dp/1942069049/

www.goodreads.com/book/show/95210207-running-away

If you want to do more, you can:

> Talk it up – encourage your friends and your local library or book club to get the book.

> If you do social media, post your picture with the book.

If you want to know more, you can check out my website. If you have questions, there's a contact form and I do answer messages.

Thanks. Sheri

www.sherimcguinn.com

sherimcguinn.substack.com

Behind the Story

My first "real" job after college was as a probation officer. Most of my caseload was teenage girls on probation for petty offenses, but the main concern was that they were out of control, lying all the time, and flaunting their sexuality. At least one girl claimed to have been sexually abused by a male in the household when she was younger, but no one believed her.

Later, I became a child protection investigator/caseworker. One of my first cases was a teenage girl who was completely out of control. She flaunted her promiscuity, stayed out all night, and lied a lot. Numerous times the night shift got a call from her father asking for help getting her to come home. Two women in our department had taken specialized training in sexual abuse; when they were on night shift and got her, they knew how to put her at ease and she disclosed she had run away from her mother to live with her father due to sexual abuse by her step-father. It was severe enough there would be criminal charges against him, so I was instructed not to ask her about it. Repeating the story too often would make it sound rehearsed and she might not be believed.

Well, I hoped they knew what they were doing, because I wasn't inclined to believe anything she said – until the day it went to family court and the step-father's attorney asked why there was no hospital report. I told him, as far as I knew, there had been no hospital visit. (It was too long after the abuse when she disclosed for that kind of evidence.) The relief on the step-father's face told me everything she said was true. I used that moment for Peg.

Sexualized and "out of control" behaviors are a common reaction to sexual abuse. By the time the victim discloses, their credibility is in question. And what parent wants to believe the choices they've made led to that kind of trauma? I told this story in both voices, hoping moms and daughters in this situation will read and understand each other a little better and start communicating.

Acknowledgments

I started writing Maggie's story in 2003. My children, Trevor, Katie, and Brian, helped make Maggie's voice and experiences real. Duane Wooters, Kari Thompson, Linda Smith, Carol Kumpu, Norma Green, Linda McCarty, and "E" listened to each chapter and gave thoughtful input. Mike Elder of Philadelphia updated me on the runaway life in Pennsylvania and Lee Rabold answered technical questions on Maggie's injuries.

In 2007 I stopped pitching to agents and publishers and "self-published" with one of the many companies that target writers. They didn't even use the final proof for printing! Despite that, *Running Away* was a prize winner in Writer's Digest's International Self-Published Book Awards.

A school librarian told me the swear words made it impossible for her to have in the school library, so, in 2012, when I managed to cancel the original contract, I revised the manuscript using ** for all swear words. I didn't like the way that read, so in 2014 I put out an uncensored edition using language true to the characters. Again I had the support of other writers: Barbara Hockabout, Carol Sletten, Mary Stuever, and Karen Alderson. My first radio interviews were with Barbara Bruce of White Mountain Radio and Apache Radio KNNB.

When I finished writing *Peg's Story: Detours,* I realized Peg's journal entries had changed, including some Maggie read in *Running Away.* I decided to change them there and make the two books align better. I also edited some of Lizzie's part, as her story is developing. Thus evolved *Running Away: Maggie's Story.*

Maggie's story has remained essentially the same through all of the versions. I expect a traditional publisher would have told me to leave it alone long ago. It's definitely time to move on now.

Sheri McGuinn
www.sherimcguinn.com
September 11, 2020

Also by Sheri McGuinn

Peg's Story: Detours

A novel that reads like memoir; one woman's journey. Asked for by readers of *Running Away,* this is the full story of Maggie's mother.

"In some ways, the novel is a brutal cautionary tale, showing how one mistake can spiral into a life-changing series of events. In another, however, it is a moving coming-of-age narrative about a girl who discovers herself amid extreme circumstances. A nuanced yet plainly told novel. " **Kirkus Reviews**

All for One: Love, War, & Ghosts

Youthful decisions changed the course of their lives and estranged lifelong friends. Decades later they think they've put 'Nam and PTSD behind them, until the past shoves its way into the present, bringing fear and uncertainty. By the end of the deadly month, their lives again change forever.

Tough Times

"Stay together." Michael knows they'll be split up by the system, so he decides to take his young siblings to the white grandparents they've never known – because *his* father was black. While Michael deals with responsibility, grief, prejudice, fear, his first romantic relationship, and hormones, the police find his mother and label it murder. They think Michael did it, but the killer is stalking the kids.

2023 KINDLE BEST OF INDIE BOOK AWARDS FINALIST YOUNG ADULT

Alice

Thirteen-year-old Nina narrates the story of her mother, Alice, who has always been responsible, proper, and totally uptight. The school eliminates Alice's teaching position, then her hippie father drops into their lives, and then the bank sends a letter threatening their home – and Nina suddenly sees another side to her mother.

Discussion Questions

1. Why does Maggie not tell right away? Maggie did not know about her mother's past before reading the journal. Do you think she would have told her mother about Richard's abuse if she'd known what had happened to her mom? Do you think Peg will tell the girls *everything* about her past now?

2. When Maggie first starts reading Peg's journal, she says the omelet reminds her more of her mother than the journal. Why? Maggie is reading what Peg wrote as a teenager. Peg tells Lizzie about some of the same things. What differences are there in the two versions of events? Why?

3. There are parallels between Maggie's story and what she reads in Peg's diary. Peg, like many sexually abused people, went on to be sexually exploited. Can Maggie learn from her mother's experience? Do you think Maggie will recover from her traumas more quickly than Peg recovered from hers?

4. Peg isn't sure at first whether Maggie's diary is true. Why would Maggie lie? Then Peg decides "Either way the answer is the same. Maggie needs our help." Why would Maggie need their help if she made it all up?

5. Peg wonders if Richard knew his job was in jeopardy. Financially, they'd have been better off if he had sold his house and moved in with Peg and the girls. What advantages are there for Richard in having them move into is house in the city? How has he manipulated each of them – Maggie, Peg, and Lizzie?

6. What circumstances made it possible for Peg to go look for Maggie? The novel takes place in just over a week. What would have happened if she had waited until the end of the school year?

7. What about Lizzie? Is she at risk? Will she benefit from counseling with Maggie and Peg? Or will it leave her shy of relationships?

My website has:

Supplemental Materials

Puchasing Links

A Contact Form (ask questions or set up an author visit)

Media Resources

www.sherimcguinn.com

My newsletter caters to readers and writers:

sherimcguinn.substack.com

Review links for *Running Away: Maggie's Story*:

www.goodreads.com/book/show/95210207

www.amazon.com/dp/1942069049

Every review helps – thank you.

Thanks for reading!

www.ingramcontent.com/pod-product-compliance
Lightning Source LLC
Chambersburg PA
CBHW020820260626
47169CB00003B/754